WHITE HELL OF PITY

The Bacons live in Swything — a charming little village with a Saxon church, green lanes and comfortable farmhouses. But the Bacons themselves are anything but charming. They are slovenly, dirty and poor. There are too many children, and Mrs. Bacon cordially resents them all. But she hates Emmie the most — because Emmie offends the most. Emmie is different. Then, when Emmie turns twelve, the miracle happens. The chance arrives for her to learn about a world the other Bacons do not know of. For when Emmie is twelve, she meets Miss Stanton . . .

WHITE HELL OF PITY

NORAH LOFTS

LARGE
PRINT

First published in Great Britain 1937
by
Methuen Publishing Ltd.

First Isis Edition
published 2018
by arrangement with
Clive Lofts

The moral right of the author has been asserted

A catalogue record for this book is available
from the British Library.

ISBN 978–1–78541–611–8 (hb)
ISBN 978–1–78541–617–0 (pb)

Published by
F. A. Thorpe (Publishing)
Anstey, Leicestershire

Set by Words & Graphics Ltd.
Anstey, Leicestershire
Printed and bound in Great Britain by
T. J. International Ltd., Padstow, Cornwall

This book is printed on acid-free paper

For
My Mother
To Whom Adversity Was Always A
Stimulus

Part One

1

The Bacons lived at Swything, one of the loveliest villages in England. There is a Saxon church there, standing high on a green mound. There is the white-fronted hall shining at the end of its avenue of beeches. There is the little street with the schoolhouse, the smithy and four shops. Down green lanes and across the tilled fields stand the comfortable farmhouses surrounded by mossy-tiled barns and thatched stacks.

The Bacons lived in a cottage that stood by itself in a lane that led to a farm called Fairacre where Mr. Bacon was stockman. It might have been a very pretty cottage; there was a low hawthorn hedge in front of it and some woods close behind. It had a garden, narrow in front and widening at the sides and a well that stood under the bowed branches of some ancient apple trees. In the late spring when the woods were green and the hawthorn hedge was snowed over with blossom and the apple trees were massed with pink flowers, the cottage came as more of a shock to the eye than it did in the winter when everything was bare and bleak. For the cottage was always bare and bleak. The gate was off its hinges; the garden space was a wilderness of weeds and old tins, broken-down perambulators, boxes, bottles, and sacks. Most of the windows showed a broken pane and there were no curtains.

Very few people passed it; but those who did could hardly escape noticing that at least one of the children was always crying, and that Mrs. Bacon was always shouting about something. Few people passed it without becoming aware of contempt for William Bacon, dislike for his wife and pity for his children. There were six of them alive. One of them had been very imperfectly concealed by the dress of shiny satin that Mrs. Bacon had worn at her wedding. Without him there would have been no wedding, for Violet Taylor was quite content with her job at the Stoney Market Three Kings: and she had all the contempt for William Bacon that a woman can feel for a man who allows her to bully him.

However, when Freddie persisted in coming despite her best efforts to rid herself of the encumbrance, Violet decided to become Mrs. Bacon and mistress of the cottage where William had lived alone since the death of his father. Freddie in Nature's, not Society's, due time was born, and possibly because of Mrs. Bacon's early efforts, proved weakly in his body and what was known in kind local parlance as "simple" in his mind. After that, two other children had been born and one had succumbed either to an attack of croup or to the croup cure recommended by a crony of Mrs. Bacon's at The Pot of Flowers. Edna, who had a sturdier disposition, took several such doses without visible ill-effect. The fourth child was Emmie. Mrs. Bacon by this time was a trifle tired, not so much of bearing the

4

children as of the tiresome if well-meant efforts of interfering busybodies who criticized the upbringing of Freddie and Edna. Quite soon after her discovery of her state she had begged some old clothes from Mrs. Briggs, the doctor's wife, and sold them to an itinerant wardrobe dealer and with the proceeds sent away for certain "Female Pills, guaranteed to remove all irregularities". Emmie may, even at that early stage, have been an irregularity, but removed she failed to be and so was born upon a blustering March morning in the year 1918. After that Mrs. Bacon lost all faith in female pills and produced William, Alice, Johnny, George, Winnie and Phyllis. George and Phyllis, like the earlier baby, gave up the struggle very soon. Nobody missed them. Edna and Emmie from the time when they could stagger about unaided were burdened with the "young 'uns". They clutched them to their waists or dragged them by the hand. They staunched their tears, wiped their noses on the ragged hems of their own petticoats, fed them green apples and took them for brain-addling rides in the broken-down perambulators. They all fell victim to, and survived, heavy colds, whooping-cough, ringworm and mumps. They were all thin and pale, and in the winter they all had red wet noses and dreadful chilblains.

William Bacon was stockman to a well-known breeder of Suffolk Punches and he was thorough and competent in his job. He was completely unaware of the irony in his being part of the system which so carefully supervised the matings of the great glossy creatures, and the rearing of the leggy little foals that resulted from them. Any comparison between his charges and his children would have drawn from him the comment that the Punches were valuable.

During the summer he was frequently absent from home, for it was his duty and his delight to accompany Swything Monarch and Swything Supremacy on their victorious rounds of the County Shows: and though he had no real reason to suspect that he had not fathered the whole of his brood he had been known to voice such suspicions to Mrs. Bacon, especially when he had received a generous share of the Monarch's prize money and had visited The Pot of Flowers. Such remarks naturally led to quarrels which often ended in blows and sent the innocent causes of the uproar scuttling upstairs or out of doors, whichever happened to be nearer.

2

Mrs. Bacon resented her children when they were in a state of gestation, she disliked them in infancy, but it was not until they were obliged to attend school that she thoroughly hated them. Trouble really began then. If they didn't attend, the Attendance Officer called at the cottage and threatened action. If they did attend, the School Nurse called and complained that they were "dirty", meaning "lousy". That word was avoided by the authorities in these dealings for fear of hurting the delicate feelings of Mrs. Bacon and others like her. The Medical Officer declared that Freddie, Edna and

Emmie were under-nourished: and when he discovered that William Bacon, as stockman, earned much more than the average agricultural labourer, he offered Mrs. Bacon not pity, but censure, on that score. Then Freddie and Edna were provided with glasses, at State expense certainly, but if the glasses were absent from their noses for so much as half a day inquiries were set on foot. There was some question too about Edna's tonsils, but there Mrs. Bacon struck. "I'll give you tonsils," she said to the School Nurse. And the School Nurse, looking from one to another of the open-mouthed children, didn't doubt that Mrs. Bacon had an adequate supply.

Another, and deeper grudge that Mrs. Bacon held against the school authorities was that they would repeat that question about what William earned before they would issue boots and clothing from the Children's Care Committee which existed to supply as far as possible the deficiencies caused by poverty. Once that question was answered the Bacons' broken shoes and dirty clothing came in for more criticism than sympathy. Edna and Emmie once managed to exist for three weeks with one pair of shoes between them, going to school on alternate days. The excuses of the baby being ill, mother having been called away, having sickness and pains oneself were just about exhausted when Mrs. Briggs included in a parcel of casts-off a pair of shoes with high, wrung-over heels and wide silk laces. Both girls clamoured for them. Edna's indeed was the prior claim since the communal pair was Emmie's: but Edna had inherited her mother's lethargy

7

without her strong right arm; there was a wordy battle; blows were struck; and the shoes were Emmie's. Next morning both the girls were in school and Emmie proudly kept her feet in the gangway until the teacher, Miss Stanton, fell over them. She looked sharply at Emmie's blushing face and then down at the ugly shoes. She saw the cracks in the patent leather, the jaunty bows of the crumpled laces. She said nothing about "sitting like a crab", or "elephant feet", as Emmie had feared she might, for Miss Stanton was often sharp of tongue, especially in Arithmetic time. She said mildly, "Your feet would be safer inside the desk, Emmie," and sat down beside her to mark the sums which were, miraculously enough, all right. Nobody expected a Bacon to get a sum or anything else right. In the two elder children their mother's attitude to school was dutifully reflected; they were not only stupid, they were sullen and troublesome as well. Freddie couldn't read yet. Despite his age, at the moment almost thirteen years, he was quite unable to pick out such simple sentences as "The cat is on the mat", or "My bat is red". These and other illuminating remarks were written on cards that bore a picture of the subject of the sentence. Sometimes this picture, showing an extremely fat smug cat or an incredibly incarnadined bat, would rouse some memory in Freddie's foggy mind and he would reel off the sentence with deceptive glibness. Then Miss Deal, the teacher of the juniors, who loathed Freddie's face, odour and manners, would suggest moving him up to Miss Stanton for reading. Miss Stanton would produce

8

another card, with an unfamiliar picture, and Freddie would stand dumb and staring before the legend "That is a big bun" below a bun the size of a haystack. So though he gardened and drew and sat through lessons known as istry and jogfry with his peers amongst whom he held his own by spitefulness and cunning, Freddie did his reading and sums with the dewy-eyed seven-year-olds who feared and loathed him. Edna, just under thirteen, and Emmie, rising twelve, were in the same class. Next year Emmie would be promoted and Edna would stay behind, but that wouldn't worry Edna. She would be glad because their work wouldn't always be compared then, and Tommy Levick was bound to stay behind too, and free from Emmie's scornful eye, Edna felt that she could make better headway with this, her first affair. Edna had already the solid figure, which, given any encouragement, would be as heavy and loose as her mother's; and she had pale eyes with scanty white lashes, periodically adorned with styes. But neither her face, nor her figure, nor her stupidity, nor her clothes could undermine her belief in her own attractiveness. And certainly she was far more popular than Emmie who had a mop of black curls which she combed every morning with an almost toothless comb, and yellow eyes and a white face usually well washed for a face of that family. Emmie's ablutions had begun very suddenly and were a matter for a great deal of mockery from Edna and her mother. She was afraid that they would discover the reason and embark upon remarks that would really sting as the present ones didn't. But Edna was not perspicacious enough to notice that Emmie's washings and combings and cobbly mendings had begun on the day after she moved into Miss Stanton's class at the phenomenal age of eleven.

Swything was the typical village school of between fifty and sixty children. A young, unqualified teacher taught the babies from the time they arrived at varying ages until they were seven. Miss Deal had the eight-, nine-, ten- and eleven-year-olds. Miss Stanton, who was also the head, dealt with all the twelve- and thirteen-year-olds and the brightest of the elevens.

"Emmie Bacon is fit to come up to you though she's only eleven," said Miss Deal one day when they were discussing promotions. "You won't have to degrade her for reading," she added, bitterly conscious that Freddie was not to be promoted.

Miss Stanton understood the addition and said sweetly, "I'm sorry about Freddie, I am really, Miss Deal, I know he's a trial. But you do see, don't you, what a hullabaloo there'd be if an inspector walked in and found him trying to read out of a book. One day you'll have a school of your own and then you'll realize that it is very difficult to please everybody in this job."

Miss Deal, like many people who enjoy throwing out a challenge, was nervous when it was taken up. She reddened and looked confused. So Miss Stanton, kind of heart, sought for something to say and landed on Emmie. "She's much the best of them, isn't she?"

"Infinitely the best of them. She'd get a scholarship I think, but of course that hag of a mother wouldn't let her sit! I mentioned it to her once when she came up to the school about some boots. She carried on abominably. They ought to afford it, poorer people have. Look at the Longs. She's a drunken old beast and ought to be shot."

"Yes, it does make you sick, especially when you look at Freddie, and that poor little Johnny in the baby room. Still, when you take glands and heredity into consideration perhaps she should be pitied too. Really these days you can't tell right from wrong."

"You'll put Emmie on your register then?" asked Miss Deal who had a swollen gland in her own neck and thought that the conversation should be changed.

So Emmie went into Miss Stanton's class and the great illusion began.

First there was Miss Stanton. She was one of those women who, owning curly hair, a decent skin and an intelligent expression, manage to convey an impression of prettiness. In repose her face wore a look of discontent that was likely to deepen with the passing of the years. It was a discontent easily traced to its source. She was thirty years old, and she was isolated. Her independent nature and her need for self-expression had made her choose rather to be head of a country school than to walk delicately as an assistant in a town one, waiting for promotion that might never come. And, (as a rule to which exceptions are known), the village school mistress cannot stoop to marry a labourer. Farmers seldom stoop to marry school teachers. Add to this social difficulty that there is a strange prejudice against marrying a teacher at all and it is easy to understand that pretty and intelligent as

Miss Stanton might be, she was doomed to celibacy almost as certainly as if she had taken the veil.

She was not completely conscious of this; would perhaps have been startled and annoyed if some one had pointed to this as a cause for her preference for romantic literature, her occasional bursts of ungovernable temper, her out-of-school lassitude. She read a great deal of poetry, deriving strange satisfaction from such phrases as,

> I shall not have him at my feet,
> And yet my feet are on the flowers.

Taxed to explain what that meant to her she would have boggled badly. Still, boggle or no, the Miss Stantons of this world are not to be disparaged. They at least avoid the nymphomania that overtakes their less intelligent sisters. Denied the apples they declare the turnip to be the fruit of paradise, the indigestion consequent upon the consumption thereof, divine ecstasy. And they are kind, especially when it ministers to their self-importance to be kind. They support charities and reform societies. And in many an outlying village a Miss Stanton is at this moment holding an outpost of civilization, expressing views, giving advice, guiding public opinion, stopping the dyke against superstition and ignorance.

When she cared to bid for it, that is when she was teaching something that she felt strongly about, Emmie's Miss Stanton had complete control and enormous influence over her mixed and apathetic classes. She could put as much enthusiasm and life into a public reading of *Treasure Island* as into her private perusal of the *Hound of Heaven*. (Perhaps no description of this woman would convey as much as a glance at the marked passages of that poem. "By many a hearted casement curtained red." "When she lit her glimmering tapers round the day's dead sanctities." And other such.)

She had "discovered" a book called *Precious Bane* before even Mr. Baldwin had heard of it. She adored it. Apart from its evident and genuine beauty it appealed to her (though she did not realize this) because it was that most ancient story of Cinderella, redressed. And how lovely was its new guise. She could not bear to think that all these girls would never know Sarn, and the Mere, and the market town: so on Friday afternoons she would read it aloud to a selected group of the oldest girls. Who knew? There might be a Prue Sarn hidden there somewhere; some one to whom the perception of beauty might compensate for the poverty of her lot. And indeed there was Emmie Bacon with her arms folded on her desk and her eyes fixed on the reader's face and her own pinched little countenance changing with every changing scene in the story, dreamy, indignant, wondering, amused, sorrowful.

Oh, the Friday afternoons of that her twelfth summer: the scent of wild flowers and chalk from the classroom mingling with the scent of the lime-trees outside: the faint sound of the cuckoo's call: the annoyance of the bee trapped in the window. The knowing that the last precious moments of the school week were running through your fingers like water and that for two whole days after this you would neither see her face nor hear her voice. What poignancy did these lend to the story! All life was altered. Fields and woods, birds and dragonflies ceased to be a lovely haphazard backcloth to a squalid life in the cottage: they became life itself.

The flowering of the acacia-trees by Dr. Brigg's gate became a spiritual experience. Emmie slipped out of the house at night in order to walk alone where the fallen petals whitened the path. She thought — a pale pool of broken blossom; she toyed with the alternative — spilled blossom. She became in that summer a poet.

A poet who went home to a mother who had seen her slip away and suspected the worst. "Sneaking out to muck about with boys. You're beginning early, you little bitch."

A poet who went to bed on a pile of verminous rags, shared with Freddie who had a weakness of the bladder, and Edna and Willie in a room whose window had only one pane that opened. And she had lately read in Miss Stanton's *Rupert Brooke*, so kindly lent, "In some cool room that's open to the night", and "green leaves in a darkened chamber".

All the things that she had hitherto taken for granted began to show themselves in their true horror: how could she have been blind to them so long?

And if Miss Stanton could have seen the leaven at work in the child's mind she would have been glad. For like those who shouted "Crucify Him!" and many others since, she knew not what she did.

14

3

A year passed. Freddie reached his fourteenth birthday and promptly gave up the struggle to read about fat cats or big buns, or to guide a pen through the intricacies of "fredy baken". Dr. Briggs, who had always been very pleasant to Freddie, having some notion of how early and heavily he had been handicapped, gave him a job as "boot and stick" boy at his house. Very soon Edna would reach the magic age and Mrs. Bacon was looking forward to the time when she too could leave "that bloody school".

It hadn't taken Mrs. Bacon a year to discover what school and Miss Stanton meant to Emmie, therefore she never failed to apply the foulest terms of her limited vocabulary to both. There had been the most sickening row over "Poems of Today" which Miss Stanton had lent Emmie and which Mrs. Bacon had thrust under the kettle saying, "I'll find a use for the mucky rubbish". Emmie had shrieked and tried to snatch the book from the fire, but the flames licked round it and caused her unwillingly to withdraw her hand. Mrs. Bacon laughed and Emmie, with a bellow of rage, launched herself scratching and kicking upon her mother. Mrs. Bacon shook herself free and aimed a blow, left and right, at Emmie's head. She staggered backward, caught her foot in the leg of a chair and crashed to the floor. Mrs. Bacon laughed again. After that Emmie never brought a book home and was in the house as little as possible herself.

In that summer, the one following Emmie's twelfth birthday, Mr. Bacon met with an accident. Taken from his usual sphere to lend a hand with the haying he managed to transfix his foot with the prong of a fork. Tetanus set in, and in a remarkably short time his employer was advertising for a stockman and his wife was looking about her in search of profitable diversion. Her bereavement did not distress her. She had exhausted all entertainment that William Bacon had to offer long before Freddie's thoughtlessness had thrust her upon his bed and board. For over fourteen years they had lived in active enmity to one another and now there was the compensation money to spend and her widow's pension to look forward to.

It occurred to her that what she needed was a lodger, and she began looking about for him (no doubt of the sex!). She did not announce her intention by word of mouth, advertisement, or sign in the window; her method was at once more simple and more subtle. She took a good portion of her "club money", and boarded the bus for Stoney Market. There she bought a satin dress, black, but redeemed from any danger of dowdiness by the lavish application of scarlet braid. It was very tight and shiny. At Woolworth's she matched the braid with a pair of large glass earrings and completed her purchases with a sixpenny bottle of perfume, "Lily of the Valley". She then went home and took what was for her an extremely comprehensive wash. She unplaited and brushed out her hair which was a living contradiction to everything that hygiene and beauty culture teach about hair. She brushed it with a very dirty brush about once a week. Generally it hung down her back in a tangled plait, making a dirtier patch upon the back of her filthy blouse. It had never been known to be washed. Sometimes, after a more than usually bitter complaint from the School Nurse it was dressed, with the rest of the family heads, with white precipitate powder and combed with a comb dipped in a solution reputed to remove nits. Yet now, brushed out, it was plentiful and shiny and untouched with grey. She plaited it again and wound the plait round her crown. She put on a satin frock, ripped off a strip of almost black vest which persisted in poking up beyond the braided collar, powdered her red face with white powder that made it look mauve, screwed in the earrings, splashed on the scent and was ready to make her way to The Pot of Flowers.

For a little while, as the bar filled up, she was very subdued. There was no point in alienating any sympathy that was to be had. A man or two, dazzled by the dress and the earrings and the powder, found an answer to the old village question, "What ever made William marry her?" The tight satin dress revealed the heavy bosom and the thick thighs: the black plait shone: her shallow brown eyes darted here and there, or veiled themselves when awkward sympathy was offered her. She admitted that she was feeling "low" (as if to excuse the red braid). But there was no point in "giving way" (as if to explain the earrings). A few cronies of the late William's treated her to a drink or two, and by the time her real quarry arrived she was in fine fettle.

17

All the newcomers were strangers and Mrs. Bacon could tell when they drifted in without turning her head, for the North Country speech sounded harsh and brisk through the drawling East Anglican voices of the natives. They were all strangers and they were almost all skilled men, engaged at the moment in rearing the gaunt ugly walls of the new beet-sugar factory. The Town Council of Stoney Market had refused to allow the erection of the factory in the borough and there was no other suitable water supply nearer to the town than the outskirts of Swything. So there had been these strange faces and voices in the neighbourhood for some weeks and Mrs. Bacon had every reason to hope that somewhere amongst them there might be one who would be willing, even eager, to take advantage of the hospitality that she was offering.

The men, who had been working late and making overtime pay, crowded into the bar and ordered drinks for themselves and one another. It was Saturday night and gradually the slight atmosphere of tension that sprang into being wherever the Swything people and the strangers met, gave way before the influence of the week-end potations. Mrs. Bacon sidled into a strategic position and accepted a Guinness from one of William's fellow-workmen. And then, coming through her powder like the sun on a misty morning, she said distinctly, "Oh yes, I miss 'im. We 'ad our ups and downs like everybody else, but on the 'ole 'e was a good 'usband. Still, no use mopin', gotta be father 'n mother too, to my pore kids, I 'ave. Thinking of taking a lodger I am.

18

There isn't much that a pore woman can do to make ends meet on her own."

She addressed the words to William's friend, but they were not meant for him, he had a wife and family in the village. She was watching the faces of the "sugar beet" men. One of them, a bricklayer named Ted Gibson, looked at her steadily and calculatingly for a moment, and then went on drinking. He had heard, he had noticed, but had he bitten? She wondered. But by the time that her glass was empty and the workman had said "Goo' night" and left the bar, somehow Ted Gibson was at her elbow and it was he who paid for her next drink. She examined him with little sly fluttering glances. A big man, she liked them big; William had been small and wiry. He had a face that looked as though it had been cut with some blunt tool from one of his own bricks, a close, cruel mouth and a bold eye. Attractive, thought Mrs. Bacon.

"I s'pose ye was meanin' bit ye said about takin' lodger?" he asked presently. "Happens I'm lookin' for place mysel'. What would terms be?"

Mrs. Bacon dropped her eyes to the wet-ringed counter. "You could make your own," she said, "it'd depend on what you wanted."

Ted Gibson dropped his eyes too, as far as the thick red throat and the bosom swelling in the tight satin frock, "All ye got, lovey, all ye got," he said, lowering his loud voice.

Mrs. Bacon, despite William, and his suspicions, and the ten little Bacons, was breathing like a girl as she asked, "When'll you come?"

"Monday night, when we knock off. That suit ye? Now what'll ye have? There's time to wet bargain."

They drank together and parted at the door.

"See ye Monday then," he said, "if ye can wait that long."

"I can if you can," said Mrs. Bacon with a giggle.

She went home well pleased.

The never comfortable home life in the cottage was violently disturbed during the next forty-eight hours. Mrs. Bacon, for once, bestirred herself, and in doing so started a great deal of grudging activity among the children. Indescribable rags were routed out of corners and flung upon a bonfire that was still smouldering when the neighbours hung out their washing on Monday. Boots, past even the Bacons' wear, were added to it, and foul smells arose. Mrs. Bacon even went to the length of bringing about a reform which she had idly contemplated ever since that nosey bitch of a School Nurse had inquired how the children slept — namely of separating her boys and girls at night. She cleared the shed and made up a bed of all the better rags and pieces there for Freddie, Willie and Johnny. She was, perhaps, quite unaware that Freddie's habits by now rendered him as unsuitable a bedfellow for his brothers as for his sisters. Her own bed she decorated with a pair of new sheets and a vivid counterpane purchased with the tail end of the "club money". She made no secret of the fact that it was to be the lodger's bed as well.

20

On Monday afternoon, discarding her custom of sending Edna or Emmie to the shop, she dressed herself and went into the store where she bought a jar of very scarlet raspberry jam, plentifully bepipped, a tin of herrrings in tomato sauce, a pound of bacon and a packet of cigarettes like those she had seen Ted Gibson smoking on Saturday. He was certainly going to have all she'd got.

4

The school had broken up for the summer holiday on the previous Friday, and Emmie, fleeing from the discomfort of her mother's mysterious, ten-years' deferred cleaning, took herself off on a melancholy pilgrimage that included the beloved school building and the cottage where Miss Stanton lived. They would both be empty and deserted no doubt, but the mere sight of them would comfort one cast into the outer darkness for five long weeks. However, she found the schoolroom door open, and pausing to discover the reason for this phenomenal thing, she saw that Miss Stanton was darting about inside. A step or two brought Emmie to the door, and showed her, ranged along the nearest desk, a pile of examination papers, some needlework bags, six ragged library books and a fern in a pot.

Miss Stanton, turning from locking a cupboard, saw her shadow against the sunny door and peeped out. "Oh, Emmie," she said, "I wondered who it could be."

"I was passing and I saw the door open. I wondered who was here." Her voice was as good an imitation of Miss Stanton's as loving care could make it.

"I went out to tea last Friday, so I couldn't take home all the things I wanted to," said Miss Stanton, eyeing the unpleasant pile. "I doubt if I shall get them all home now."

"I'll carry some."

"Will you really? Are you sure you can spare the time?"

Emmie nodded.

"I should be grateful. I don't want to make two journeys. I've got such a lot to do, and I'm going away tomorrow morning." She began loading Emmie's outstretched arms with the lightest of the things.

"People yap about teachers' holidays," she continued, as she rammed some knitting-needles into a grubby bag; "they don't think what there is to do in them. I must cover those books though they're hardly worth it. And there're these papers to mark and the lists to make, and all this awful needlework to set up." She lifted the fern to the top of the books, balanced them against her chest and waved to Emmie to go ahead through the door. As she locked it behind her her mood changed and the depression caused by the empty classrooms shed away. They walked together along the dusty road in the hot afternoon sun, the woman aware with lifting heart that for five weeks she would be free of simple interest and tables and Martin Luther's reforms: the child miserably conscious that there'd be no school tomorrow or any tomorrow for thirty-five days; that she wouldn't see Miss Stanton for as long as that, and that there'd be nothing to read.

"Where are you going for your holiday, Miss Stanton?" she asked timidly.

"To Guernsey," said Miss Stanton brightly. "You know where that is?"

"Channel Islands," replied Emmie promptly. "Have you ever been there before?"

"No; but I've heard that it's very lovely. On a clear day you can look out and the water is the colour of blue hyacinths, and the sea has other islands in it, ringed with white where the waves hit them."

"Sounds lovely," said Emmie.

"Doesn't it?" Then she remembered that Emmie was unlikely ever to see it, so continued, "Still, most things are lovelier as you imagine them, I think. And it's got to be a beautiful sight to beat that." They were passing Dr. Briggs's garden and she waved towards it with her less encumbered hand. Through the iron gates set in a yew hedge they could see a stretch of path, paved with dim red tiles and bordered with lavender bushes, delphiniums, and great white daisies. They peered through the gates for a moment and then tramped on in the dust.

"Seems odd, doesn't it?" said Emmie.

"What does?" asked Miss Stanton, smiling at her.

"Such lovely things, and such nasty ones, in the same world."

"That's a problem that has baffled wiser heads than yours, my dear."

"You don't understand it either?"

"Gracious no. And people are even odder. You'll find one person who'll spend a lifetime cleaning up a mess another has made."

"Like Wilberforce," Emmie said, pleased to mention something that she knew.

Miss Stanton nodded. Her mind had gone off wondering if anybody would ever clear up the mess that Mrs. Bacon, and others like her, had made of the gift of procreation. For as Emmie had looked at her and said, "Like Wilberforce," something had stirred in her. The child was so thin and pale, so badly dressed, and yet so patient and sweet and intelligent. What chance would she ever have? The State might try. Mrs. Bacon stood firm in its path, with a citizen's rights but none of a citizen's responsibility.

"Come in and have some tea with me, Emmie," she said as they reached the gate of her cottage. I'll steal an hour from my packing, she thought to herself as she unlocked the door.

They stepped into the cool, almost musty shade of the cottage's one room. To Emmie, whose knowledge of interiors had been gained in the Bacon cottage and the back-kitchens of houses whither she had been sent on errands, the low, whitewashed room, with its bright chintzes and stained floor, was like a glimpse into another world. A bowl of sweet peas stood on the gate-legged table, and another filled the space between the little frilled curtains at the window. The fireplace was hidden by a hydrangea in full flower.

"Dump the things down there, child, and if you want to wash your hands come into the kitchen."

The kitchen was a lean-to building with a red flagged floor, and a number of shelves covered with white paper. An oil stove stood on an up-ended sugar box in one corner and over this Miss Stanton busied herself. To the faint cheery hissing that preceded the kettle's singing they washed their hands in an enamel bowl and dried them on a rough roller towel, striped with yellow, that hung behind the door.

The shelves were full of coloured pots and jars. Emmie would have loved to look into each one, but she only stared at their outsides while Miss Stanton uncovered a tray and reached down another cup, saucer and plate from the shelf. Then she made the tea in a flowered teapot and they went back into the sitting-room. All Emmie's soul was in her roving eyes. For years, for her lifetime indeed, that humble little room remained in her mind, representative of a state, rather than a place, to be remembered and longed for, as some men say we remember and sicken for Heaven. There was a shelf of books, other books by Mary Webb ranged by the familiar faded cover of *Precious Bane*. There were bright pictures of flowers on the white walls; a blue and rose coloured rug underfoot. She thought of her own home with a shudder of deadly repulsion. Miss Stanton's voice broke in on it, "How much sugar, Emmie?"

"One, miss, please," said Emmie politely.

"Only one?"

"Well, miss, two is nicer, really." Then she went perfectly crimson; should she have said, "Two *are*

25

nicer"? But Miss Stanton seemed not to notice, "I should think so," she said, and slipped in three.

They were such dainty little cups, all matching, and with silver spoons in the saucers. It was the first time that Emmie had ever handled a saucer. She took an appreciative and noisy sloop at her tea, observed Miss Stanton drinking silently, and drank silently too. They ate thin bread and butter and strawberry jam and generous slices of dark shop cake. And Emmie thought that this would end in a moment: it was a pity that she couldn't just die now, in some easy and untroublesome fashion and never have to say good-bye, or see her mother any more. And Miss Stanton thought, I'd like to adopt you, Emmie, but I can't afford it, and at heart I'm as selfish as everybody else. And very soon she mentioned her packing, and the necessity of having a bath, a lengthy business when water has to be lifted by pailsful into the copper and out again into a hipbath and finally baled out and emptied down the drain.

"I'll go now," said Emmie, taking the hint and getting to her feet. She went to replace the book she had been holding and Miss Stanton, moved by the same impulse that had made her issue the invitation to tea, said, "Keep it, dear, it'll be something to read in the holidays."

"Have you forgotten your other book?" Emmie said darkly.

Miss Stanton's face coloured with her quick vivid blush. "I had forgotten, as a matter of fact. Anyway try with that one. You might have better luck, and it's a cheap one. It wouldn't matter."

"I wouldn't give her the pleasure," said Emmie bitterly as she drove the book into the tightly packed shelf.

"Parents can be a trial." There was a forced lightness about Miss Stanton's voice. "You'll have to look forward to the time when you'll leave school and be able to do as you like." She accompanied Emmie to the door and stooped to kiss her as she said good-bye. She was aware that the light holiday feeling that had fallen upon her as they left the school that afternoon had vanished completely. I wouldn't feel like this if I'd asked some other brat to help me home with the things, she thought. But perhaps all their homes are like that, and all their mothers, only Emmie is more articulate than the others. No, that was an unfair thought, she reflected, remembering most of the Swything women, gallantly struggling to make ends meet on thirty shillings a week, or less; cheerful, humorous, uncomplaining. She cursed Mrs. Bacon as she set about the preparations for her bath.

Meanwhile Emmie was hurrying back through the summer dust. The sun was still hot and she panted as she went, but she had been away longer than she had intended. It would be dreadful if mother started inquiries that would reveal that she had been wasting her time with "that bitch of a teacher".

By the pond in the middle of the Green a group of boys were catching frogs, destined to a death better not described. Emmie averted her eyes as she hurried past.

" 'I come in the little things,' saith the Lord." Why the hell, Emmie wondered, in Bacon idiom, couldn't He do something to stop that kind of beastly business? He could fool about with fire on Mount Carmel and wine in Cana. Never anything very useful. Never a martyr had been salvaged from the stake: though surely a miracle at such a crisis would have done more good than all the blood of all the martyrs. God, of course, couldn't be expected to understand pain. He was a spirit. He had never had any suffering flesh to endure. But you might have hoped for something from Jesus Christ. His death had been horrible too. And no miracle had delivered Him, though the midday darkness and the torn veil of the Temple proved that God had been watching. Yet there was the fact that Miss Stanton was always impressing during the Scripture lessons, the fact that Christ was God too. So God had known pain, everything in fact that the grown-up counterparts of the boys by the pond could devise. Perhaps He suffered, as Emmie did, with every blown-up frog. Perhaps the secret was there. The bitterness was melting in her heart. She paused to consider the profundity of that thought, and then remembered her mother. She ran the last couple of hundred yards to the cottage. Freddie and Edna were not to be seen, but Willie and Johnny and little toddling Winnie were in the yard, cautiously peering in at the window like hungry sparrows.

"Can't go in," observed Willie, as Emmie joined them, "lodger there."

Emmie took a peep through the window. Mrs. Bacon and the lodger had just finished tea. He was leaning back in his chair with his coat off and the leather belt loosened about his middle. Mrs. Bacon held a smouldering cigarette between her thick thumb and finger. She was listening to something that he was saying, and burst into a hearty laugh when his strange yelping voice was silent. The lodger took up the fork that he had used for the herrings and began systematically to pick his teeth with it. Emmie's hatred of him dated from that moment.

5

And went on increasing. For it was plain that the Bacon children had lost rather than gained by their mother's queer attempt to be "father 'n mother both". William had been a poor father, but he was seldom at home and seldom angry with them. On the rare occasions when he had "fetched one a clout" Mrs. Bacon, from sheer perversity, had rushed to the defence. Now, however, she had eyes and ears for no one but her new bedfellow. If he complained of the children's noise she picked up the nearest weapon and chased them out of the house. Unless this happened at mealtimes it was no great hardship in summer when out of doors was far more pleasant than in. But when the evenings grew cold and damp they were obliged to beg humbly for admission to the shed that was the boys' bedroom, and sometimes Freddie and Willie, warned of the impending invasion, derived great pleasure from barricading the door against the other four. Ted Gibson often struck blows on his own account, and he was very heavy-handed. Mrs. Bacon, deep in the infatuation that overtakes many, and better, women at her age, never lifted even a whisper of protest. The little Bacons, fortunately, were not particularly depressed by this treatment: they expected very little in the way of comfort and by being quiet and nimble they managed to escape much actual ill-treatment. Emmie, indeed, preferred Ted Gibson when he was cross. Sometimes in a goodnatured or maudlin moment he would call her "bonnie" and pull her down on to his knees, twist his thick fingers in her hair and try to give her kisses that smelt of stale tobacco and beer. That roused in her a panic that his roughest word or blow could never do. However she quickly realized that her mother's presence was a sure preventive of such behaviour, and she took pains to avoid the house if her mother were out and Ted Gibson in. On one occasion when he had been into Stoney for something he had brought back a large bag of cheap toffees, and meeting her at the gate, said, very pleasantly, "There's summat for a bonnie lass in my pocket." Emmie had stood, stricken with that paralytic chill that came over her whenever he was available to her.

"Go on, pull them out," he said, thrusting his hips towards her. There was something in his voice and eye that presaged a sudden change of mood. To avoid an outbreak of irritability that might last all the rest of the evening she inserted a hand into the pocket of his coat and drew out the paper bag. But not swiftly enough. That time she was soundly kissed. His rough chin rasped her face, and her lips were damped by his. She thrust the toffees into Winnie's hands as soon as she was in the kitchen, and rushed to the sink to wash her outraged face.

The next time he tried that trick (and his uninventive mind could think of none better), Winnie was with her. She lifted the child up before her and said, "Feel in Uncle Ted's pocket, Winnie." Winnie felt. "Kiss him for the sweeties," said Emmie, very pleasantly. Ted Gibson backed away, and that was the end of the sweet business.

Early in December the last brick was laid at the beet-sugar factory and Ted, who was at least not averse to work, gathered his things together and went back "to t' North" where he had heard that temporary work was to be had. Mrs. Bacon stormed and raved when he announced his intention, but she might have saved her breath. She had no hold at all upon her lodger. After he had gone she relapsed into melancholy. The black dress, very shabby now, hung upon a nail behind the lonely bedroom door. Her hair swung down her back almost all the time. Despite the buns and oranges provided for the school-children by Mrs. Briggs and a few other charitable ladies, the Bacons had but a poor Christmas. They hung round the windows of other cottages where other, luckier children had Christmas trees, and they sang carols so often and so dolefully at the doors of the farmhouses that at last even the kindly who had given them pennies and oranges at first, came out and bade them begone. The very first notes of "Good King Wenceslas" caused people to say, "Oh Lord, the Bacons again."

6

The New Year came, the New Year that every one had hoped would be so happy for every one else. Chilblains and cracked lips were added to the troubles of life: but at least, with Ted Gibson gone, the children could crowd round the fire in the evenings and enjoy the blazing of the sticks that they had gathered during the day. And with Winnie back in mother's bed, Emmie and Edna had no longer to balance themselves on the edge of their narrow one.

But in February the factory authorities commenced to build a colony of houses for their workpeople: and Ted Gibson duly reappeared at the cottage.

Absence had not improved him. He arrived back in the worst of tempers, declaring that he was ill, and certainly looking it. The brick-red colour had gone from his face and some livid red spots showed up startlingly upon his pallor.

On the very first evening he and Mrs. Bacon had a row that sent the children helter-skelter to the shed where they huddled together to keep warm and rubbed their chilblains.

"It won't last," said Emmie, who remembered other quarrels. "They'll make it up and probably go down to

The Pot of Flowers tomorrow night and we'll have the house to ourselves."

But, unlike the other quarrels this one continued. Some "lousy dirty tart" was connected with it: that phrase was for ever upon Mrs. Bacon's tongue. And Emmie, wise in the ways of her sordid world, assumed that Ted had "lodged" with the person thus described during his absence from Swything. Altercations rang loud through the house. More and more often the children spent the evenings in the shed. Even The Pot of Flowers seemed to have lost its attraction, though Mrs. Bacon occasionally visited it with a jug.

Presently, for no reason at all, Emmie began to imagine that she was, in some mysterious fashion, mixed up in the trouble. Stray words and sentences that didn't make any sense stuck in her mind and convinced her.

"I've seen you making sheep's eyes at her. What about Edna?"

"Ye couldn't be sure of Edna."

And, "That's the latest way to get a girl I've ever heard of." To which Ted Gibson replied, "It's t' God's truth. It's t' only cure. Doctors is all my eye."

She wasn't mentioned in these fragments, but the talk had stopped when she showed herself on the stairs. And once again she heard her mother say, "I never been on the wrong side of the law before. You'll get us both a stretch."

What was it all about? She found herself having to switch her mind away from the puzzle in order to pay attention to her lessons.

There came the night when her mother stopped her on her way up to bed and offered her a cup of cocoa. The very surprise of the offer might have warned her — but of what? And the night was cold. Ted Gibson moved back from his place in front of the fire and she dragged the stool forward, sat down, accepted the cocoa and tried not to mind the way he was looking at her, or his distinct personal odour. It was very strong cocoa and not at all nice. Under its extreme sweetness there was a stealthy taste of something that she vaguely remembered but could not name. Not to drink it, or to complain of the taste, would only result in being sent to bed with a tingling ear, and she concluded that her mother had been using the mug for some strange purpose of her own before making the cocoa in it.

She drank it slowly, making it last out because it was so comfortable here by the fire. Warm, warm, warm and drowsy. She swirled the last drops of the thick dregs round the mug to collect what was left of the sugar; and as she did so she sniffed and remembered what the cocoa had reminded her of. That time when she had toothache so badly and Cissie Grey's grandmother had given her some laudanum in an eggcup to rub on her gum. But that was nonsense, laudanum was poison, even mother wouldn't put it into cocoa! Anyway it was too late now, whatever it was she had drunk it: and she was most blissfully comfortable. The room was swaying and fading. She was falling, falling, falling, asleep upon a stool. From an immense distance she heard her mother say, "You sure it'll be all right?" And Ted Gibson said "As right as rain, and all t' good times back again eh?" But the words had no significance for her. She did not know what was wrong with the man, nor what was commonly supposed to be a cure, nor why Edna wouldn't do.

They carried her up on to Mrs. Bacon's bed, and went down to finish the beer that was left in the jug.

Possibly they sat too long; or perhaps Mrs. Bacon, anxious to avoid a murder, had not been sufficiently liberal with the dose. Emmie woke, just soon enough. Her mother's bed. Herself without her frock, laid out on the bed alone and helpless. Ted Gibson getting undressed by the dancing light of the candle. For a moment the fear that had come in small measure when he had touched her hair or hand, flooded over her, so that she was pressed to the bed, unable even to breathe. Then that wild unreasoning thing that we call instinct woke and took control. From what she fled she hardly knew: and action, when it came, was not what she would, in her senses, have chosen. With hardly a sound she flung herself off the bed, across the strip of floor, full at the crazy little window. Ted Gibson with his trousers dropped round his feet took a step and stumbled just as the whole fabric of the window gave way with a splintering of rotten wood, and Emmie, shaken and bruised but uninjured, scrambled to her feet in the yard below.

It was raining and she was soaked through in five minutes. The water poured down her face and made a waterfall between her shoulders and another over her quaking stomach. The wind stopped her breath, and her heart too, when it seemed to bring sounds of pursuit from behind. The road hurt her feet, and there was a stitch in her side that at any other time would have demanded that she stop and touch her toes. But she ran on and on, stopping only once, to hear the church clock drop one solemn boom and then another into the night. Half past, but half past what? "From Mechlin church steeple we heard the half-chime, and Joris broke silence with, 'Yet there is time'." But was there? How long had she slept? If it was later than half past eleven Miss Stanton would be in bed. And would Emmie dare to wake her? What alternative? She might lie down in a ditch. Then she would die of exposure. But already she was exposed, half-naked and half-drowned, and she had never felt less like dying in her life. Her pounding heart, her aching but swiftly moving limbs urged on her the need for haste, but not the need for rest. She must live: and to do that she must get to the one person who could help her. The one person who would see in this, not the end of a childhood, but the beginning of something. What Miss Stanton would make of it Emmie did not know, but something.

With a moan of relief she saw, while she was yet some distance away, that a light was burning in Miss Stanton's cottage. She opened the gate and almost immediately a voice cried sharply from within, "Who's there?" Emmie drew in her breath carefully, and said, "Me, Emmie Bacon, please, miss." But the words were all lost in her gasping, and the next instant Miss Stanton flung open the door, so that a long streak of light fell on the wet path, and Emmie could see her outlined in the doorway. She was wearing pyjamas and a dressing-gown and a cigarette glowed in her hand. That spark of light against the dark of Miss Stanton's body made Emmie think of pistols, and she gasped, after another careful breath, "Don't shoot me, miss. It's only Emmie Bacon."

"Emmie Bacon," said Miss Stanton in an astounded voice. "What ever are you here for? Is something the matter?" And immediately she knew that something was, for, her eyes accustoming themselves to the dimness, she could see in the faint light from the door the child's bare shoulders gleaming white, and her hands, dripping water, held out in an unconscious gesture of appeal. She thought inconsequently of that awful "Rock of Ages" picture, even as she said, "Come in, child. Has some one been trying to drown you?" And at that question Emmie was tempted to turn round and run back into the darkness, for it opened up a problem that she had not considered as she ran . . . in what words could she possibly tell Miss Stanton what had happened, or rather what would have happened had she not waked just then; had Ted Gibson not been stepping carefully out of his trousers; had the window not given way so easily? There were ways of saying it, of course, but could one use them to Miss Stanton? By the time that she had thought this Miss Stanton's arm was round her and she was being hustled up the path into the house.

"Pull off every stitch you've got on. I've been having a bath, and the copper's still hot. I'll have one ready for you in just one minute."

Emmie stripped, glad that Miss Stanton's rapid dashes to and from the kitchen gave her no chance to see the torn and dirty vest and knickers which she took off and screwed into as small a ball as possible. As if at the bidding of a genius a rubber bath-mat was spread before the fire, and on it stood a bath of steaming water, soft water, dark and greenish, and Miss Stanton poked up the fire and threw on an armful of logs and handed Emmie a big cake of pink soap and said, "Hop in quickly", and then ran upstairs so swiftly that the whole cottage seemed to rock. She came down again with a huge white towel and a pair of pyjamas exactly like her own and laid them in the corner of the hearth. Then, observing Emmie energetically soaping her toes, she picked up the discarded clothes and thrust them into the dying copper fire. Next she hurried Emmie out of the bath and gave her a brisk towelling and helped her into the pyjamas. By that time the effort and the shock and the laudanum had taken their toll and Emmie dropped back into the easy chair like a doll that had lost most of its sawdust.

Miss Stanton cleared away the bath things as quickly as she had prepared them, then she lighted a fresh cigarette and crouched down on the fender, picking up the poker as she did so, and idly prodding the fire with it as she said, "Now, would you like to tell me all about it, or leave it till the morning?"

Emmie started to speak and cry at the same moment. Words and sobs struggled against one another, then the sobs won and she was crying bitterly. Miss Stanton remembered the way in which she had said that her mother enjoyed putting books under the kettle, and imagined that something like that had happened again. She was utterly unprepared for what Emmie at last brought out. She turned white and then red and said "God" under her breath. Then some sixth sense sprang to life within her, and she realized that Emmie had, fortunately, missed some of the horror of the affair, and that by right, immediate treatment she might prevent the incident from leaving an ineffable scar. She controlled herself, and said with commendable lightness, "Well, that was nasty. But people do funny things when they're drunk. And you weren't hurt, were you?"

"No, only just where I cut myself on the glass. You see, only one pane broke at first, then it all dropped out into the yard."

"And you with it. That must have looked rather funny. Would you like some hot milk? I was just going to have it when you came."

She slipped an aspirin into Emmie's share of it, they sipped together by the glowing fire and then went up to bed.

Emmie slept the deep sleep of exhaustion: Miss Stanton lay awake until the clock struck four. In that space of time she had settled on several courses of action. She had written about ten letters to the inspector of the N.S.P.C.C., she had given evidence before twenty different magistrates; she had thrashed Ted Gibson with a horsewhip (she enjoyed that thought); and she had severely mauled and pummelled Mrs. Bacon. But every one of these procedures had the same single draw-back. They would only impress upon Emmie that something awful had happened. The less made of the affair, the better, thought Miss Stanton as she turned first her head and then her pillow. A crime had been attempted, somebody ought to pay; but it looked as if it might be Emmie who would pay. She'd be taken away, that was certain, and put in a Home, possibly.

Here Miss Stanton reached for her torch, looked at her watch, felt Emmie's forehead for signs of fever, which she did not find, switched off the torch and lay down to go through the whole thing again in her mind, until she, too, fell asleep from sheer exhaustion.

She was awakened by a sound that she associated with being away on holiday, the chink of a cup in its saucer. Emmie was standing by the bedside with a cup of tea that she was steadying with both hands. "Hullo," said Miss Stanton.

Emmie returned the greeting in her prim little imitation of her teacher's voice and added, "I made it properly, miss, warmed the teapot and everything."

"Well, this is a treat," said Miss Stanton, sitting up in bed and reaching for the tea. She felt tired and depressed. This was the tomorrow that had caused her so much anxious thought. What was the first . . . and the best . . . thing to do? This was the peaceful English village that people raved about. This was God's good green earth that everything was right with. Christ! muttered Miss Stanton to her tea.

"Did you have one yourself, child? Well, go and get one. You'd better put on that coat, no, the checked one, over those pyjamas. Aren't they huge? I can't think how you found your hands and feet this morning at all."

Emmie smiled, slipped into the coat and pattered away downstairs. She hummed softly to herself as she set the table with a lace tea-cloth. The loveliness of waking up beside Miss Stanton, admiring her hair spread out on the pillow, the joy of being able to surprise her with a cup of tea, and now to be getting the breakfast ready in this dear little room, were sufficient to obliterate the thought of either last night's horror, or this joy's transience. She was not yet fourteen.

Miss Stanton came down soon and helped with the eggs and toast. She praised Emmie's fire and the table. They kept up a stream of chatter through the meal, and then Miss Stanton said, rather gravely, "You can't come to school this morning, Emmie, because of your clothes. I want you to lock the door, and not go outside. Well, of course, out at the back, if you want to, but don't stand about. Your mother may have guessed where you are. She may even come here, but you're not to answer the door. Lock the back as well. There's a dress and a petticoat on the bed upstairs, if you want a job you can unpick the hems and cut off about a foot and turn up fresh hems. Or rather you needn't unpick them, just slice off a piece. I'll be back at half past twelve, and I'll bring you some shoes. What size do you take?"

"You are good to me," said Emmie, misty-eyed.

"Not a bit. Oh, by the way, Mrs. Steggles will be coming in to clean up. I must write her a note and tell her not to."

"I'll clean it up, miss."

She watched Miss Stanton pull her hat down over one eye, turn up her collar and tuck her bag under her arm. There she was, just as Emmie had seen her on the morning of every school day for nearly three years. It was a sight to which she looked forward from one evening until the next morning. Today, although she was seeing it, it was different. She was being left behind. In the sudden silence after Miss Stanton's departure she began to feel sad, to remember her terrified running through the rain, and to wonder what would happen next. She shed a few tears as she swept and dusted. In the middle of her sewing she stopped, stricken by the thought that her mother might be at school. If she guessed, as Miss Stanton had supposed she would, she would go there and be abusive. A step on the path made her hold her breath. The step sounded all round the cottage, then retreated down the path, and Emmie, peering from the bedroom window, saw Mrs. Steggles turn into the lane. She had come at once upon receiving Miss Stanton's note. She could not understand why her services were not required that morning. She could only conclude that there was a visitor who mustn't be seen: that meant a man, and it was worth putting on your outdoor things and walking that far to see if you could catch a sight of him.

Emmie finished her sewing and put on the underclothes that had been left out for her. She lifted the blue dress over her head and buttoned it down the front. Accustomed to be dressed in anything that came to hand she did not mind the shoulder seams that came half-way to her elbows, or the curious pelican pouch that resulted from the tightened belt. She preened happily before the strip of mirror that ran down the inner side of the bedroom door. Then she peeled and boiled some potatoes and set the cold beef on the table, frowning over the knives and forks. Sooner than had seemed possible she heard Miss Stanton calling at the front door, and ran to open it.

"Anybody been?" asked Miss Stanton at once.

"Only Mrs. Steggles. She prowled round the house."

"Like Satan, seeking what she might discover. Well, I've seen your mother."

"What was she like? Very angry?"

"Only at first. How nicely you've set the table, child. Oh, and potatoes. How nice, I never have them at midday."

She washed her hands and sat down to the table as if she were very hungry, but Emmie, watching closely, could see that she ate her food as if it were so much tasteless material that had to be disposed of as neatly and quickly as possible. As soon as the last morsel disappeared she lit a cigarette, and kicking over a log that lay smouldering on the fire, threw herself into the armchair and gave herself over to her thoughts. Emmie moved her fork more and more slowly until it stopped altogether. Something had upset Miss Stanton. She could only conclude that it had been her mother's visit to the school. She could imagine the scene, and she could not imagine a row in which the person who shouted and swore wouldn't come off victor. She couldn't possibly imagine, and would hardly have believed what had taken place: how Mrs. Bacon, all black satin and bluster, had arrived at the school, secretly hoping to find Emmie in her place. It was almost twelve and Miss Stanton had dismissed the children and hurried them away, all except those who stayed for dinner, whom she banished to the Infants room. Then she shut the door and began on Mrs. Bacon.

It was no fair fight, for Mrs. Bacon, under the bluster, had been deadly scared. And the school-teacher was fired with real indignation. She had only to imagine what would have happened if the window had not given way . . . quite vaguely, but horribly to imagine . . . and her blood boiled.

Nevertheless she began calmly, "Do you know where Emmie is?"

"No," said Emmie's mother, "do you?"

"Do you want the police in on this?" was the next question, and Mrs. Bacon replied with a foolishly emphatic negative.

Then Miss Stanton began. She lashed Mrs. Bacon with words that penetrated even her layers of self-deceit and fat and bluster and ignorance. She talked till words failed her, and then, with a pang of delight shooting through her rage, she leaned forward, took Mrs. Bacon's fat shoulders in her hands and shook her violently to and fro until her teeth rattled in her head and her head lolled. Only breathlessness made her stop: she finished with a smart slap of the plump red cheek and a push that sent the heavy woman reeling amongst the desks.

All the rude messages she had ever received, all the pity that she had ever felt for the Bacon children, all the worry of the present situation were avenged in delicious violence. She leaned back against her own table and thought ridiculously of Arnold's words, "The gods are happy." Sure they were. Hadn't one of them said, "Vengeance is mine"? Mrs. Bacon recovered her balance, but not her poise. If her own tin kettle had turned and bitten her she would have felt no more surprise. That this little thin pale bitch of a teacher should dare! Anger momentarily replaced fear: she came towards Miss Stanton, menace in her eye.

"Don't open your mouth to me," cried the teacher breathlessly. "Make a sound and I'll raise such a row that you'll never forget it. I'll see you in gaol. I'd send for a policeman now if it weren't for Emmie. The laudanum in the cocoa would condemn you, apart from anything else. Get out, and keep out. I know where Emmie is, and she'll stay there. Lift a finger to find her, mention her name and you're for it. I mean that." Two pairs of furious eyes met and did battle for a moment, and then, without a word, Mrs. Bacon turned and lumbered out of the schoolroom. When she reached the cottage she found that Ted Gibson had taken advantage of her absence and gone, taking all his things with him. There would be no more good old times. And that in itself was almost punishment enough for Mrs. Bacon.

Emmie watched Miss Stanton's face for a few moments and then flung herself down on the rug at her feet, crying, "You're worried. It's all my fault. I didn't ought to have come here."

45

"Don't say 'didn't ought'", said her teacher mechanically, and then, "Oh, child, don't fret so. I'm only thinking. Of course you were right to come. I'm very glad you did. It's the future I'm thinking of. You can't leave school yet, anyway, and I think you deserve a bit extra in the way of education. There's just a chance that I might get you into a place that belongs to a woman who was at college with me. We'll try that first, anyway. We'll go and let her see what a nice little girl you are. We'll go to Stoney Market early tomorrow and get you some clothes and then go on by train."

"Won't it . . . I mean it's going to cost a lot," said Emmie doubtfully. "I think I'd better get a place. I'm quite tall for my age."

"That's against the law," said Miss Stanton firmly.

"But the money . . ." said Emmie.

"I can afford it. Haven't you ever read or heard what a colossal amount teachers earn? And if you go to school and work hard you might even be one yourself. Then you can pay me back."

"I'll do the very best I can," said Emmie, from her heart.

7

The friend whom Miss Stanton remembered at this crisis had spent the first twenty years of her life as Alice Stokes. As Alice Stokes she had been known during her first year of training at the college, where with Helen Stanton and ninety-eight other young females she had gone through a course of arduous, if unambitious study. But she had been christened Alison Frances Stokes and during her second year she had become very particular about the "Alison"! and after she had left college she realized the possibility of the "Frances". How easily did it become "Francis": how smoothly link itself with that undistinguished "Stokes".

She had been the very worst student of her year; not because she was lazy or stupid, but because she had absolutely no brain for abstractions. She had been obliged to take the examination that qualified her for entry four times. And therein lay her difference. Three failures had not persuaded her that college was not for her. She had the persistence and the blind perseverance of a rat undermining a warehouse wall. And having at last attained her desire, how she worked! She burned her midnight oil: she scraped acquaintance with any girl who was reputed to be specially good at any subject. She toadied to lecturers, so that when the question of sending her down as hopeless arose, she did not lack for voices that said, "Though she may not be clever she has character which is what the elementary teacher needs far more than intelligence." So she stayed and in the end failed to take her certificate. No student, no lecturer was there to supply the answers to the terrible questions that faced her; her papers went in almost blank.

Twenty-one years spent in pursuing something that had eluded her at the end. She went back to her humble home and fretted and sulked and upset her family for almost three months. And then one of the lecturers for whom she had run errands and bought flowers from her scanty pocket-money wrote to tell her of a job in a private school that was run by a friend of hers. Would she care for that? For if so, the lecturer would commend her so warmly that there was little or no doubt that she would get it. Alison did care for that; and got it.

It was a worse-paid and more onerous job than those with which the ordinary students of her year were struggling. She went to Arlington House as the most junior and poorly remunerated member of the staff. But her unique method went with her. She never grumbled, she was never tired, she worked like ten women. The rest of the staff, almost all veterans, and torn, as are all staffs, by internecine warfare, found her a thorn in the flesh. Now on this side, now on that: toadying, blacklegging, undermining. But to the aged Head who clung to her school though she could no longer properly steer it, she became a reliable tool, a leaning-post, a trusted friend. When the dying autocrat made her will she stipulated in one clause that Alison Francis-Stokes should be offered the whole concern for the sum of one thousand pounds, and in the next left her a thousand pounds "as a token of esteem". At the age of twenty-seven Alice Stokes entered into her kingdom and saw the reward of all her labours.

The school itself was the result of almost seventy years of growth and change. In its early days, when travel was slow and difficult, it had been very high-class and exclusive, taking only the daughters of gentry, teaching them water colour, dancing and deportment. It meant something in the neighbouring country-side to have been an Arlington House girl. It still meant something, but to a slightly different set of people. For with rapid transportation it was possible for the daughters of the gentry to go farther afield: and with the growing wealth of the trading classes it became possible for the daughters of shopkeepers and farmers to take the place of the vanished great ones. Miss Stokes played the new hand cleverly. She never played down to her audience. Rules of entry were, apparently, as strict as they had ever been, rules of decorum within were as rigid. Arlington House still stood for something. Nice, earnest, rather common mothers who interviewed Miss Francis-Stokes went home subdued and yet elated, glad that their daughters were to have the advantage of her tutelage.

Miss Stokes often smiled her rather bleak smile when she thought of all the ninety-nine girls who *had* passed that examination. Now they were wiping the noses and buttoning the squalid trousers of the proletarian young. They were harassed by inspectors, paid by Burnham scales, grappling with fifties of under-nourished hooligans in dingy classrooooms, waiting every day more wearily for a pension at sixty. If they displeased a parent, the parent came up and raised hell, and there were explanations to be made to committees and apologies to be choked out of angry hearts. If Miss Stokes displeased a parent she was able to say, "There are twenty girls on my lists, any one of whom will be only too pleased to hear that you have removed your daughter." And the parent did the apologizing. She could look out on her smooth lawns with the belt of beeches beyond them, and on her scarlet tunic-ed young ladies at their tennis, and she thought of netball in a concrete playground. The race was not to the swift, it was to the determined, said the cold smile.

Fortunately for Emmie Miss Stokes had fought hard enough for her power to enjoy the feel of it, even after four years or more. And so, listening to Helen Stanton's voice, and recalling how, in the old days, Helen, as the brightest history student of the class, had helped her with her answers, she was moved to show her power by considering Helen's request.

At first she had been quite genuinely shocked at the idea of taking a slum child into her forcing-house for young ladies. "I simply couldn't do it," she had said. "The idea is absurd. Her language, her accent, and her manners, nothing could hide them. I should have complaints from the other girls' parents."

"You know quite well, Alison," Miss Stanton had retorted with guile, "that if you decided to introduce coloured pupils into Arlington House the parents would trust your judgement."

"I have five young Africans and seven Indians here now," put in Miss Stokes stiffly.

"How advanced of you! And a real service to the Empire." Miss Stokes docketed that for future use. Helen always had been bright!

"As for her language, Emmie would know well enough what and what not to say, and her accent is as like mine as she can make it, not that that's anything. But she's very intelligent, and as imitative as a monkey. And I've done nothing but drill table manners into her since I thought of this idea. Really, Alison, you're the only person to whom I can appeal. I must get her out of the village, and I do want her to have the best I can give her."

It was then that Miss Stokes made up her mind to grant the favour. Not, of course, without sufficient hesitation to impress the fact that it was a favour, but in her own good time to grant it graciously.

"She's outside, isn't she? We'll have her in and I'll look at her while we have some tea."

With what pleasure did she ring her bell and watch the prompt appearance of the parlourmaid with the tea. How brightly did the silver shine.

Emmie, with a careful eye upon Miss Stanton, got through tea without a mishap: and was dismissed to the ante-room again.

"She seems quite a nice child," Miss Stokes conceded. "And of course it is incumbent upon some of us who are more fortunate to try to compensate her for her unhappy home. For your sake, Helen, I'll try her. You must impress upon her the necessity, the utter necessity of refraining from anything, any word or gesture that would betray her past. *You* must do that, partly because it will be more acceptable from you, partly because I shall know nothing of it. There is nothing, as you know, so important in education as atmosphere. I must be part of the atmosphere, not part of the plot."

However, thought Miss Stanton, however did I think that you were stupid? You may not know a date now, but you are astute, plausible, worldly-wise.

"I shall never be able to thank you," she said.

Miss Stokes smiled and led the conversation round to their college contemporaries. She had lost touch with them all, but she loved to hear about them. Their little promotions and betrothals and marriages threw her own life into such brilliant contrast. Helen Stanton did not know as much about them as Miss Stokes could have wished, but every phrase was sweet.

"I've kept in touch with just a few of them. Do you remember Ella Frome? Dark, Eton-cropped girl, good at science."

"Oh yes," said the lady who had picked Ella's brain on more than one occasion. "I recall her."

"Well, she's my best friend. She gave up teaching after a year and went into a chemical firm. She's doing very well. We've had several holidays together but I shall have to give them up, she has too much money for me."

"Indeed? What does she make?" asked Miss Stokes, aquiver with curiosity. Had some one outraced her, after all?

"A matter of six hundred, or just over a year," said Miss Stanton, to whom the sum sounded colossal.

"Really?" said Miss Stokes, to whom it didn't sound anything of the kind. But it reminded her of something.

"By the way, about terms. What could you pay for this poor child?"

"It's a question of what you charge, Alison." After all, even a poor elementary teacher must have her pride, especially over her hobby.

"Would twenty guineas a term ruin you, Helen?"

"It's frightfully good of you to take her for so little."

And Miss Stokes, who had been prepared to say, "Well, let's say fifteen and we'll share the burden of the poor child," was very disappointed. She wished she had said thirty and come down to twenty with a gesture. After all, it was the gesture, not the money, that was important. For if she had taken Emmie for nothing she could have made it up by charging some more than usually illiterate parents double for the privilege of saying, "Our Floss, you know, she's at Arlington House".

Helen Stanton spent five more minutes very usefully in telling Alison all the things she liked hearing. How even in her rural fastness she had heard of the wonders of Arlington House. How queer it was what different paths people took. Gladys Mitchell, for instance, had married a blacksmith, and Dora Copping had had an illegitimate baby. She repeated how deeply, deeply obliged she was and ever would be. They parted most amicably. "Say good-bye to Emmie — is that her name? — out there, and then ring the bell. Bletchly will take you to the station. Oh no, no trouble at all. Good-bye, Helen, I'm delighted to see you. And of course I shall see more of you in future. Good-bye." That was how the nice winners behaved to the losers.

Outside in the ante-room Miss Stanton took one of Emmie's hands in hers and sat down beside her on the chintz-covered sofa. "Now, child, I've a lot to say and not much time to say it in. Miss Francis-Stokes is going to have you here. She has lots of girls who would like to come here, but she taking you ahead of them as a favour. You're lucky really, Emmie, but there may be

53

one or two things that you'll find rather difficult. We all have to learn, and some people get a chance to learn earlier than others. Most of the girls at this school have been lucky and learned early . . ." She realized that she wasn't making much headway. "Remember at first to keep your eyes open and your mouth shut and . . ." She went on with a list of things that Emmie might do or say and was on no account to do or say.

"You're pretty bright, Emmie, or I wouldn't have brought you here. Remember that if there's anything you don't understand you can write to me, or go to Miss Francis-Stokes. She's my friend and will be yours, I think, if you're always polite to her. Anything you want of course you will ask me for. Don't hesitate about that. There, I must go." She stood up and Emmie got up too, giving her hand a convulsive clasp before she let her pull it free. Miss Stanton was conscious of a slight thickening in her throat. "Good-bye," she said, with her hand on the bell. God send that the child didn't break down, that she couldn't bear. "Try to be happy, dear, here's your chance. It won't be long till the holidays and we'll have lots of fun then."

8

Except for the fact that she missed Miss Stanton, Emmie was perfectly happy at Arlington House. Uniform is more than half the battle in the struggle for uniformity as all good dictators know. The wearer of a shirt of a certain colour becomes, not "a man in a

54

coloured shirt" but "a coloured Shirt". And Emmie with clean body and hair, and the first underclothes that had ever been bought for her, wearing the scarlet tunic that had been ordered to her measure, was not so very different from the rest of Miss Stokes's young ladies. She kept her eyes, as Miss Stanton had advised, open, and her mouth shut until she had learned the jargon of the moment. Things were all perfectly marvellous or too foul for words, if you judged them from casual conversation. Several of Mrs. Bacon's favourite words were quite at home there. The food was often terminologically as well as literally bloody, and the gym mistress was unanimously voted a bitch. Nobody persecuted her, or asked uncomfortable questions. Her arrival in the middle of the term provoked a little curiosity. "Have you been to school before?" could be answered truthfully with "Yes, but not at a boarding school". The fact that she lacked things that the better-equipped ones owned was tacitly understood to be the result of changing schools in the middle of the term, and after she had turned the possible handicap of being very good at some lessons into an asset by being free with her knowledge, there were always people who were willing to lend her things. On the whole she liked the girls very well. But they did not make Arlington House for her. Far more important were the books. More books than she could read if she stayed there until she was twenty, as one girl actually did. There were gardens too. Every girl who wished might have a plot of her own. Miss Stokes had discovered that this was one way of assuring a supply of blooms for her private rooms without denuding the general garden. There was a good deal of competition amongst the girls to offer the Boss, as she was known, the first roses, the finest sweet peas.

And beyond the garden there was a belt of beeches that screened it from the road. In the autumn they blazed through the pale air of October, bribing the sun to linger with promises of kinship. In the spring they loosed green nets to catch the rain. They were always there, a lovelier background for the livelier things one read. They were the woods of Sarn: the outskirts of Arden: Héloïse and Abélard walked there.

For the first time in her life since the day that she had become conscious of her surroundings, Emmie was free of the misery of having to make sudden adjustments between sharply contrasting environments. Man is so very adjustable. In the tropics he is black and lives upon bananas: in the Arctic he is fat and lives upon blubber. The city man is keen and brisk, the countryman slow and patient. They are adjusted. But when one can, as Emmie had done, step from one world into another by crossing a threshold, go from the scent of limes to the reek of the seldom-cleaned earth closet, go from Miss Stanton's voice reading poetry to Mrs. Bacon's voice shouting obscenities, what then can one's adjustment be?

Here she was free of that trouble. Life moved gently from sleeping to waking, from learning to playing, from eating to walking and so to sleeping again. Then there were the holidays spent in Miss Stanton's beloved presence, the short ones at Swything and the long ones in a cottage near the sea. The holidays at Swything had the air of an adventure, for Emmie never ventured out-of-doors until after dark. Whether, despite these precautions, Mrs. Bacon ever guessed at her whereabouts was a question that Miss Stanton often discussed but never decided. "Anyway, until I'm fourteen and can go out to work she won't bother about me. She doesn't like me, and now she won't have me to feed," said Emmie with unintentional bitterness. After her fourteenth birthday she expected Mrs. Bacon to besiege the cottage at any minute, but she never came. Mrs. Bacon had quite enough to bother her without crossing swords with Miss Stanton again.

After that fourteenth birthday, however, a certain unrest fell upon Emmie. Sometimes in her happiest moments at school the thought would strike her — I have no right to be here. I ought to be out at work. This is costing Miss Stanton a great deal of money and it isn't necessary now.

But Miss Stanton, timidly tackled about the matter was firm and brusque. "You must let me know best about this, Emmie. People who start work too soon earn least in the long run, unless they're geniuses. Now, I don't want to hear any more about it." After that Emmie would sink back into another brief period of content.

9

It was the summer vacation after Emmie's fifteenth birthday. For the fifth time she had come home to spend her holiday with Miss Stanton. They were going, as soon as the council schools broke up, to spend a month in a bungalow at Overstrand. Until then Emmie was, as she had done in the previous holidays, keeping indoors as much as possible and doing Mrs. Steggles's chores about the cottage. On the last day of the term, Miss Stanton's term, which was so much longer than Miss Stokes's, there came a telegram for Miss Stanton. Emmie opened it, prepared to brave the curious eyes in the village if it should contain news that could not wait Miss Stanton's return. It said, "Coming this afternoon. Stay the night. Ella."

There was nothing to be arranged or altered in that. Even in a telegram Ella Frome managed to be her definite self.

Emmie hunted up and hung out in the sun the narrow little sheets and blankets that were used on the camp-bed in the spare room. Then she dusted everything a second time, and went on with the packing until Miss Stanton arrived, hot and tired, laden with the usual end-of-term gear.

She read the telegram with a slight frown which pleased Emmie because it seemed to show that this invasion was as unwelcome to her as it was to her permanent guest. But she only said, "Oh dear, I don't feel like entertaining anybody. Or grappling with that bed thing." Emmie took great pleasure in pointing out the bedclothes already airing on the line. Miss Stanton said, "Good kid. This is the friend who used to go holidays with me. I guess she's come down to row me.

Be a dear and pop off to bed early and leave us to it, will you?"

Emmie promised. She later discovered that to go to bed early when Miss Frome was about was a privilege rather than a deprivation.

Ella Frome, who had been a plain and dowdy student, noticeable only for her style of hairdressing, had become an elegant combination of masculine trimness and feminine touches. Her hair was still cut short, but her nails were brilliantly laquered. She wore a severe tailored suit and over it, when she arrived in her car, a mannish camel-hair coat: but she had large pearl earrings in her ears, and a sweet subtle perfume rose from her hair and her clothes. Her voice was hybrid too. Generally it was deep and abrupt, but now and then it sank unexpectedly into a caressing dulcet murmur. She was obviously extremely fond of Helen Stanton. For Emmie she had only the flintiest of stares, the most strident voice.

Emmie went, thankfully, to bed as soon as she had washed the supper things. From below her she could hear the voices of the two women, it seemed in argument. Miss Stanton's voice lost all power, opposed to that deep bark or velvety whisper.

After about half an hour Miss Stanton dashed upstairs to fetch something. She paused by the bed and laid her hand on Emmie's shoulder. "Not asleep yet, child? I'm in the thick of it." She ran down again in the way that shook the whole house; and she left both the bedroom door and the one at the foot of the stairs just ajar. Now, as well as the tones, Emmie could distinguish the voices. The idea of not listening, of burying her head in the clothes, an idea that Miss Francis-Stokes would have approved, did not occur to her. In fact she sat up in bed in order to hear. And she heard only too well.

". . . time somebody talked a little sense to you, Helen. Have you ever thought what a responsibility you're shouldering?"

"Who should know that better than I, Ella? If I think it's worth it, that's all there is to it. I'm sorry about the holidays and the week-ends and things, but I can't help it. Sixty pounds is the hell of a lot when you only earn two-forty. And there're the holidays and various extras on top of that. But I don't mind."

"Then you should. You must be completely crazy. Or else your maternal instinct has gone to seed early. You're ruining your life. All very well to live amongst yobs and yokels if you get away every now and then, but to chain yourself down here, with a yob in your very house and never have a penny . . . it's crazy."

"Emmie's not a yob, as you term it. She's a sweet child, and to abandon her now would be criminal."

"Well, look at it this way. Your grandmother brought you up, didn't she? Suppose some eccentric lady who believed that no child could live without its dose of violet rays and a daily pint of pasteurized milk, had seen you. She'd have said, 'I must rescue this child.' How much better would you have been? It's exactly the same. Their surroundings suit them. They're no better, or happier, for being torn away and washed and taught. Besides, what stock! If you must indulge your primitive instincts wait till you're ready to settle down and then adopt an orphan of decent parentage. You're wronging the child too. Giving her tastes that she'll never be able to gratify legally. She'll be on the streets six months after leaving Alice Stokes's snobbery."

"That's all nonsense."

"Maybe. But it isn't nonsense to say that you're saddling yourself with an intolerable burden. I can't bear to see you spoil your life."

"Well, in that case, help me. Smoke Players for a change, and give me the difference."

"Damned if I do. This life is a dog fight. We're entitled to all we can scrap. Why should I, or you, give up a single moment's pleasure for somebody who'd spit in our eye for a nickel? You haven't gone all moral, have you, Helen?"

"God, no! I'm as material as you. Only in your dog fight I want to stand outside, like God, and see that one poor little puppy has fair play."

"Power complex. Oh, Helen, can't you see that it's because I'm fond of you . . ."

There was no need to listen any more.

When Miss Stanton came up to bed Emmie was sleeping soundly; for by that time she had reached a solution to the problem presented by her eavesdropping, and it is indecision rather than misery that banishes sleep.

In the morning she rose as usual and prepared the breakfast, scowling at the third place laid at the table, and yet shrinking from Ella Frome's stare. Half-way through breakfast Miss Stanton said, almost apologetically, "Emmie, you wouldn't mind being left today, would you?"

Emmie shook her head and smiled, "Not a bit, Miss Stanton. Is there anything you'd like me to do, specially?"

"There are some stockings . . ." said Miss Stanton coaxingly, smiling over her admitted hatred of darning.

"I'll do them," said Emmie, rejoiced that Miss Frome might see that she had her uses. Miss Stanton kissed her when she said good-bye, and the kiss was eloquent of something that could not be spoken. The two friends drove away: no doubt last night's discussion would be continued, and dropped, and taken up again. Emmie did the housework, smoothing out the dent that the sleek black head had made in the pillow, setting straight the alien, expensive things that strewed the small spare bedroom. The hatred that she felt, partly by reason and partly by instinct, against Miss Frome, was uncomfortably leavened by the memory of the velvety voice saying, ". . . can't you see that it's because I'm fond of you?"

Yes, the interloper loved Miss Stanton too. Differently — from above, as it were — patronizingly, protectively, without worship; still, she loved her, wanted her company, wanted her exclusive company. It eased Emmie in some obscure way, gave her a queer sense of power to realize that she could at least understand Ella Frome's bitterness towards herself.

She darned the stockings, lingeringly, attending even to the thin places that otherwise would be holes some time in the future when she would not be here. Then, when they were finished and rolled into neat balls and laid away, she took up the local paper, which by a kind coincidence had been delivered that morning. There was a long list of advertisements, as there was every week. Emmie worked through them, methodically. Many of the places were too near home . . . there must be no chance of her mother discovering where she was and coming round, making a row, demanding a share of her wages. Others demanded experience, or "some cooking". Her heart was falling as she drew near the bottom of the long column: and then she found it. A Mrs. Fincham, of Fincham's Farm, Denshall, was advertising for a strong country girl, willing to help in the house and dairy. "Fond of children" was the only stipulation, and with that Emmie felt she might comply.

Once, long ago, at the village school, Emmie's class had spent a term studying "local geography", and she remembered that Denshall was almost thirty miles on the other side of Stoney Market. Safe enough. She was glad that she was not required to apply to a box number, it would have held things up so much. Actually the Editor of the paper disapproved of such "new-fangled" ideas. It would have meant having people call at his office, and providing pigeon-holes for letters and a clerk to dole them out. If people wanted to advertise a vacant place, or a cow for sale, they were at liberty to say so in his paper, and then they could look out for the rest. Otherwise, Mrs. Fincham would gladly have hidden her identity. For she knew quite well that the country-side was peppered with strong country girls

63

who had tried to help her with her house and her dairy and her children, and were now expressing their opinion of all three, and of Mrs. Fincham, in strong country language. It was, as she dolefully admitted to herself, almost useless to advertise, but there was always a chance that the paper might be seen by some girl who wanted a job and who didn't know anybody who knew somebody who knew somebody who knew Fincham's. And for once her hope was justified. Her advertisement leaped at Emmie, and although Emmie did not know it the job was hers from that moment. She looked at the clock. Half past eleven, time to catch the bus to Stoney if she hurried across the fields, because even in a crisis like this, one must avoid the village. She ripped the Arlington House band from her plain panama hat, looked in the drawer where Miss Stanton kept loose change for household purposes, collected two half-crowns, a shilling, and several coppers, locked the front-door, hid the key in a pot of fuchsia that stood by the path — a recognized hiding-place — slipped round to the back and set off at a trot across the field path.

10

She had to change buses twice, losing time at each change, and when, late in the afternoon, she reached Denshall and inquired for Fincham's she was told that it was a "good half-hour's walk". She was hot and dusty and her head ached from the jolting of the buses and there was an empty feeling in her stomach, for she had not felt justified in spending any of the borrowed money on refreshments at Stoney or the other bus stop. However, she set off at a run again, and reached Fincham's in under twenty minutes. It was very remote, even from the lane that led to it, for upon a decaying gate-post was a letter-box, placed for the convenience of the postman, and labelled with white paint, "S. Fincham". Emmie turned in at the gateway and hurried over the dried cart-track, deeply rutted, that would be a sea of mud in the winter-time. The track ran uphill for a time and Emmie panted and wiped her wet face on her handkerchief: then it took a slant downward and in the hollow below she could see the farmhouse, long and rambling, white from this distance, and pleasant in this sunshine.

On either side the fields were spread, sloping as the track did, and Emmie's country eyes recognized them without conscious thought, wheat, sugar-beet, barley, seed-clover. She did notice — and laid it to S. Fincham's credit — the remarkable absence of weeds in these crops: hardly a poppy or thistle or knapweed as far as eye could see. S. Fincham was evidently a good farmer. The house, however, as she drew nearer, did not display the same neat aspect. Most of the windows were uncurtained, and a few upper ones were broken. The walls that had looked white from the distance were actually peeling and discoloured from age and dampness, and the thatch, once elegantly scalloped, was ragged and full of holes. There were lime-trees behind it, however, and their fragrance reached Emmie as she stood for a moment to compose herself and to recover her breath. The silence of the place, and the remoteness and its air of having fallen on evil days made a certain romantic appeal. Sarn, she thought, Sarn after Prue had left it, and somebody found it again. Heartened by that thought she walked on to where the track divided, half going on to the buildings and the yard at the back, half swooping round to the front of the house. Emmie hesitated for a moment, and then decided to go to the back: after all, servants used the back door. It was just as well that she did, for the front door was only used for funerals and had not been opened since old Mrs. Fincham had been carried through it on the only occasion that any honour was accorded her.

To get to the back door one had to screw oneself into as small a compass as possible in order to pass a huge black dog that was chained to a kennel. It sprang to the extremity of its short chain and stood there alternately barking and snarling and ignored Emmie's placating clucks and snapped fingers. It was evidently a reliable watch-dog, for in response to its noise, before Emmie could tap on the paintless door, the door opened and a tall pale woman said, in a voice in which patience and exasperation warred oddly, "Well, what do you want?"

"I would like to see Mrs. Fincham."

"I am Mrs. Fincham. What is it?"

"You advertised . . ." Emmie began.

In Mrs. Fincham's eyes appeared a gleam that might have warned a more experienced job seeker. Picking up the edge of her checked apron, she wiped her wet hands, pushed back three little figures that crowded the doorway behind her and said, quite warmly, "Come in."

The kitchen, Emmie saw at a glance, was both muddled and dirty, but there was a pleasant scent of baking bread.

"Come into the dairy, will you?" said Mrs. Fincham, leading the way. "My butter has just turned, I daren't leave it a minute. I've had such a job with it, the weather is so hot."

The three children, tow-headed, dirty-faced, grubby pinafored, followed in gaping silence, and Mrs. Fincham went on draining off buttermilk salting and shaping the butter while she talked to Emmie over her shoulder.

"I'm in rather a muddle today; my last girl had to go home, her mother was ill." That was a lie, but Mrs. Fincham had said it so many times that it had become conventional, like saying, "Very well, thank you", to someone who inquires after your health on a day when you feel you may die at any minute.

"You were looking for a place?"

"Yes."

"Been out before?"

"No, but I've done housework since I was very young."

"Know anything about dairy work?"

"No, but I could learn. I mean, if you'd teach me I'd try awfully hard to do what you told me."

It seemed to Emmie that the conversation was taking a perilous turn. Evidently Mrs. Fincham wanted as much as the other advertisers, only she hadn't said so. Mrs. Fincham's silence after that last answer smacked of dissatisfaction. Actually Mrs. Fincham was holding her breath: if they hadn't been busy she would probably have held her thumbs. Here was a girl who seemed really anxious for a job, who wanted to come, wanted to learn.

"How old are you?"

"Over fifteen."

"Not sixteen?"

"N . . . no, not quite yet," said Emmie, wishing that she had lied.

"No insurance yet, then," said Mrs. Fincham in a relieved voice.

Emmie caught the significance.

"When could you come in?"

"Tomorrow."

"That would suit me very well. Could you come early?" Then, fearing that she was sounding too eager, Mrs. Fincham added, "It's so much easier to work early, this hot weather."

"I'll come as soon as I can . . . but I don't mind the heat," said Emmie. "And I'll bring a testimonial with me then. Will that do?"

"That'll do very nicely. What is your name?"

"Emmie, Emmie Bacon."

"Then I'll see you tomorrow." She laid down the wooden "Scotch hands" with which she was moulding the butter and accompanied Emmie to the door. Something, perhaps distrust of her luck, or a desire to forestall any second thoughts that might come to

Emmie in the night, made her add, "Of course, it's rather a lonely place: but we're homely people and I'll be working with you all the time. I hope you'll be happy."

Emmie mustered her best smile. "I'll try to be," she said, "I'm so glad you'll have me."

Mrs. Fincham's face took on a smile which was quite obviously not at home there. "Don't mind the dog, he'll soon get used to you. Good-bye."

Emmie started running back to Denshall.

It was more difficult to fit in the buses going back and Emmie had, in the end, to walk from Stoney Market, so that the soft unterrifying darkness of July had fallen before she reached Swything again. She chose the field path, not for concealment now, but because it was shorter, and as she scrambled through the hedge at the back of the cottage she could see the sidelights of the car shining in the lane. That was a pity, for now when Miss Stanton asked where she had been she would have to explain it all in Miss Frome's paralysing presence.

They had finished supper and the used plates had been cleared away. Emmie's supper, covered with a cloth to protect it from the flies, stood on the end of the table. The friends were sitting together on the settee that in summer was pushed beneath the window. Miss Frome looked cross and was drawing hard at her cigarette: Miss Stanton had a book on her lap and her face was worried and slightly flushed. She jumped up when she saw Emmie, and the book fell to the ground.

"Wherever have you been, child? I've been *so* anxious. Has anything happened?"

"I'm sorry," said Emmie, "I've been to Denshall, and there wasn't a late bus from Stoney. I'm *awfully* sorry, I'd hoped to be back first."

"Why have you been to Denshall?"

"I've been getting a job."

"A job?"

Emmie nodded. She was aware that Miss Frome was regarding her with interest, that the flush had deepened upon Miss Stanton's cheeks, that her own knees were shaking, and that despite the emptiness of her stomach she felt a little sick. A jug of lemonade stood on the table with cool wheels of lemon floating in it. She must have a drink or die. She sat down at her place at the table and directed an apologetic smile to Miss Stanton as she lifted the jug. "Do you mind?" she asked, "I haven't had anything since breakfast."

"Go ahead," said Miss Stanton, "but talk as you eat. What job is it?"

Emmie set down the glass, drained to the last drop, and lifted the cloth. Pale pink slices of succulent ham, tomatoes, cucumber, crisp lettuce. Lovely . . . but she must explain first.

"In a house, a farmhouse. I saw the advertisement and went over so I could get it settled at once."

"Very nice," said Miss Stanton harshly. "But I thought you were still at school! May I ask what put this into your head?"

"I've thought about it ever since I was fourteen. It isn't right that I should be a burden on you any longer. You've been too good as it is and . . ."

Miss Stanton whipped round to her friend.

70

"Ella," she said furiously, "you've been getting at this child. How dare you?"

"You're quite wrong, Helen," said the calm voice, most velvety now. "Ask Emmie if you don't believe me. I've never addressed a word to her except in your presence."

"I don't believe you."

"It's perfectly true, Miss Stanton. It was entirely my own idea."

"But *why*, Emmie? I thought you were so happy at Arlington House. I thought you were going to take School Certificate next year and really try to make something of your life. Now you want to throw it all away, waste it all. Well you shan't do it. I shall write to this woman and tell her it was all a mistake." She picked up the local paper which Emmie had left neatly folded and turned towards the advertisement page with fingers so uncertain that the middle pages slipped and fell to the floor. Miss Frome leaned forward and picked them up.

"Don't be so absurd, Helen. Emmie is quite right, and you'll realize it later. She can at least see the truth that I was trying to persuade you to see last night."

Miss Stanton threw down the paper.

"'Last night'," she cried, in a sudden burst of illumination. "Of course. Emmie overheard all the poisonous things you said. That's it, isn't it, Emmie? Well, don't you take any notice of it. It's all nonsense, spiteful nonsense because she was disappointed that I wasn't going a holiday with her. Forget it, Emmie. If

71

you heard what *she* said you heard *me* too. You know how I feel about it, don't you?"

Emmie swallowed a piece of cucumber with difficulty.

"Last night?" she asked. "I don't know what either of you said last night. I only know how I feel. I want to leave school and begin keeping myself." A positive burst of inspiration came to her, "You see, Miss Stanton, it's quite different for you, you belong to a class of people who go on being educated until they're eighteen or even older, but I don't. Once we're — people like us, I mean — once we're fourteen we're sort of grown up. It seems right for us to start working then."

"But you're not like that," protested Miss Stanton, and Emmie saw with horror that tears had gathered in her eyes and were beginning to spill, unchecked, over her flushed cheeks. "You aren't like that. You're so clever. You've got on so marvellously. You're so clever you'd Matriculate easily. And if you did I was going to send you to College."

Miss Frome snorted.

"You're absolutely mad. Helen. Here, take this handkerchief, you look like something out of *East Lynne*. The child has more sense than you. After all it *is* her life. I respect her for knowing how to run it."

Emmie said with a hardness that had been born in her quite suddenly, "After all, if I'm so clever a year more or less at school won't make all that difference."

"You utter little fool," cried Miss Stanton, frankly sobbing now. "That's just what it will do. You'll sink into being a housemaid. You'll waste your brains. Who

72

cares whether a housemaid has brains or not? Besides it isn't fair to me. If you don't finish your education it's a waste of all I've tried to do for you already."

"That shan't be wasted, I promise you."

"But, Emmie, if you want a job, wait. Perhaps you could get into an office, or something; the Shire Hall, perhaps. I'd ask the Director."

"It wouldn't be any good, Miss Stanton, please," said Emmie earnestly. "I wouldn't be keeping myself. They start you off at about seven-and-sixpence a week. Jobs like that are just for girls with homes and parents who can afford to keep them in essentials."

"This is your home," said Miss Stanton stubbornly.

Miss Frome stirred uneasily.

Emmie repeated, "I can't be a burden to you any longer."

And that brought the conversation round to its beginning again. Evidently Miss Frome was afraid that it was going to start from there a second time. She interrupted, "When will you start?"

"Tomorrow."

"Tomorrow," Miss Stanton exclaimed. "Then you won't have any holiday."

"I've had a lovely fortnight here," said Emmie reasonably.

"I'll drive you over tomorrow," said Miss Frome in a voice that she had never used to Emmie before. "You'd better get your things together, hadn't you?" That, she trusted, would put a stop to this fruitless discussion.

Long after Emmie had packed her bag and climbed into her side of the bed, she could hear the voices carrying on, ding-dong, downstairs. Words were indistinguishable, for all the doors were closed tonight. Nothing that was said downstairs concerned her now, her course was set. She felt older, years older than the child who had lain in this bed last night. She had ceased to float, steered by other people's charts. She had made a choice and stuck to it. Even without Miss Frome's support — which, indeed, had inclined her, through perversity, to side, mentally, with Miss Stanton — even without that she had proved stronger than Miss Stanton. Weary and hungry and sad, with the depressing back premises of Fincham's hung like a backcloth in her mind, she had not weakened or wept.

They came upstairs at last. Miss Stanton said in a sodden, unfriendly voice, "Good night, Ella."

Miss Frome replied, "You're hating me quite causelessly, Helen, but you'll get over it. Good night, darling."

Miss Stanton made no answer. She came into the room and shut the door. In silence she undressed, put on her pyjamas, brushed her hair and then sat down on the bed, reaching out so that her hand fell on Emmie's shoulder. "Are you asleep?" she said softly, "because if you are, wake up. I've lots to say to you."

Emmie sat up. Miss Stanton began to talk.

It was the same talk, but more intimate and detailed, that Emmie had heard her address to big girls who were about to leave the village school. It might mean little or much, according to the mind of the listener. It was vague, but earnest; uninformative in a way, but suggestive.

74

A listening cynic might, with justification, at the end, have asked whether Miss Stanton regarded kindness, love of reading, cleanliness of body, or chastity of sexual relationships as the supreme virtue. And he would have received no satisfactory answer, for to her these things were one. Emmie, listening to the voice she loved, found no difficulty in gathering Miss Stanton's meaning. The muddled outpouring of a bookish, sentimental, yet not unworldly-wise mind was to her just what it was meant to be — a shield against the world that tomorrow she was to face.

Before she fell asleep she renewed her resolve to be the kind of person that Miss Stanton would like her to be, the kind of person that Miss Stanton was herself — that is, Emmie's Miss Stanton, a very different person from Ella Frome's Miss Stanton, or even Helen Stanton's own.

Emmie rose early, as usual, prepared the breakfast, washed up afterwards and tidied the kitchen. Then she fetched down her bag, took her hat in her hand and announced that she was ready. Miss Frome went out for her car, and then Emmie remembered the testimonial. Meekly, because she was asking a favour, she requested Miss Stanton to write her one. Miss Stanton hunted up a piece of school paper and wrote a testimonial that would have led a reader to believe that Emmie had been her personal and trusted maid for several years. Incidentally, Mrs. Fincham never asked for it, and Emmie never bothered her with it, so it remained amongst her most treasured possessions, revered not for its sentiments, but for its writer's sake.

"I'm not coming with you, Emmie. You understand, don't you, dear? And do remember to write to me, and come and see me if you can. And do look on this as your home . . . and if ever you're in any kind of trouble . . ." She held Emmie close, and kissed her. Ella Frome revved up her engine fiercely and then stilled it to call, "Now make haste, Helen, I expect you to be ready when I come back."

"I am not," said Miss Stanton, "going on a holiday with you, Ella." She half-turned in at the open door and then out again to call to Emmie:

"Darling, if anyone tries to bully you, tell them to go to hell, and come straight back here."

"All right," said Emmie. She raised one hand to wave as the car jerked forward, but Miss Stanton had gone indoors.

She took one last look at the little flagged path and the pots of shrubs and the rose bush that climbed up to the sill of the bedroom window. A thought of Eden flashed through her mind, and without turning her head she eyed Ella Frome sideways — a strange new kind of fire-sworded angel.

She asked Miss Frome to stop the car at the gate that bore the letter-box. They had exchanged about six words on the swift smooth journey, and those all about directions.

"That's all right," said Miss Frome, preparing to change gear to negotiate the turning. "I'll run you up to the house. There's your bag, you know."

"I'd rather you didn't really. The bag isn't very heavy, and the road is bad, bad for the car, I mean."

"All right."

The car turned in and then backed out again, and came to a stop in the lane. Emmie got out.

"Thank you," she said gravely, "good-bye."

"Here, wait a jiffy," said Miss Frome, fumbling with the clasp of her bag. She dived into it and brought out a piece of thin white paper. "You'll need some money till you get your wages." Emmie guessed that it must be a five-pound note. She had never seen one, but it was money, and it was neither pound nor ten-shilling note. She did not take it.

"Thank you, Miss Frome, but Miss Stanton gave me enough to last until the end of the month."

"Never mind, you can find a use for this, I'm sure."

"I don't want it, thank you. But . . ." she said, voicing the idea as it came to her, "if you want to give it to me you can give it to Miss Stanton. I've cost her a great deal."

There was just the faintest sparkle in Emmie's eyes as she spoke. Ella Frome, with the rejected note still folded between her fingers, looked at her. Thin childish figure, like a tall doll, limp cotton frock cut down from Helen's size, pale pointed little face crowned by a mop of short black curls, odd yellowish eyes fixed on her own . . . she took in all that was visible of the human being known as Emmie Bacon. Dignity is here, she thought unwillingly, dignity even in the awkward position of being offered money and confessing an obligation.

"I can't very well give it to her," she said at last, dropping the note into her capacious bag, "but I tell you what I'll do I'll buy her something."

"That'll be lovely," said Emmie. "Thank you again for bringing me. Good-bye."

"Good-bye, good luck," said the voice of honey. The car started forward gently, grew louder, changed its note and went humming down the lane. Emmie turned in at the gateway.

Part Two

1

Emmie achieved the distinction of being the only maid to stay at Fincham's for more than two months and to be dismissed. Generally girls gave notice at the end of the first month and left at the end of the second. Or they left suddenly, giving some trumped-up excuse, or none at all: and at the end of a week Emmie fully understood and envied the giving of notice in which other, luckier girls, girls with homes, could indulge. She stayed from the end of July until the following March, and she was hungry all the time.

Hunger, of course, was no very new experience, though since her flight from her mother's house she had been full fed. Possibly that, indeed, made the present hunger more noticeable. But even in the Bacon cottage there had been times when, if not well nourished, she had at least felt full. And that pleasant feeling was denied to any creature, animal or human, whose diet Saul Fincham supervised: pigs might be an exception, since the virtue of a pig lies in its fatness.

Mrs. Fincham was thin; the children were thin; Emmie, at the leggy stage of early adolescence, stuck there and lost rather than gained weight. The cows that gave the milk were bony, even for cows, and as starved-looking as the horses that dragged the milk carts into the town. It took Emmie very little time to detect that the blame for this scarcity of food lay at the master's door rather than that of the mistress.

Mrs. Fincham was harmless, and suffered as much from Mr. Fincham's meanness as anybody. Most farmers, as Emmie well knew, having lived in the country all her life, allowed their wives the "egg and butter" money, since the hens and the dairy were traditionally the wife's province. But Mrs. Fincham never handled a penny of her own. Even the bills for food went to Mr. Fincham, and he paid them direct.

Emmie soon saw in Mrs. Fincham a fellow-slave, not a mistress, and pitied her accordingly. Had she known all Mrs. Fincham's story she would have pitied her even more. She had been an assistant in a draper's shop in the town. She had always been tired there. The law might demand that a chair stood there for her use, but it could not see that she was given time to sit down on it for a moment, even on the days when she most needed to. Wearily she had reached up and handed down the heavy rolls of serge and towelling, coarse calico and flannel that made the bulk of the country trade. Wearily she had laid them out for inspection, and wearily returned them to their places. She knew that her only hope of escape lay in marriage, and she knew that the hope was slight; for she was too pale for beauty, though she had in her youth a certain fragile charm, and she was always too tired to display any vivacity or sex-appeal. Then it seemed that a miracle happened. Saul Fincham came clumsily into the shop one market day to buy butter muslin. His mother who had hitherto performed the thankless task of looking after the dairy at Fincham's had recently died, and Saul was already looking about him for a substitute. What it was about the pale, wilting girl who served the butter muslin that he should pick on her, who could say? Possibly he could detect in her the "meek and quiet spirit", which, the hymn assures us, "shines so fair". Whatever it was, it worked. He carried on an awkward courtship, grudging every moment and every penny he spent on it, and in six months had married her. Perhaps he behaved unnaturally during that courtship, perhaps he was mean and bullying all the time. Poor Vera was in no state to be critical . . . a first admirer . . . a genuine farmer farming his own land . . . a big, burly, full-blooded male creature . . . what more could a pallid shop assistant, past her first youth, hope for? By what standard could she judge him? She thought of a farm as a cheerful place, flowing with milk and honey, redolent of bacon, paved with eggs. All these desirable things that one bought in small quantities with small, hard-earned sums of money were to be had on a farm for nothing. And she would be a wage slave no more.

So she came to Fincham's, where the eggs were all known and numbered, the milk dedicated to "the round", the cream to butter-making, and where the only bacon was a green lump of home-cured streaky, cut off in thick slices for the master's breakfast and his alone. And now she was a wageless slave with miles of stone flooring to scrub, a number of implements whose names she barely knew, to master and clean with scalding hot water; and an insatiable monster called the separator now took toll of her aching back; and from this slavery there was no discharge. Saul, whose big burliness she had admired, seeing protection in it, was not above shaking or striking her in those early days when she was slow or stupid about her new duties, or on the few occasions, also early, when she tried to stick up for herself. Then the children came. Saul wanted boys, but two of the three were girls and he seemed to attribute that to some fault in her.

She was resigned now, and when Emmie made her acquaintance she was a thin pale woman with her lips pressed together in patience, and large restless eyes that seemed always to be trying to look behind her. Her hair, always fair, was turning grey imperceptibly and thinning so that her pale skull shone through it. There were faint brown patches that matched her hair under her skin. She had advertised for help because she was in the fourth month of pregnancy, and although she could have carried on her multifarious duties alone a little longer, it was inadvisable to leave her search for a maid until autumn when Fincham's looked at its worst.

Emmie made her master's acquaintance on the first day when she bent over the black range in the kitchen, looking to see whether the kettle boiled for the six o'clock tea that was the last meal of the day. She was conscious, almost simultaneously, of a heavy step behind her, a shadow cast over the stove, and a strong scent of human sweat. Then a reddish brown arm, heavily muscled and hairy, stretched over her head and pushed in one of the flue draughts.

84

"You'd better learn early not to waste the fuel," said a hard voice. Emmie straightened herself and turned, took one look at Mr. Fincham, and hated all she saw. The low frowning forehead, the pale eyes, like blue marbles, the over-developed muscles that widened his jaw, all repelled her instantly.

Her dislike of his face, however, did not render her oblivious to the fact that it was his stove and his fuel. She said, "I'm sorry," meekly, placatingly. He went on, with his heavy tread, towards the general living-room that adjoined the kitchen. She heard him address Mrs. Fincham, "You'll have to watch that girl. She's extravagant, like the rest of the hussies."

For a moment or two Emmie wondered . . . she was inexperienced with big cooking ranges, perhaps she had done something wasteful; yet the stove had been burning like that all afternoon under Mrs. Fincham's eye. And mingled with her doubt there was a shred of respect for the alertness of an eye that could, in passing, detect something wrong in a matter not generally considered a man's business. She was soon to learn, though, that every candle, every crumb, every stick that was used in that house was emphatically Saul Fincham's business.

He had evidently, perhaps long ago, arrived at a nice decision as to the minimum that might be spent upon food. Variety was not considered. Every morning Emmie made a large panful of porridge, which, milkless and sprinkled with salt, provided breakfast for everyone except the master for whom it was followed by a plateful of the home-cured bacon. Dinner was almost as monotonous, cold salt brisket of beef, or stew. The stews were made of rabbit or shin beef, and often Emmie failed to draw from them anything but vegetables and gravy, or on lucky, exceptional days, a dumpling. The six o'clock meal consisted of bread, smeared with butter, or home-made jam, never both, and there were eggs for the master, if eggs were cheap, or cheese if they were dear.

Perhaps Mr. Fincham in his passion for economy had arrived at the ideal diet; for many doctors and philosophers believe that we eat too much, and it is certain that the family at Fincham's continued to live though they did not fatten, and Saul himself was an extraordinarily strong and energetic man. He turned out far more work in a day than any of the men he employed, and found time to sit on several committees, including the Board of Guardians, where the accounts for the food in the workhouse must have given him grave concern. He generally came home in a good mood from meetings, for he enjoyed asserting himself; and would sit retailing to Vera what he had said and what had been said to him, and when he repeated his own shrewd remarks there was on his face a cramped, sly smile, less attractive even, than its usual gloom.

Once he directed that smile at Emmie. It was in August when she had been at Fincham's three weeks and had had time to make friends with the big black yard dog.

She was sorry for him because he was always chained and never noticed. She began by fussing him, and he responded extravagantly. One evening, when she felt that she knew him well enough, she went out with a piece of cord, slipped it through the ring of his collar, and unhooked the clasp of the chain. She meant to take him for a walk. But the mere prospect of semi-freedom sent him into such a frenzy of excitement that his barking convinced his master that thieves were at the coal heap. He came out in his slippers and harshly bade Emmie chain the dog again.

"I'm only going to take him for a little walk," Emmie faltered, "I'd hold the string. I wouldn't lose him."

"You heard what I said, chain him up."

She saw the uselessness of further appeal, and slowly and sadly stooped and fastened the chain to the collar. The dog, not yet relinquishing hope, went on barking. Saul Fincham stooped and picked up a half-brick which he hurled in the dog's direction. Emmie stepped forward, and with a skill learned long ago in the village cricket on the green, caught the missile in her hand.

"Can't you find anything to do?" Saul asked furiously.

"I've finished for the night."

"Oh, have you? Well, tomorrow night you can go gleaning." The nasty smile crept out and widened as he added, "Gleanings are good for hens."

He went in and slammed the door. Emmie nursed her thumb for a bit, and then tried to comfort the dog with a strip of bacon rind, the only edible thing she could find. He ate it, but his eyes reproached her as one who had promised much and performed little. Long after her thumb regained its normal hue Emmie cherished resentment over that little affair. Indoors Saul

Fincham said to his wife, "I don't like that girl. I never did from the moment I set eyes on her." Insolent, interfering little baggage. Best get rid of her."

"Oh dear, and she's the best I've had, and the only one for ever so long who has settled down."

"Well, keep her out of my way then."

And that, Mrs. Fincham found, wasn't in the least difficult.

2

The house at Fincham's made Emmie think of Mrs. Poyser's farm in *Adam Bede*. It needed a bustling mistress of Mrs. Poyser's kind, with a grown-up daughter or two, or several sturdy maids to do her bidding. It was meant for more spacious times and more spacious people. Often, especially in the evenings and early mornings, Emmie was oppressed by the size and chilliness, the dim silence of the enormous kitchen, the scullery, the long back passage and the dairy. They took so long to "scrub through" that the pail of water, hot to start with, was cold before she had finished. And hot water was never plentiful at Fincham's.

It added to her work too, that Mrs. Fincham, crushed and resigned as she was, clung to some remnant of her shopgirl refinement and insisted upon keeping a spare bedroom, where no guest ever slept, and the parlour, where no visitor ever sat, swept and garnished. Fortunately Emmie never resented the time spent in these two musty, heavily furnished apartments.

It was nice to have places that only needed to be swept and dusted and have their windows and grates polished occasionally. The rest of the house was marked with the track of hobnailed boots and muddy Wellingtons that shed clods of soil everywhere: the rest of the furniture was sticky with the finger-marks of children. Emmie gained as much satisfaction from setting straight the plush cloth beneath the jar of everlastings, puffing up the ancient fat cushions and closing the door on the oases of peace as Mrs. Fincham did from thinking of them.

Harvest began soon after Emmie's arrival at the farm, and it became part of her duty to carry jugs of hot tea and piles of sandwiches, locally known as "fourses", to her master. The children loved to go with her into the fields, and by balancing another jug and cutting a few more chunks of bread thinly smeared with butter, Emmie was able to add frivolity to these occasions by turning them into picnics. Having delivered Saul's tea they would betake themselves to a place in the hedge where even he could not say they were in the way, and drink their tea and eat their bread and talk to other people who had come on the same errand. Emmie enjoyed that as long as there was a good deal of corn still standing. But when the wedge-shaped piece in the middle of the field was thinning and the boys in the widening stubble began to handle their sticks, Emmie began to think of the rabbits, cowering there in their insecure and doomed retreats. Generally then she would gather up her jugs and baskets, call the unwilling little Finchams and make for the house, rather as though she were a rabbit herself. Sometimes, however, it was her fate to arrive in the middle of the slaughter, and then every thudding, too often non-fatal blow seemed to fall on her shrinking flesh; the thin, almost human cries of the rabbits would ring for hours in her ears and the sight of the blood and mangled bodies would come between her and the desire for food. Harvest meant heavy work for the thin horses, too. Altogether she was glad when it was over.

At the end of her first month Mrs. Fincham presented her with twenty-five shillings, and apologized in her vague but not unkindly way for having forgotten about "half days".

"I'm sorry, Emmie, I've only just realized that you haven't had any time off this month. I've been so busy with the harvest and the job this hot weather has made of the butter, and generally girls are only too ready to speak up for themselves. Would you like all day next Tuesday? It's Ipswich Market and you can get a bus at Denshall Green."

Emmie, clinging to her wealth, thought of her dearth of underclothes and much-cobbled stockings, and was tempted. But "sixty pounds is the hell of a lot when you only earn two-forty" rang in her ears. She folded the note over the two half-crowns and smiled upon Mrs. Fincham.

"It's all right, thank you. I'll go a walk on Tuesday afternoon perhaps, but I don't want to go to Ipswich."

In sixty months at most she would be in a position to pay Miss Stanton back. Sixty months . . . five years, a hell of a time . . . but then, perhaps she could save the five shillings sometimes too; or ask for a rise; or get another job. Life was full of possibilities.

3

Autumn came on step by step. The mornings and the evenings grew chilly and touched by mist. The lower and outer edges of the trees began to flame, and then suddenly all the woods were ablaze. Emmie came back from her walks on Tuesday afternoons dazed and dreamy, with her hands full of spindleberry and her head full of tags remembered from the academic days.

But now in autumn with the black and outcast
   crows
Share we the spacious world . . .
I hear a dead man's cry from autumn long since
   gone.
I cry to you beyond upon this bitter air.

As though Anchises the olden
cried to Aeneas in the shade
and the leafy dead blew golden
and were no more afraid.

She had no idea who Anchises was, or who Aeneas. Sufficient that the lines held the magic of the time, for there is always a day of harebell sky and burning leaves when the "leafy dead" stir again; when Richard rides for his far crusade, Joan mounts her white horse and Drake turns westward.

And through all the autumn, she heard, as the young do, the whisper of the spring: saw behind the torn and faded banners of this year's chestnut leaves the black bud that the spring would break "in one green stride".

Life was not bounded by Fincham's, by greasy dishes and gritty stone floors. The coral berries of the rowan, a bird busy in a hawthorn hedge, the prodigal gold cast by the trees for reverent feet to walk on were all sureties, hostages, promising — but what? Life, love, fortune, fair company, what?

Oh, Miss Stanton, you cried on Ella Frome's shoulder after Emmie had gone. You said that you had betrayed her, wronged her, let her down. Then you quarrelled, for her sake with Ella, of whom you were fond, who had been one of your links with the life you had missed. But you were repenting the small sin, Miss Stanton, and ignoring the great. You, with your poetry, and your *Precious Bane*, your pious little remarks about cultivating refinement and sensitiveness, you had made this one poor soul, who was clay in your hands, vulnerable as she should never have been. She should by now have been a tawdry imitation of her favourite screen star; her few poor shillings should have been buying the trappings of sex-appeal. So she would have been happy, with a coarse hard heart to face a coarse hard world with. You promised her something — but what? Something you hoped for yourself? Something that trees and flowers and romantic poetry promised you? Perhaps. And perhaps you, too, are to be pitied.

92

Saul Fincham was dissatisfied with his harvest and with the prices offered by the corn chandlers. He stopped threshing half-way through, and stored the corn already threshed in the end of the big barn. Other men might accept the wicked prices because they were in need of ready money, he said, but he, although he did not say this, was a "warm" man and could afford to wait for the rise in price that was bound to come after Christmas. As for ready money there was the sugar-beet harvest to look to. Unfortunately this neat and apparently satisfactory solution to his problem did not improve his temper, and the cheeseparing that went on at Fincham's became more and more severe. Indoors and out the winter set in with an economy campaign.

Sugar-beet harvest is unlovely, associated with fog, and slight frost and plentiful rain falling on the damp and mud-coloured remnants of the last leaves. Mrs. Fincham, growing every day heavier of body and more palely pinched of face, moved slowly about in a daze of hopeless, helpless misery. Colds began and the first chilblains appeared on Emmie's hands that still bore the discoloured reminders of last year's similar affliction. Emmie discovered the tiny branch of the Public Library attached to the village school. The books were often soiled, from careless handling, and redolent of the unsavoury places where they had shed their light, but they were readable, and a delight. She could lie in her hard little bed, with her feet wrapped in her vest, still warm from her body, with a twopenny cake of

Snowfire waiting to solace her chilblains, and by the draught-driven light of her candle she could make her escape. All Galsworthy she read that winter, all Kipling, all Charles Reade. She discovered Humbert Wolfe with delight, and Drinkwater with tears.

But not all by the light of Saul Fincham's candles. For he, quite early in the season, called out to a sick cow, discovered upon his return that there was still a light in "that girl's' room. He hammered on the door and shouted, "Put out that light. If I catch you wasting it again you'll go to bed in the dark."

In the morning he made loud and bitter complaint to Vera, who turned away her aching head and wept. When the children were in bed that night Emmie ran through the dark and the mire to the village shop, and with trepidation at her own extravagance, purchased a pound of candles. She had them in her hand when she presented her master with his slippers. "I've bought myself some candles," she said in her most dignified voice, "I suppose that will be all right?"

"None of your insolence," Saul retorted, "and don't go setting the place alight, that'll be the next thing."

"When other beauty governs other lips,
And snowdrops come to strange and happy springs,
When seas renewed bear yet unbuilded ships,
And alien hearts know all familiar things,
How will it be with you and you . . ."

read Emmie through her tears. She saw the snowdrops pushing their white heads through the dark

94

soil on some far January day that whispered a false and premature promise of spring; she saw her own dead, buried, sightless face turned up towards them. She thought a little of the man, Drinkwater. How did he know so exactly what the passing seasons did to you? Was he alive still? Did the people who knew him feel themselves fortunate? Did many people think like that? Where were they? Would she ever meet one? Reaching out for the Snowfire, blowing out the candle made no breach in her thoughts. They ran on strongly and mingled with her dreams.

Just before Christmas, however, she gave up her reading, and devoted the time to a far more perilous pastime, not even guessing that the substitute was one that the poets would, most of them, highly approve.

Ever since she had come to Fincham's the state of the horses had worried her. Now, in the rush "to get all the beet in", she was worried all day. The horses were thin and weak, the farmways thick with retarding mud, the loads heavy. It was bang-bang, bang, chuck, chuck, chuck, shout, shout, shout, all day long. It wasn't, her shrinking ears assured her, the bang of sticks on well-padded flanks, it was on the bone. It hurt her, more than the cracked chilblains that she plunged unthinking into the strong soda water. She even thought of leaving Fincham's to escape the strain of listening avidly for what she wanted not to hear: of looking for evidence that she hated to see. But a better, she thought, idea occurred to her. She could feed the horses in the night. There were only six, four big that pulled the waggons, two small that divided their toilsome days between the milk-carts and the tumbrils. She marked, with consummate care, the position of the haystack that was already in use, cut, like a cheese, on one side. She tried, in the daytime, when Saul was out, to find her way with her eyes shut from the barn where the oatbin stood, into the stable. The experiment taught her that she must use a lantern. The yard dog knew her and would make no sound.

Christmas Eve, she decided, would be a good night to start on, for, for all her godlessness, she felt that there was something special about the baby Christ in a manger. He had at least been kind, which God wasn't. God had let Him down in the end, had let Him die on the cross crying, "Why hast thou forsaken me?" but there was something special about Him still. And the thought of the stable birth bore her up on the cold and creepy journey that she made for the first time on Christmas Eve. She dared not take much — two armsful of hay and a pailful of oats, but it meant three journeys through the cold night, in a silence that might be broken at any minute, by anything . . . anything from Saul Fincham's justifiably bull-like bellow to the crying of a banshee.

Victoria Crosses have been pinned on breasts that have braved no more. Even in the stable she was afraid of the horses; much as she loved them all, in the abstract, much as she pitied these, the thought of their hoofs and their teeth terrified her. And around them, too, in their scent and their presence hung the thought of their hunger and the blows that they had uncomplainingly taken that day.

That thought made her shrink from them, she could not understand why. She ground it down, however, and forced herself to touch them, one by one. That reassured her, for they were all too tired, too dispirited to resent her presence, strange though it was. Their warmth and thinness moved her to tears: but as she left the stable for the last time and closed the door softly behind her, there came to her ears the little shuffling and crunching noises of the feeding creatures, and for all her tears a warm happiness curled round her heart. It wasn't much . . . but it would take the edge off, like when you were peeling swedes for dinner and slipped a slice into your mouth. Perhaps if she wasn't discovered, she might see them get a tiny bit fatter.

She continued the practice for well over two months. Once she was badly frightened, and once nearly caught.

A week after Christmas she was barely in bed again with the vest round her feet and her coat spread over the thin quilt, when there was a banging at the door. The master's voice:

"Emmie, Emmie, you gotta get up. The Missus is taken bad, I gotta get a doctor."

Hell, thought Emmie, without replying. He'll go into the stable and find them feeding; he'll find the lantern is warm. I am undone, as they used to say.

She made no sound; let him call again. That would save a minute in which the lantern would grow cooler. And simultaneously came the thought of Mrs. Fincham who had cried out and turned paper-white that morning after she had tried to move the mangle from the wall. She had dropped down on the wooden bench where the washing-bath stood and held her back for a moment or two. Perhaps she had really hurt herself, though she had gone about uncomplainingly for the rest of the day. Perhaps it was something to do with the baby. Poor Mrs. Fincham, she would have to wait for the doctor, anyway, for he lived six miles away and it would take Mr. Fincham some time to get there. He had never bought a car; because, Emmie suspected, there was no way of making a car run on less than its adequate allowance of petrol and oil.

She called, just as her master laid his hand on the latch of the door, "All right, I'm coming." Horses and lantern must take their chance. She pulled on her knickers and tucked her nightgown into them as though she were preparing to paddle, and put on her overcoat while her feet were fumbling into her hard cold shoes. Saul Fincham, with his face flickering and darkening grotesquely in the light of the blown candle, was waiting in the passage. Beyond him Mrs. Fincham's bedroom door showed as a pale oblong of light. A sound of moaning came to Emmie's terrified ears.

"There's a light in there. You just stay with her. She's more frightened than hurt and there's no call for the doctor till morning, but I can't stand this fuss."

Emmie stepped into the bedroom.

Under the faded patchwork quilt, the work of some long-dead industrious female Fincham, Mrs. Fincham was stirring uneasily. Her face was damp and dirty white against the pillows, and her eyes, as Emmie entered, were screwed tight shut. But she spoke in her usual voice.

"I guess I left it too late. I had a twinge or two before bedtime. I hoped I'd hold out and send a message by the milk-cart for the doctor. Mr. Fincham does so hate to be put out."

So it was the baby.

Emmie's heart began to flutter. She had been at home when her mother had had the babies, but Mrs. Bacon seemed never to have any trouble. The nurse came in, and the children were driven out, and when at the end of some hours they had come creeping back there had been a new baby, and that was all. This crisis found Emmie utterly unprepared.

"Is there anything I can do?" she asked. Her voice was very small.

Mrs. Fincham opened her eyes again and said hurriedly, "Yes, clear all those clothes off the chairs and make the room look a bit tidy. I hate for the doctor to find me like this." The hurried words ended in a moan: but almost immediately she added, "And the good counterpane is in the drawer, second drawer down."

Emmie moved softly about, making the room ready for the doctor, who, when he came, would have no eyes for anything except the woman on the bed. How long did it take babies to be born?

Mrs. Fincham moaned again, and said immediately afterwards, "Go get the stove going, Emmie. There must be some hot water."

"I don't like to leave you."

"I'll be all right. Do as you're told."

Emmie lighted one candle from the other and ran down to the kitchen. Would the stove be dead? Yes, not a spark. She crumpled some paper and threw in the sticks with a reckless, extravagant hand. The flames began to crackle and she drew out the flue controller to its fullest extent before filling the biggest of the kettles. Oh, why had Mrs. Fincham delayed? The doctor would be asleep; he would have to dress. Horrible thought, he might not even be at home! She filled the yawning gap of the stove with more sticks and lumps of coal and set on the kettle. Then she ran upstairs again.

The children were awake, and she was obliged to stop by the door of the room where they slept and bully them into bed again. "I'll slap you all, harder than you've ever been slapped if you get out of bed or make a sound," she said with fierceness bred of strain. There was no time for coaxing or explanations, and coming from the usually kind and gentle Emmie, the threat had great effect.

Mrs. Fincham was really screeching now, though she took a fold of the sheet between her two shaking hands and stuffed it between her teeth. Emmie wiped her wet palms on her coat and tried to draw a steady breath, but her throat was constricted. She could only stand, breathless and agitated, hating herself. I'm not suffering, she's suffering. I must mind about her, not about my breath.

There was a violent agitation in the bed. Mrs. Fincham let go the sheet, cried, "Help me," and screamed.

As Emmie moved forward a wave of dizzy horror struck and for a moment threatened to fell her. But by the time she had reached the bed and lifted the tumbled clothes, it had receded, leaving her calm and steady.

Writhing white limbs, strangely white, like those of a statue. The gates of birth.

More screams.

"We are born in another's pain and perish in our own."

Nakedness. "Thou shalt not look," but then, who would wish to? Swollen blue veins mapping the taut white stomach.

Scream after scream, and again that cry for help.

But what could one do? Oh, why was all this so hidden away, whispered about, draped with the folds of ignorance and purient silence? Why weren't people taught about this, instead of about how fish spawn?

Blood.

The other children, driven to disobedience by terror at the screaming, appeared at the door. Born children, all born this way, but they mustn't know yet. They mustn't know. She pushed them roughly into the passage and dragged a chair against the door.

Hurry back to the bed.

The blind, thrusting head of a baby with all the forces of nature behind it. Relentless. Seeming to demand help, and yet needing none.

Will Mrs. Fincham die? All through my ignorance? Yet there is a strength in her that one would never suspect; straining; pushing, even as she screams. And there is the cord that either must, or must not, be touched. God help me! God help me! God help me! Of course. I can at least wipe Its face.

★ ★ ★

Two hours later the doctor, on his way out, paused in the kitchen where Emmie crouched by the roaring stove. With a finger under her chin he tilted up her drained white face with the heavy shadowy eyes.

"You've been a very good girl," he said. "How old are you?"

"Fifteen."

He was silent for a moment, still holding her chin on his finger. There was a scent about him . . . hospital? . . . carbolic soap?

"It isn't always like that, you know. With help. And she'd hurt herself." He dropped his finger. "I'm going now to knock up a woman in the village. You keep the fire going and carry on as usual. Everything will be all right."

That was kind, thought Emmie. He was afraid that I should remember it, and mind, if ever, if ever that happened to me. Oh, but it never could . . . I could never . . . and yet it was so tiny and, well, so tiny.

5

After that Mrs. Fincham was ill for a long time. At the end of the second day the doctor brought with him a proper nurse from the town. The village woman stayed too — at the doctor's order. Emmie heard him say to Saul Fincham, in a cold, determined voice, "It's absurd to expect a child to look after a house, a man, three children, an invalid and a nurse."

Saul had retorted in his most unpleasant manner, "Why does the nurse need looking after?"

"She must have her meals prepared. Be reasonable, man. It won't be for long."

Fincham's became a small hell on earth. Saul was maddened, quite literally maddened by the thought of the expenses he was incurring. The nurse, who complained of the food, and then finding complaint useless, ordered in a supply of luxuries in his name. Special food for the baby because its mother had no milk. The doctor. Medicines. The woman's wages. Fires in the bedroom. And that ignorant, insolent little devil messing about in the dairy. It was enough to craze any man. He made no attempt to conceal his feelings from Mrs. Fincham, who, utterly broken at last, could cry and beg the nurse to keep him out of her room.

The village woman resented the nurse's presence and would have gone home in a huff but that she feared the doctor who often gave her employment in simple cases. She was as unhelpful as she could be, and took out her own feeling of inferiority before the professional by bullying Emmie who hadn't any standing at all.

The nurse hated the country and didn't consider Fincham's a fit place to put pigs in: dripping candles, smoking stoves, cold passages, common people.

Emmie was put upon by everybody, and obliged to grapple with the dairy work under the lash of Saul Fincham's jaundiced eye and bullying tongue. One day, as he flung out of the dairy after a bitter tirade about the house being full of lousy women and squalling brats, Emmie muttered after him.

"You helped to make them, didn't you?" He didn't hear her, but it was a relief to have said it, all the same.

At last the day came when a fire could be lighted in the parlour, that Holy of Holies, and Mrs. Fincham came down and lay on the shiny horsehair sofa. Soon after that the nurse departed, pleased and flaunting. The hired woman stayed another week, doing everything for Mrs. Fincham and the baby in her own way at last, the exact opposite of the nurse's. Then she, too, departed to another case and life fell into its regular pattern, except that there was now the baby, another girl, to look after, and that Mrs. Fincham must never lift or pull anything heavy. And an even more rigorous economy campaign set in, to make up for the wicked extravagance to which Mr. Fincham had been put.

6

And then, in rapid sequence, came the fire, and Emmie's dismissal.

The fire broke out in the night, some time after Emmie had returned from the stable; for she had resumed her nightly expeditions as soon as people left off popping about the passages at all sorts of odd hours. It burned down three stacks of unthreshed corn and the barn where the threshed corn, that Mr. Fincham hadn't sold, stood in sacks, before the fire brigade got it under control. Emmie, watching from the kitchen window with Mrs. Fincham, tried to see in the conflagration the drama and significance that there was in the fire at Sarn, but that was impossible for several reasons: the main one being that one could not be sorry for Mr. Fincham. It was only his stacks, not his hopes, that soared to the sky in a cloud of flame and smoke. Besides, after that, he had many papers to fill in, and the man from the insurance company came down and surveyed the scene of the fire, and asked questions and took notes. And presently Emmie heard Saul tell his wife at breakfast that the company was "going to pay up".

Emmie said nothing. She went on with her work all day; and every night, when the house was still, she crept down and fed the horses. They were fatter; she wondered whether any one else had noticed. Saul had grumbled in her hearing at the way "the feed" was going this winter, but so far he seemed not to have suspected. They had a little more "pull" too, Emmie noticed, with the kind of loving eye that people turn upon growing children. Sometimes when they broke, the milk-cart ones, into a trot of their own accord, her eyes moistened with the sorrow of it. That just that little extra should make such a difference, should lend them that little bit of extra spirit that saved them from the blow; and that that little should be, legally, denied them. It was very unjust. So when she and Saul came into battle over her depredations his was not the only temper involved.

He caught her, one night, red-handed. She had the lantern swinging from her wrist and her arms full of hay, and as she came out of the stackyard the darkness took shape and substance suddenly in a way that she had secretly dreaded that it might. She clutched the hay

105

to her leaping heart, the lantern shuddered; and it was with a certain amount of real relief that she heard the apparition say, in Saul Fincham's voice, "What the bloody hell do you think you're doing?"

"I'm feeding your horses, Mr. Fincham. They don't get enough to eat."

"Well, I'll be damned."

To that, something unknown in Emmie heretofore, yearned to cry out,

"Yes, you will. I hope there's a hell for people like you." But something else warned, prompted her. Don't annoy him any more . . . apologize . . . then you can go on doing it somehow. And if you let him know how you feel he'll have a weapon against you, in them, like the boys with the frogs. They were always worse when you were about.

She said meekly, "It was only a little . . . I didn't think you'd mind."

"You're a blasted little thief, that's what you are. I knew it the moment I set eyes on you, with your smarmy voice and butter-wouldn't-melt-in-your-mouth face. Are you going to tell me how to feed horses? The hell you are. Out you go tomorrow morning, neck and crop. And I'll tell you another thing . . . every bit of extra fodder that's been wasted this winter, *wasted*, you hear me, is going to be made up. If you don't pay it back they'll go without. To think of you, you snotty little thief! How long have you been doing this?"

"Not long," said Emmie, still, from long training, meek in the face of abuse.

"Anyway, once is too often. You go tomorrow, and not a penny wages do you get — nor a character," he added vindictively.

The last breakwater of patience gave way in Emmie; anger rushed in at full flood. There was even a definite physical relief, she stopped trembling for the first time since the shock of his appearance, and her breath came easily. She felt bigger too, and her voice rang out strong and menacing as she said,

"Actually I've been doing it a long time . . . since before the fire, Mr. Fincham."

He missed the menace and the point.

"All the worse," he said. "And if you've any money saved you'll pay me before you go."

"Oh no."

"What do you mean, oh no? Do you realize that I could get a policeman to you?"

"You would be silly," said Emmie. "You see, I saw you fire the ricks."

There was another moment's silence: she could hear the owl whose cry had often chilled her by its eeriness. She was not frightened now.

Then Saul Fincham said, "You bloody little bitch, you're lying."

"All right, I'm lying. But why was the insurance man a bit puzzled about the barn catching? It was supposed to be the wind, wasn't it? But there wasn't any wind that night. I was out in it, and I know. I know in what order you lit the stacks. I saw you. You gave me the fright of my life."

"Nobody will believe you. You're making it up because you're caught thieving and you're sacked."

"All right," said Emmie again, "you test it. The reason why I was thieving as you call it will sound well, too, won't it? It'll prove that I had a chance of seeing you. It hangs together well. I don't mind the police knowing. I haven't gained anything. You have."

Saul Fincham was not over-gifted with imagination; but he had sufficient to enable him to look forward and to see that Emmie could, if she liked, call into being a very awkward situation. He played a weak card.

"Look here," he began, "I've been a good master to you . . ."

"You're nobody's good master," said Emmie fiercely, feeling the prick of the clutched hay at her breast and thinking of its destination. "You ought to be a slave." She would have liked to have handed Saul over to the infamous Simon Legree; there were limits to even her kind-heartedness.

"We'll talk things over in the morning," said Saul, who was beginning to feel the bite of the cold through his déshabille. He had been roused by a noise suspiciously like the closing of the kitchen door, and looking out, had presently seen a light moving in the yard. He had come down, all agog, to find somebody at his coal heap. And now the situation that had promised so well at the start had gone all wrong. He wanted his warm bed, and time to think.

Emmie made one of the greatest efforts of her life. It was also, to her crafty little mind, a test.

"I've stolen this now," she said, with emphasis on the verb, "so I might as well do what I meant with it."

She turned towards the stable. Saul Fincham, completely stunned, stared after the retreating light. By God, she was sure, the little viper. He would have liked to have wrung her neck.

Next morning, after breakfast, while Emmie was washing the crockery at the kitchen sink, she heard the door of the living-room close with a bang: heavy footsteps came along the slate-tiled passage, the kitchen door opened and slammed, and Saul Fincham stood by the draining-board. Emmie drew a deep careful breath and went on dipping the things in and out. Forces were not so even as they had been last night; she knew that. He would not be surprised this morning, and his size and fierceness would count. She had the curious feeling that she would always be much braver if she could wear coloured glasses, so that any timidity or embarrassment that shone from her eyes would be invisible to her opponent. She did not realize that just as her adversary had grown in the night, so had Saul's. She had no means of knowing, no experience that might lead her to guess, that he had spent the greater part of the night thinking over her story: how well it fitted: with what assurance she spoke: how even her midnight expeditions would reflect discredit upon him. So she was quite unprepared for his opening remarks.

"I've been talking you over with the Missus and she's a bit upset at the thought of your going. So for her sake, her being poorly, I'm willing to overlook your tricks so long as you promise to stop them, and I'll try to forget

109

that wicked nonsensical yarn that you've got into your head about me. See?"

The white flag, not openly waved, but plucked, as it were from a pocket, and hastily returned again! She could turn now and look at him. Red scrubbed face scored with lines of ill-temper: little pig's eyes, watching her warily: cruel mean rat-trap of a mouth. Great hulking lump, standing there pretending to forgive her.

"I don't want you to overlook or forgive anything, Mr. Fincham." She spoke primly, taking pleasure in the little separate words that fell neatly from her lips as beads fall from a fingered necklace. "I'm quite willing to leave today, as you suggested. In fact I shall be glad to . . . especially if I can't feed the horses any more." And then, quite suddenly, between her face and his, there floated another face, pale, pretty, discontented, with wavy hair and lips that had opened and shaped around many lovely words, saying now, "Sixty pounds is the hell of a lot." Miss Stanton. I may not get another job as quickly as I think; I've saved only five pounds.

She focused her eyes once more upon that ugly face and said, very firmly and clearly, "As for the nonsensical story, you seem to have forgotten it, and I'm willing to — for fifty pounds."

Be glad, Saul Fincham, that you are dealing with a novice, one who has only heard one sum bigger than that mentioned in actual money. Clive's story she has heard, and there were lakhs of rupees in that, and some fantastic sums are mentioned in *Treasure Island*: but so far Emmie has only come to grips with little sums, sixty pounds the limit. Ten she may conceivably find for

110

herself some time, so now she asks for fifty. Be glad, Saul Fincham, it might so easily have been a hundred. His red scrubbed face turned a dangerous blackish crimson.

"Blackmail," he gasped at last, "you can go to quod for that."

"And for firing ricks and drawing the insurance." A comical thought, even at this tense moment, made her smile as she said, "If we don't come to some arrangement, it looks as if we might both go." He mistook the smile. This was a deep one, deeper than he'd ever imagined; smiling there now in that crafty manner. Perhaps she had something else up her sleeve. Perhaps some one had been with her. God, who would have thought it? Little, spindly, mealy-mouthed handful of — ! What a mistake ever to have offered to keep her. He should have taken the upper hand last night, boxed her bloody little ears and pushed her off to bed, not talked to her.

Emmie pounced on the mistake too, at the very moment. "Besides that," she said, looking with interest at a spot on the wall just above and behind his left shoulder, "if I am a thief and a liar, why do you offer to keep me on?"

"Look here," he said, dropping all bluster, "this tale of yours is all poppycock, and you know it. But if you get spreading it about there'll be a lot of inquiries that'll waste my time. I won't have my time wasted, you understand. On the other hand, if I give you fifty pounds, and why the hell you stopped there I shall never understand, it looks as if there was something in it . . ."

"It's very awkward," said Emmie, "but it's either your time or fifty pounds, isn't it?"

She turned back to the bowl of cooling water where a greyish scum was already forming. With one last venomous look at her narrow back, stooped over the low sink, he went out of the kitchen. She heard him go upstairs, there was a pause. He was opening his safe. Presently he came down again. A little brown bag, with "Silver £5" printed heavily upon it, was clenched in one of his huge hands. He was breathing audibly and a good deal of his colour had deserted his face. With lamentable lack of sympathy Emmie perceived that he was suffering; she had attacked him at the one sensitive point in his make-up.

"This is to be the end," he said hoarsely. "It's no good coming this game again. It's only to save time and talk that I'm doing it now." He put the bag, with the crumpled ends of the treasury notes protruding from its top, down on the corner of the kitchen table and walked heavily away.

7

There were tears in Mrs. Fincham's eyes. She had not made even a pretence of siding with her husband, though Emmie had told her exactly why she was being sent away.

"I used always to keep on at him when I first came here and saw how he kept things." She sighed heavily, from the heart. "But I soon found out that it wasn't any good. That's the way he is, and nothing can change him. But I'm sorry you're going. You can't think how I shall miss you. You've seemed like a friend." They were in the dairy, and at the end of the speech Mrs. Fincham glanced into the handleless jug that held the money for the butter sold at the door. Then she went softly out and upstairs, returning with her thin black bag, a remnant of her unmarried days, a pathetic pretence of a woman's companion, since it never contained anything but a copper or two, a comb and a handkerchief. She opened it as though she expected to find something in it, sighed, and snapped it to again. A faint dull colour rose in her thin cheeks.

"I wish I could give you a little present, Emmie, but you know how I'm placed. Will you have this?"

She held out the bag. The paper money that Emmie had thrust into the neck of her frock lay suddenly heavy and hot upon her heart . . . fifty pounds! But it wasn't Mrs. Fincham's money: she'd never see a penny of it if Emmie gave it back.

She put out her chapped, chilblained hand and laid it, not on the bag, but on Mrs. Fincham's thin blue-veined wrist.

"I don't want a present," she said gently. "I've been paid for what I've done. And I shan't forget you."

"I know it isn't very nice," said Mrs. Fincham, looking at the bag again.

Oh, the pathos of it.

"It is," cried Emmie, feeling the tears in her throat. "It's far too nice to give away."

"Have it then." Emmie let her hand slide down Mrs. Fincham's and laid hold of the bag. Then she flung her arm over Mrs. Fincham's shoulder and burst into tears.

"You're so much nicer than he is," she sobbed. "Why should he treat you like this? It isn't fair."

Mrs. Fincham hesitated for a moment, then she turned towards the churn, escaping from Emmie's arm.

"I'm being paid for being a fool," she said in a hard voice, quite unlike her usual patient one. "Mind you don't get caught the same way."

What did that mean? Could there be another Saul Fincham in the world?

"You'd better go now, Emmie. And don't let him see the bag. He'd recognize it."

"Good-bye, Mrs. Fincham. And thank you."

"Good-bye, Emmie, I hope you'll get a good job, I've given you a nice reference."

She lifted the lid of the churn. The emotional moment might never have been. But it had spoilt the morning for Emmie. All the way to the station, through fields where the young, silky wheat was ruffled into waves by the young spring wind, she thought of Mrs. Fincham. She, Emmie, was escaping. Saul Fincham might not exist for all he mattered now. But Mrs. Fincham was chained to him; and so long as he housed her, and didn't actually beat her, there was no escape for her.

There was something wrong somewhere. The sun was shining, catkins were blowing yellow by the side of the wood. It was spring. She was young. She had a substantial instalment of her debt to Miss Stanton,

114

dropped unexpectedly as it were from Heaven. She had five pounds and some odd shillings of her own saving. She could hardly be going to a more unpleasant job than the one she had left. But she wasn't happy. Mrs. Fincham, the thin horses, the chained dog . . . still in Saul Fincham's power.

She made for the station rather than the bus stop because she felt vaguely that the station offered more variety of destination. A time-table or a poster might give her some idea of where to go. The station was small and homely; there were well-pruned rose trees and the green spears of bulbs in the raked beds beside the platform. Emmie put her bag on a bench and walked the length of the platform looking at the advertisements and the notices that urged you to take your bicycle or your dog on your contemplated journey.

The poster that finally caught her eye, and so shaped her life, was on the other side and she had to cross over to get a better view of it. It showed an old stone arch, a gateway, and beyond it a stretch of greensward with some pieces of ruins standing upon it. It was drawn in posterish, futuristic style and was more attractive when seen from a distance, though you could get the same effect by looking at it through half-closed eyes. Underneath it said in bold black letters, "Visit the site of the famous Abbey of St. Petersbury. Day excursions every Saturday and Thursday throughout the summer 5s." Emmie recrossed the line and looked at the poster again. There was a charm about it. Ancient peace brooded in the purple shadow of the gateway; the green was urgent. Well, it was all the same to her. "Ever let the

115

fancy roam," she thought. A single ticket to St. Petersbury was more than five shillings, the clerk at the office told her. That seemed harsh, since on certain days they could take you and bring you back for that sum. She bought the ticket and sat down by her bag to wait for the train.

Part Three

Part Three

1

St. Petersbury was an ancient town that had grown naturally into three roughly concentric circles. There was the still green centre with the Cathedral church, the Abbey Ruins, St. Michael's Church, two squares of fine old houses and three old but respectable shopping streets; that was the original town. Beyond that was a circle of poorer houses, slums, mean shops, three cinemas, the station and one or two factories that made agricultural implements, mineral waters, ice-cream. And outside, a multi-coloured girdle, lay the new housing estates, cheap or expensive according to the depth of the second circle between them and the centre.

Emmie alighted from the train in the late afternoon. The sun had gone in, but the wind was left, piling up drifts of dirty paper that was always scattered over the second circle, in the gutters and the angles made by the worn stone steps of houses where they met the pavement. She had asked a porter at the station whether he could direct her to some place where she could stay for a day or so. He knew nowhere, but a Miss Trappit who kept a little general store, "just along the street to your left", would know of somewhere. The name was over the door. So Emmie walked along

119

slowly, looking at the shops until she reached a small double-fronted one with "M. Trappit, licensed to sell tobacco", painted in dim white letters over the door. It was indeed very "general". A row of newspaper hoardings sloped beneath its windows; and a rack of film magazines and pattern books for the home dressmaker swung on one side of the door. The left-hand, wider window was filled with boxes of stationery, lisle stockings, woollen vests, tin kettles, cretonne overalls and scrubbing brushes. The narrow window on the right was devoted to cigarettes and tobacco, jars of sweets and packets of chocolates. White enamelled letters, fixed to the panes, indicated that cocoa, metal polish and Oxo could also be obtained there. Emmie pushed open the door, and to the accompaniment of the loud jangling of a bell, entered the shop. Behind the counter a small, middle-aged woman was fixing price tickets to a number of cloth berets, grass-green, scarlet, bright blue and brown. She lifted her head inquiringly, slightly on one side, like a bird.

She evidently looked upon Emmie as a customer, and Emmie hadn't the heart to ask straightway for information, so she bought a packet of notepaper, a pen, a bottle of ink, and then, when the woman was putting them together in a parcel, said, "Do you know anywhere where I could stay for a day or two? The porter at the station advised me to ask you."

Miss Trappit put her head rather more on one side and looked at Emmie consideringly.

"For how long?"

120

"A little time, a day or so, till I can get a job."

"I see. What would you require?"

"A bed . . . and something to eat, of course. I wouldn't be any bother."

"Well," said Miss Trappit, very slowly, "as a matter of fact I sometimes have people myself. I've plenty of room. The only thing is . . . my brother and sister live with me . . . and they're a trifle queer. Some people object to that. Would you?"

"Not a bit," said Emmie, wondering what "queer" might mean.

"What could you pay?"

"What would you want? You see, I've never lodged anywhere before. I wouldn't know how much."

"Would four shillings a day be too much?"

"I don't think so. No." Twenty-eight shillings a week. An awful lot — but then, she might get a job straight away.

Miss Trappit let her eyes travel slowly over Emmie from head to foot and back again. Very young. Poorish, but nicely spoken. Better be on the safe side. "Paid in advance, of course."

Emmie selected two florins from her money and laid them on the counter. Miss Trappit brightened visibly. She lifted the flap in the counter and stood aside so that Emmie might come through the gap, lowered it again and opened a door on the side of the shop farthest from the window. Propping this door open with a metal cat, no doubt that she might hear any one who entered the shop more easily, she said, "Come with me."

The passage and the stairs that led from it surprised Emmie. The shop was poor and crowded, unpainted and cheap-looking, but there had evidently been a time when it was prosperous, when the people who owned it had lived in surroundings of comfort and a degree of beauty. The passage was floored and panelled in oak, darkened with age and shiny; the stairs were solid and shallow and wide, with massive carved newel posts. The upper landing was wide too, and the oak floor was polished as smooth and bright as glass. There were plaster mouldings, yellowed with passing years, over each door that led off it. Miss Trappit opened one of the doors, and crossing the room thus revealed, pulled up a blind. "This is the room. You see it looks out on the garden. My brother does the garden. It'll be a mass of bloom soon."

Emmie crossed to the window and looked out. Immediately below, bounded by high walls with higher buildings looming over them, was a garden about the size of a tennis court. A chestnut tree, just freckled with green, stood at its farther end, masking a tall building that rose behind it. The whole garden was laid down with crazy paving, broken here and there by patches of soil filled at the moment with the green heads of bulbs. Crocuses were beginning to break already, mauve and white and yellow.

"It's a lovely garden," she said appreciatively.

"And so sheltered," said Miss Trappit joyfully, "that we have often gathered roses on Christmas Day."

She turned briskly from the window.

122

"I must run down to the shop. I'll tell them downstairs about you and we'll soon have a cup of tea. I'll come up for you." She trotted to the door, half closed it, and then put her head round to say, "Bathroom *etcetera* across the way."

Emmie unpacked her washing materials and went across to the bathroom where the bath, almost nude of paint and cased in mahogany, told the same tale as the architecture of the house. Then she brushed her hair and laid her nightgown under the fat eiderdown with its faded Paisley cover.

And now she could write to Miss Stanton.

In the writing that had been a slow and painful imitation of Miss Stanton's own, but which had become quickened and individual through scribbling long essays at Arlington House, she set down the name of the town and the date, realizing that she did not know the name of the street, nor the number of the shop — and anyway would be there for so short a time that neither mattered. Then,

"DEAR MISS STANTON," she wrote, "I have left Fincham's and am looking for a job here. It seems quite a busy place and I expect to find a place soon, especially as I am not particular. I am sending you a little of what I owe you. I expect you will wonder where I obtained so large a sum in so short a time. I assure you it is quite all right. I didn't steal it or anything. The whole story would take too long to tell." And anyway she doubted whether Miss Stanton would approve. She might share Saul Fincham's views on blackmail. She paused with her pen poised, remembering the scanty meals, and the long hours, and the gleaning at Fincham's and added, "Some of it I saved. The rest came by a stroke of luck. I hope you are well. As soon as I am settled I will send you my address. I am staying for a day or so with some people who keep a shop. The shop is small and sells almost anything, but the house is lovely and makes me think of merchants and guilds in the Middle Ages. Mrs. Fincham is better than when I wrote to you last. She was sorry when I came away, and gave me a handbag; I feel sorry for her, left there with Mr. Fincham; longer acquaintance did not improve my opinion of him. I will write again soon and hope then to have a letter from you. Your loving and grateful EMMIE."

She put the folded sheet in the thin handbag beside the fifty pounds and determined that after tea she would find a post office and buy either a registered envelope or a postal order. She was a little vague about the best way to send so large a sum of money.

Very soon Miss Trappit came along and tapped on the door. "We're just going to have tea," she called. Emmie joined her on the landing and was met by the mouth-watering scent of cooking kippers. Miss Trappit led the way downstairs and through a door at the end of the lower passage. Emmie followed her into a room where three people were already seated round a large square table covered by a fine white cloth with crocheted lace around the edges. Emmie eyed them

124

shyly. At the head of the table, behind a tray also covered by a lace-edged cloth, sat a tiny old woman with thin white hair drawn tightly back from a brown, indescribably wrinkled face. From sunken sockets there gleamed a pair of bright black boot-button eyes that peered out just above the level of the massive silver teapot. On her right hand sat a woman and on her left, a man, whose complete similarity gave the impression that they were two versions of the same person. The "queer" brother and sister.

"My aunt, Mrs. Meadows, and my brother and sister," said Miss Trappit, indicating them in turn. "And let me see, I don't know your name, do I?"

"Emmie Bacon," said Emmie softly.

"This is Miss Bacon," said Miss Trappit, relaying the information. Mrs. Meadows stretched her neck so that the whole of her face was visible and gave Emmie a toothless smile. The other pair stared at her a moment without smiling and then returned to their plates where the hot kippers smoked.

"I trust you like kippers," said Miss Trappit. "We generally have a high tea, then we are satisfied with Ovaltine before we go to bed." Emmie, whose last meal had been taken at seven that morning and made of porridge, and whose last kipper had been eaten long ago, last summer, nodded, smiling, and plunged her fork into the most fleshy portion. A thin piping voice from behind the teatray inquired whether she took milk and sugar, and she was unable to do justice to the first lovely mouthful because she was obliged to swallow quickly in order to reply. The tea was hot and strong,

125

sweet and creamy, and for a little time, while she took the first edge off her hunger, she paid little attention to the other occupants of the table. Gradually, however, she became aware of just how queer Miss Trappit's brother and sister were. They were called Carrie and Alfred, and a blind person at the table would have come to the conclusion that they were very young children, so constantly did they require admonition.

"Carrie, you're slopping tea all over the cloth."

"Alfred, a lump of butter fell on your waistcoat."

"You can't eat cake with kipper. The bread is right in front of you."

Dozens of rebukes like these fell from the aunt's lips. Miss Trappit went calmly on with her tea, only addressing a remark now and then to Emmie or Mrs. Meadows. At first Emmie wondered whether Carrie and Alfred were dumb, neither spoke for a long time. Mrs. Meadows kept her eye on their cups and refilled them when they were empty, and said, "That'll do now," as she moved their kipper plates aside when nothing but bones remained. Then suddenly Alfred said. "The clock's wrong again," and rose, opened the front of the black marble clock that stood on the velvet-shrouded mantelpiece and pushed the long hand back from twenty-five minutes past six to a quarter past. Nobody rebuked him, and for a moment Emmie believed that the clock had been ten minutes fast. But on his way back to the table, where Mrs. Meadows had placed a slice of cake upon his plate, he paused by Emmie's chair and said in a confidential voice, "Perhaps you don't know it, but clock hands always slip down when they're going that way. They come down much too fast, and go up much too slowly. I'm always having to set them right."

Emmie went bright red from embarrassment. Ought she to take no notice? Or to agree with him? How did the others treat the matter? She gave a feeble, she hoped understanding, smile. Miss Trappit came to the rescue. "Yes, she knows, I told her." He sat down, satisfied, and Miss Trappit said softly to Emmie, "It's the one thing you mustn't argue about. I think somebody tried to teach him to tell the time when he was very young before we found out that he was queer. He'll alter the clock twice every hour, once to put it back ten minutes. Once to put it on. Between quarter to and quarter past it's generally all right."

"I see," said Emmie.

"Well, aunt," continued Miss Trappit, raising her voice, "I must get back to the shop. I haven't been disturbed once in half an hour. That'll show how trade is." She leaned over the back of Emmie's chair. "I should sit down here in the warm, if I were you. They're quite harmless, you know."

"Oh yes. Thank you. I want to go to post first."

"I'll tell you the way when you come through the shop," said Miss Trappit, and bustled away.

At once Carrie jumped to her feet and said, "Shall I take the things away?" Her speech was far more childish than her brother's. Mrs. Meadows nodded, moved over to the huge curly armchair by the fire, turned up the gas a little higher and drew some mending from a cretonne bag. She seemed quite happy to leave Carrie to deal with the silver teapot and the delicate china. And indeed, as Emmie watched, she was amazed to see that Carrie, so clumsy over the matter of feeding herself, was carrying and piling and folding things with the most earnest and the most delicate care.

When she had gone out with the last trayload, Alfred, who had been sitting quite still in his place at the table, turned to his aunt and said, "Have I time to help her with the washing up?"

Mrs. Meadows said calmly, without looking up, "I think so, just about."

He went out with a pleased expression.

Emmie, conscious of lessened tension, moved over to a stool on the hearth and sat down with her hand stretched to the blaze. What comfort. A stomach full of food: a seat by an open fire upstairs that big bed and fat eiderdown waiting for her. All for twenty-eight shillings a week. If only there were some way of earning that sum and staying here.

"They're twins, you know," said Mrs. Meadows, drawing out a strand of wool and matching it on a sock. "They were lovely little babies, too, and nobody thought they were funny until they were about six; they seemed just like other children. But it seems as though their senses got split up. They've been an awful burden on Meggie, Miss Trappit, you know; though she never makes a burden of them. I must say. What she'll do when I'm not here to look after them, I don't know. Of course, in a way they're useful. Alfred works for hours in the garden and Carrie can wash and scrub and polish with the best; only they have to be minded, and taken for walks, and looked after." Mrs. Meadows looked steadfastly into the fire for a moment as though she was recalling to herself the long hours of minding and dull, dutiful walking that she had endured. Then, with another bird-like movement, she pulled herself together and thrust one of her fleshless claws, knotted with rheumatism out of all resemblance to a hand, into a sock and began weaving the long foundation strands across an enormous hole.

Emmie watched her, and the words, "when I'm not here", echoed in her mind. How strange and awful to be old: to have no future: to be able to look back and see all the mysteries of your life laid bare, lived through. All the things one longed for, pleasant scenes, pretty things, money, would be useless then. Even friends and good company would count no more: the ultimate action of dying must be done alone, and after that there was the silence and loneliness of the grave for ever.

And they were all bound for that end, the poets, Miss Stanton, the Finchams, Miss Trappit, the two idiots in the kitchen, this old woman and herself. And beyond that, outside, in other countries, millions of people, white, brown, black, and yellow, all hurrying into the grave. And yet one wished away the days, blind to the thought, the true thought, that when the moment for the last breath came one would cry out (and nobody would mind it), "Give me a day, just any day, even the day when my head ached so badly and I had to wash all morning and churn all afternoon, any day so that I had twenty-four hours more here in the light and the company."

129

Hideous thought, unbidden and unwelcome, but never to be quite banished again; although tonight she shook it off, thinking, this is the first time that I've been idle since I was old enough to think. I really must keep busy.

Nor did she recognize, in that resolution, the secret of half the activity of the world; the need that drove people to the cinemas, the dance halls, the taverns; the need that set people playing cards and driving fast cars and travelling the world: the urgent need to hide from themselves the fact they were sentenced.

The thin old voice was making a claim on her attention. Mrs. Meadows was glad of a new listener.

"Meggie has had a very hard life," she was saying, "since the family came down in the world. Her grandfather, that is my father, was a leather merchant and sadler here. He was Mayor of the town eight times. It was a good business then. He used to have as many as eighteen men all working in that tall building at the back, behind the chestnut tree. He had his saddle horse, and grandma her carriage and three help in the house. Then it all went, and when Meggie's father had the shop he sold dog-leads and suchlike trumpery rubbish. And he did what jobs of mending the farmers needed with his own hands. Of course, Meggie couldn't carry that on, so she started the general shop, but what with Woolworth's and Marks and Spencer's she has a job to make ends meet. I often wonder how it will all end. Don't ever, while you're staying here, mention it if you go into one of those shops. It upsets her so. Though

I know they're very attractive to young people, so cheap and gay, and such variety."

"I've never seen one," said Emmie. "But I won't go in one while I'm here."

"Oh, I wouldn't ask that. Don't mention it, that's all. As a matter of fact I get quite a lot of household things there myself, cheaper than Meggie can get them wholesale. But I never tell her."

Just as Emmie was smiling her appreciation of this confession Alfred threw open the door and dashed towards the clock.

"I'm late again," he said, "I knew I would be." He pushed the clock forward from quarter to seven to five minutes to, gave a sigh of relief and sat down, waiting apparently until it was time to push back the down-hurrying hand again.

"What time does the post office close?" asked Emmie.

"Seven," said Mrs. Meadows. She, too, looked up at the clock and then turned over the gold watch that she wore pinned to bosom on a true lover's knot. "It's five to, now. I'm afraid you won't catch it."

"It'll do in the morning. Might I look at your paper?"

"We don't have one in the house," said Mrs. Meadows. "Meggie always tells us the news from the headlines. You get such horrid things in the papers nowadays, murders and so on."

"I really wanted a local one, to look for a job, you know."

"Ah, yes, that's different. The *Petersbury Press* will be out tomorrow. We always have that. It's a thoroughly nice paper."

Carrie came in with a plate of apples in her hand. She set it on the table, selected the rosiest of the fruit, rubbed it on her sleeve and took a big bite.

"Offer them round, Carrie," said Mrs. Meadows as though speaking to a child, and without lifting her head.

Carrie obediently held the plate, first to Alfred, who took an apple, then to Emmie. She shook her head, though they looked very attractive, partly because she wondered whether "meals" included such incidentals as these, and partly because not to have one covered up Carrie's breach of manners. She looked at the two of them, stolidly and audibly chewing, and was suddenly afflicted with the first nervous spasm of the kind she had ever known. She could not sit here and do nothing. It was only seven o'clock. The evening might last three hours more.

"Can I help you darn?" she asked. Mrs. Meadows drew out another sock, matched it with wool, selected a needle and passed them all across to Emmie. She began to darn, thankfully.

Neither Carrie nor Alfred seemed to need occupation. They ate more apples. At a quarter past seven Alfred pushed back the clock, at twenty-five minutes to eight he moved it on. He did the same between eight and nine, and nine and ten. Miss Trappit joined the party at eight o'clock, and sat down at the table with some writing. At half-past nine Mrs. Meadows served Ovaltine in tall brown beakers with silver rims. At ten o'clock she raked out the fire. Miss Trappit rose, and they all trooped upstairs. By that time Emmie had changed her mind about the desirability of being a permanent guest in the Trappit household. She must have a book before tomorrow evening or she would be "queer" herself.

2

The bed, however, was all she had imagined it, and more, and she lay in it until Miss Trappit banged at the door in the morning and called that breakfast was at eight and she had ten minutes. Ten to eight, good gracious! At Fincham's she would have been up almost two hours. Mrs. Fincham had probably risen at five to get forward with her single-handed day. There was a sigh for Mrs. Fincham on her lips as she tumbled out of the soft warm bed on to the soft old fur rug that lay beside it. She washed and dressed rapidly, ran a comb through her curls, opened the window and stripped the bed as she had been taught to do at Arlington House, and dashed downstairs.

Breakfast had started and she slid into her place with apologies directed half at Miss Trappit, half at Mrs. Meadows.

"I'm awfully sorry. I'm used to an alarm clock. And it was such a comfortable bed."

"That's all right," said Miss Trappit. "You see I get up at half-past six to start off the boy on the paper round, and by eight I'm ready for my breakfast. By the way, I've brought you a *Press* in. Aunt said you wanted one."

"Thank you," said Emmie, noticing that there were three copies of the paper on the table.

"That's all right," said Miss Trappit again, "we always read the *Press* at breakfast time on Wednesday. Two of these I shall just run through the mangle and sell later on. What kind of job are you looking for, by the way?"

"In a house . . . housemaid or something." Both Miss Trappit and Mrs. Meadows looked slightly surprised.

"Well, you won't be with us long," said Miss Trappit, folding back her paper. "Look at this, ten, twenty, twenty-eight people all needing maids. I'll see if I know any of the places."

She bent her grey head over the paper, and Emmie, relieved, for the moment, of the responsibility of choice, gave her entire attention to her breakfast. There was porridge, not the stodgy, lumpy porridge that was eaten with a grudging avidity at Fincham's, but smooth porridge, thinned with milk and sprinkled with sugar like crushed amber. And after that there were sausages. Did the Trappit family breakfast like this every day? Then how bad was business? Or was all poverty comparative? Or did they, even in poverty, refrain from stinting the table?

"Can you cook?" asked Miss Trappit, looking up and lifting her cup to her lips.

"Not much," said Emmie, "just porridge, and stew and dumplings."

"Safer to say you can't, then. You should learn, you know. There's a great demand for cooks. That wipes out a good half of these; they mostly ask for plain cooking. How old are you?"

"Seventeen." She put the year on to her age, longing to have added more, but fearing to.

"I should have thought you were much older than that."

"So should I, nineteen at least," put in Mrs. Meadows.

Suddenly Miss Trappit laid her finger on an advertisement and said, "Here's the very thing. Mrs. Clarkson, in the Close, wants a house-parlourmaid. You'd have no cooking there, her old housekeeper does it all. And Mrs. Clarkson is such a sweet lady. I know her a little. I'll write you a note to take with you, if you like."

"Thank you so much," said Emmie. She turned to her own copy of the paper to read the address. "Corner House. The Close."

The shop bell jangled and Miss Trappit jumped up. "I'll write the note in the shop," she said, and hurried away.

Emmie went up to her room, made the bed and tidied her things, and dressed herself carefully in her dark blue coat and felt hat that she had worn for winter walks at Arlington House. She looked at the seams of her stockings to see that they were straight and taut, and rubbed her shoes on yesterday's handkerchief. Then she went down to the shop where Miss Trappit handed her an envelope addressed to Mrs. Clarkson in an old-fashioned, flourishing hand.

"I've been thinking," she began, and then broke off to serve a packet of suet. "I've been thinking that perhaps it will be a hard place for you. But it would be nice for you to be with such a nice person. You see, Mrs. Clarkson has come down in the world, and has to have people in her house. All her money was invested in Russian oil wells and railways, I understand, so she's very poor. But she is a sweet person and she is a lady. That makes all the difference, doesn't it?"

"I suppose so," said Emmie, who had had little experience of ladies. "How do I get to the Close?"

"Go left from here, away from the station, and straight on till you come to the Abbey Gate. Cross the open space in front, and you'll see a little pathway with posts and chains to keep out cyclists. That takes you straight into the Close, and Mrs. Clarkson's is the house on the corner nearest the Cathedral Gate. You can't miss it."

"Thank you so much, and for this," said Emmie, brandishing the note before slipping it into her pocket.

"I hope you'll get it," said Miss Trappit. "We have lunch at one. But come back whenever you like."

Emmie smiled and went out, leaving the bell dancing behind her. She walked swiftly, for the morning was cold though bright, and the streets, emptied of the people who worked, were not yet filled by dawdling morning shoppers. In a short time she reached the Abbey Gate, whose pictured beauty was responsible for her presence in St. Petersbury, and stood for some time looking at it. She remembered enough of her history to recognize that it was a specimen of late Norman

136

architecture, and to brood over the niches that had once held the effigies of saints. Through the gateway, above which the suspended portcullis hung like a stiff fringe, she could see the green grass, some beds of breaking crocuses, and the grey ruins of the once powerful Abbey. Henry Tudor's men had arrived at this gateway. The red and white roses had shone on their tunics, halberds and pikes had gleamed in their hands. And the monks had filed out, homeless, bewildered, dismayed. There was a great deal to think about here. But not now. She crossed the open space and passed between the posts that guarded the little paved path. It was bordered on both sides by tall old houses, gabled, timbered, aslant. One of them bore a stone tablet beneath which she paused, to read, "John Freeman, last Abbot of Saint Petersbury, evicted from his Abbey in 1536, died here of a broken heart, 1537" Here, in this little gabled house! Had he just walked across the open space as she had done — and were the posts there then — and did he come to this house because somebody, perhaps somebody to whom he had been kind, lived here and would take him in? Interesting, fascinating place.

For a moment her pleasure in her first intelligent encounter with the visible remains of the past drove all thought of her errand from her mind. She held on to the rusty twisted railings that ran in front of the little house and let her imagination run backwards.

She was greatly startled when a voice near her said something in harsh, un-English syllables. The harshness of the voice and the fact that she had been clinging on to the railings and staring at the house, led her to think for a moment that an angry householder was bidding her move on. She had met with rebuffs at far too many kitchen doors in the past to be able to meet a situation like this with anything but fear and apology. "I beg your pardon," she said swiftly and raised her eyes almost imploringly to the face of the man who had spoken. His expression of half-gibing interest gave way to one of confusion.

"No. I must beg yours," he said. "Let me explain. I thought you were one of a party of students from Sweden whom I had to tote round yesterday and am just going to join today. It's the coat and the hat, and your evident interest in old Freeman's house. And those girls have so little English, I thought that if one had wandered I'd better pick her up. Do forgive me."

"It's all right," said Emmie, greatly relieved and smiling so that her yellow eyes danced. "I was afraid it was somebody annoyed by my staring."

The strange man smiled back at her and fidgeted with the belt of his shabby raincoat.

"You interested in that kind of thing?" He jerked his head at the tablet. Emmie nodded.

"Then take a look at the Corner House, if you're going through the Close. Louis Napoleon stayed there once when it was a hotel and was kicked out for not paying his bill. You'll see that the steps gave the kicker a wonderful chance. Good morning."

His hand went to the brim of his jaunty hat, and he hurried away up the path. Emmie set off at an equal rate in the opposite direction; the Corner House meant something more to her than a place of historical interest!

138

Louis Napoleon — the Crimean War — a wonderful story called *Between Two Thieves*. Not a very nice person. What a pity it hadn't been Queen Elizabeth, that much-travelled person; or Charles the Second. Still, there was always Eugenie.

> Victoria, Carlotta and Eugenie
> Were young queens once,
> Were once young Empresses . . .

> Queens have died young and fair.

She hurried into the Close and made for the Corner House.

There was an air of secrecy, of calm and of withdrawal about every house in the Close. They had no front gardens and no railings, the narrow strip of pavement alone divided them from the square of grass and shrubbery that lay in the centre. The road did not come into the Close, but ran past at the far end before the Cathedral Gate. But their windows were guarded from curious passers-by by tightly stretched fine net. Every house in the Close had net curtains. And they all had flat grey stone fronts and flights of whitened steps leading to wide white doorways. Yet they were not all alike, for some were large and some were small; on some the white paint was new and shining, on others cracked and greyish. But there was no conscious striving after individuality, no red or blue paint, no strange ornaments at the windows, no pretentious or humourous names on the doors. Even the Corner House

139

had no name. It stood on the corner, everybody knew it, that was enough. Its steps, at which Emmie glanced with interest, were not so white as some, and neither the bell handles nor the doorknob nor the plate that said, "Do not ring unless an answer is required" had been cleaned that morning. Emmie pulled the bell after she had rounded the corner to discover whether there was another door there. Far away she could hear its deep bass clanging. Nobody answered. Emmie waited, wondered whether to ring again, put out her hand, drew it back, and went on waiting. Anybody in the house must have heard the bell. Presently the door was torn open from within and Emmie had to step out of the way nimbly to avoid being knocked down by a girl who flung herself through the doorway and pulled the door to behind her before she saw that there was someone on the steps. She pulled up short at the sight of Emmie and said in a rapid, breathless voice, "Was it you ringing?"

"Yes."

"I suppose Tally is on strike again. Oh blast, and I'm late already."

She turned, opened her bag, drew out a ring of keys, selected one, opened the door and went inside, flinging "Come in" to Emmie over her shoulder. With a rapid sliding step she then crossed the hall opened a door and shouted, down some stairs by the sound, "Mrs. Tallet, Mrs. Tallet. There's somebody at the door, you'd better come up. I've asked her in." Leaving that door open the girl ran across the hall again, nodded to Emmie and let herself out with a bang.

The hall was large and square, and empty except for an oak chest and two massive chairs that flanked it on either side. Black and white tiles covered the floor, and on the side opposite the chest a wide oak stairway, with a strip of pale brown carpet in the middle, ran up and curved out of sight. That was all Emmie could gather before a ponderous tread and heavy breathing heralded Mrs. Tallet's appearance. She came through the door, wiping her hands on a checked gingham apron, a tall gaunt woman with loops of black hair falling stiffly on either side of a steep, fiercely furrowed brow. She looked extremely cross, but asked Emmie her business civilly enough.

"I've called about an advertisement — for a maid."

Mrs. Tallet's manner changed abruptly. "You should have gone to the back," she said crushingly.

"I couldn't find it."

"Oh well, now you're in, wait there." She began with more hard breathing to mount the stairs.

The housekeeper? Probably. Not the person of all those in the world that Emmie would have chosen to work for. That bad-tempered look was too deep-seated. Within a minute she appeared upon the stairs again, beckoning. Emmie joined her and followed her along a passage.

"That open door," she said, stopping and pointing.

Emmie went forward, into a room the like of which she had never seen. It was full of the oddest things. Not daring to stare much, she saw them one or two at a time. Lace antimacassars, beaded footstools, a trinity seat, wax fruit and flowers under glass, a work-table

141

with a green silk bag hanging below it, like a dropped stomach, a huge gilded harp in one corner. And in the centre of it all, seated at a kidney-shaped desk was the room's occupant, not the ancient survival of Victorian days for whom the room prepared you, but a woman of Miss Trappit's age, dressed in a grey knitted suit. Bit by bit, as she had gained knowledge of the room, Emmie gathered the details of Mrs. Clarkson's appearance. It was most pleasant. And it told at once why people thought of her as nice and a lady. She had the whitest silkiest hair, neatly cut, perfectly waved. Her skin looked soft and pink all over, so that around the eyes and mouth where wrinkles were gathering, it was like crumpled pink satin. And her eyes were so blue, a vivid clear, clean-looking blue like a healthy child's eyes. She was short, that was clear even while she was sitting, and had a neat compact figure, comfortably plump without being at all fat. She pushed her chair back from the desk and turned slightly towards Emmie, with a smile as she said in a low sweet voice in exact keeping with her appearance,

"You've come about the advertisement?"

"Yes," said Emmie, and added "madam". Something seemed to be called for, and the abbreviated "'m" that was used so much by comic characters in books, repelled her. She had never addressed Mrs. Fincham so, but the maids at Arlington House called Miss Francis-Stokes "madam" always.

"I have a note from Miss Trappit," she added, laying it on the desk. Mrs. Clarkson put a pale, plump hand on it, saying as she did so, "Miss Tappit?"

"She said you would remember her. I'm staying there just now. A shop . . ." She faltered before the blank expression in Mrs. Clarkson's extraordinary blue eyes. But recognition dawned.

"Ah yes. I remember. Meggie Trappit in the Saltgate. A little general shop, isn't it?"

Emmie was left with the impression that once, long ago, in no very creditable circumstances, Meggie had crossed Mrs. Clarkson's path. And that was the exact impression that Mrs. Clarkson intended to convey.

"Do sit down," she said, opening the envelope. Emmie chose the least comfortable chair near by and sat down rather gingerly.

"Any further reference?" asked the sweet voice.

"Yes, two, madam." She took out the paper that Miss Stanton had written and laid it beside Mrs. Fincham's hastily scribbled eulogy.

"Very satisfactory indeed. And how old are you?"

"Seventeen."

"I see. And where is your home?"

"I haven't one."

"Indeed. How sad. Well, if you decide to come here I hope that you will be able to feel that it is, in some degree, your home." Her eyes met Emmie's with an expression of deep sympathy. Actually she was delighted to hear of Emmie's homelessness. Maids with homes were so prone to run to them the moment anything went wrong.

"And when would you be able to come?"

There was a gleam in her eye curiously like that in Mrs. Fincham's when she asked the same question.

"When would you like me to?"

"Tomorrow?"

"Yes," said Emmie. "I can come in tomorrow. Directly after breakfast."

Mrs. Clarkson rose and Emmie got up hastily.

"I dare say you'll find the work rather different from that which you did at the farmhouse, but my housekeeper, Mrs. Tallet, will always be glad to show you things. And so shall I. I do quite a lot of work myself, as much as my health permits." Her sweet sad smile hinted at weakness bravely borne. "Then I shall see you tomorrow. I do hope you will be happy and comfortable here. I like to think of the household, mixed as it must be, as one big family." She paused at the door with another smile. "The stairs at the end of the passage lead straight into the kitchen. Good-bye Emmie."

Emmie hurried along the passage, extremely conscious of the noise her feet made when the carpet gave place to thin painted oilcloth. She tried to tread more lightly and achieved only a clumsy self-conscious step that was noticed, she felt sure, by Mrs. Clarkson who still stood at her door. A lady — no doubt of that. A sweet lady — but but — There was just something about that sweet smile that made it compare unfavourably with Mrs. Fincham's weary one.

Mrs. Tallet was making a pie at the large table in the kitchen. She looked up as Emmie reached the last stair, but her hands never paused in their cutting and moulding of crust.

"You staying?" she asked briefly.

"I'm coming in tomorrow, after breakfast."

"The mistress say anything about uniform?"

"No."

"Always forgets that. Have you got any?"

"Only aprons," said Emmie, calling to mind the checked ginghams bought at the village shop and laboriously stitched by the light of the smoky lamp in the kitchen at Fincham's.

"Brown print for mornings, and white caps. Brown gaberdine, or something like that, and yellow aprons with frills, and caps for afternoons. Wright's in Market Thorofare is the best place." She spoke firmly.

Thank God there was some money left. "I'll get them today," said Emmie.

She stood by the table, awaiting anything else Mrs. Tallet might choose to tell her. The kitchen, she noticed, was half underground, only the feet of the passers-by could be seen through the grated window. A large boiler stood in one corner, a gas stove in the other. She had never dealt with a gas stove before and hoped that she would have a chance to watch Mrs. Tallet at it before she was required to touch it. Dozens of cups and plates and saucers were draining on the boards that sloped towards the deep white sink.

"That is the back door," said Mrs. Tallet, at last, with a jerk of her head.

Emmie took the dismissal. "Good morning," she said.

Mrs. Tallet, stooping at the oven door, gave a grunt. Emmie opened the door and stepped out into a paved area with a coalshed on one side, an open shed containing a mangle and a bicycle on the other, and a large meat safe nailed beside the door. Some steps with a small gate at the top brought her into a passage which

145

in turn opened on to the little paved pathway where the stranger had spoken to her. The opening was between Numbers Five and Six; she mustn't miss it tomorrow.

3

It was very sunny now and there was a kind of dancing radiance in the air. Market Thorofare she found easily, it opened out of the space before the Abbey Gate, faced it in fact. Buses were stopping and setting down crowds of women with rosy faces, country faces. Their clothes were all slightly old-fashioned, their baskets capacious. It was evidently market day. Down the centre of the wide Thorofare stalls were being erected by men with mittens on their cold red hands. Pots of daffodils and hyacinths reared bright heads above wrappings of thin paper, white, lime green, cobalt. Boughs of feathery mimosa, stark yellow and faded green hung from the hoods of the stalls, telling of warmer sunshine. Where? The South of France perhaps, where they were so cruel to horses. Forget the South of France. Remember that mimosa grows in Australia too, and is called wattle. "Smells are surer than sounds or sights to make your heart-strings crack . . . Like the smell of the wattle at Lichtenberg, riding in, in the rain. Forget that too, and look about for Wright's.

A low, double-fronted shop with old-fashioned, over-crowded windows. Over the door, in tarnished gilt letters, "T. Wright", and below, "Late Spencer". Sometime then it had been known as "Spencer's", but one was left with the impression that the last Spencer had been at rest for many, many years. Emmie entered the long dim shop, hung with goods and lighted by dusty skylights. At intervals down the shiny counters on either side languid and elegant young ladies lounged, prepared for, but not yet enduring, the market-day rush. She approached the nearest of them.

"I want some dresses."

"Dress department through the archway. Miss Green."

A high voice answered from the archway. "Yes."

"Young lady for dresses."

Emmie went through. A tall girl in a black satin frock came to meet her from behind a stand hung with bright dresses. Other stands, bearing coats and evening frocks, stood around the walls. Oh, if only I were buying a brown coat with a snuggly fur collar, and a yellow jersey and a brown cap to pull down over one eye!

"Yes, madam, what can I show you?"

"A brown print dress and a brown gaberdine one."

"Maids?" asked the young lady with a sudden chill in her manner.

"Yes," said Emmie, noting the change. And why do I hate black satin so much? Of course, mother's dress for Ted Gibson. Mustn't think of that, especially now, with this girl so haughty.

She picked out, and tried on behind a casement curtain, two dresses, both brown and plain, one harsh-feeling and cold, the other woolly and warm. Gaberdine, the girl informed her, was "out".

"Spit upon my Jewish gaberdine," thought Emmie with a faint smile hidden by the folds of the garment.

147

"I want aprons too, and caps," she said, speaking firmly because she was ashamed of the shame that the girl's manner provoked.

"Main shop, nearest the door," said the girl, making out the bill in a very illiterate hand. "Pay at the desk."

Emmie paid. Eighteen and eleven for the warm frock, seven and eleven for the print.

At the counter nearest the door she bought two honey-coloured aprons and caps, boxed together in sets, pretty things in themselves, but shameful. This girl's manner, too, left no doubt of that. However, this ladylike creature could not add and Emmie enjoyed pointing out to her that twice four and eleven did not make nine and eleven.

She paid that bill, too, at the desk and then, with all her purchases in a paper carrier, left the shop. Next month when she had bought a second print frock she would be able to spend money on her private clothes, perhaps. She would buy now a pair of lighter shoes and save these for outdoor wear so that she didn't sound like a ploughboy on the oilcloth. Then perhaps she might buy two pots of flowers, one for Miss Trappit and a small one for herself. The extravagance might be justified by the old Persian saying about the two loaves of bread and hyacinths for the soul.

At last, too weighed down to take her proposed walk through the Abbey ground, she made her way back to the Saltgate and Miss Trappit's shop.

A customer was just leaving, and as the door closed Miss Trappit asked with bright interest, "Well?"

"I'm going in tomorrow. I'm sure the note helped."

"Perhaps it did. I was sure she would remember me. We were at school together at Arlington House. Of course our ways have lain apart since then . . . she made a good match, and so on. What delightful flowers!"

"The daffodils are for you," said Emmie, overcome with shyness. It was the first present she had ever made to any one. Miss Trappit's gratitude was real and vocal enough to convince her that it was very pleasant to give presents.

Next morning immediately after breakfast, dressed in the brown print, and with her case in one hand and the pot of blue hyacinths in the other, she set out for the Close. Miss Trappit had given her a pressing and open invitation to come to see them whenever she had time and nothing more exciting to do.

4

It took her a fortnight to get her bearings in the Corner House. It was all so different from anything she had ever known. But she learned a great many things each day. Almost first of all she discovered that Mrs. Tallet was a surly automaton, wholly devoted to Mrs. Clarkson whom she called "Miss Ada", and hating, it seemed, every one else in the world.

Lodgers were all "trash". She resented their presence and the need for it. Tradesmen were all rogues: errand boys, "saucy little varmints". Maids were "bone-idle rubbish". Only Miss Ada was good and sweet and gentle: to be pampered and waited upon and shielded as far as possible from the unworthy rabble that had burst (you would have thought, to hear her, unbidden) into the sacred precincts of her once comfortable and respectable home.

Mrs. Clarkson had actually suffered in all her life from nothing more serious than a bout of tonsillitis when she was sixteen, and a few headaches: Mrs. Tallet was racked with rheumatism and had severe varicose veins as well. Yet every night, at the end of her sixteen-hour day, Mrs. Tallet climbed the stairs to Miss Ada's room, bearing a chromium-plated thermos jug of malted milk. She turned on the gas fire, opened the bed, spread out the silk nightdress, filled the hot-water bottle. She then tapped on the sitting-room door, accompanied Miss Ada to her bedroom, hung up her clothes as she took them off, poured out the milk and waited while it was drunk. Then, turning off the fire and opening the window, she switched the reading lamp on and the main light off, said "Good night" and softly closed the door.

Emmie soon realized that to Mrs. Tallet (Mrs. by courtesy) Miss Ada took the place of God, family, home, personal pleasures. Mrs. Tallet appeared to own nothing except her few necessary clothes; she had gathered round her none of those small possessions that emphasize the individuality of the owner. Her small cold room at the top of the house was as bare and neutral as a cell. Everything that was hers was there within the bounds of her own gaunt and unlovely person, and that everything was at Miss Ada's service, completely. Emmie, who loved her few poor clothes because they were hers, and who clung to her fading hyacinth, and a book or two that had her name in Miss

150

Stanton's writing on the flyleaf, pitied Mrs. Tallet and was inclined to cherish this pity because it softened slightly the otherwise inhuman relationship between them. It was wasted pity. What Emmie did not realize was that Mrs. Tallet owned everything in Miss Ada's possession. Mrs. Tallet enjoyed vicariously Miss Ada's soft warm bed, her heaped fires, her fine linen, her dainty food. Miss Ada had become, in the course of years, a projection of Mrs. Tallet's self, and had Miss Ada to suffer any deprivation she would not have suffered alone.

Mrs. Tallet enjoyed, through Miss Ada, many things that she herself would have hated. For instance, she would have loathed any one else to be present when she removed her own long, fleecy-lined knickers, yet, through her projection, she nightly enjoyed slipping her hemstitched crêpe-de-chine garments to the floor and having them picked up and folded for her. Mrs. Tallet had riches and pleasures of which Emmie could know nothing: and she had them, not because she was an exceptionally imaginative woman but because every one must have something. "Man does not live by bread alone." Forgotten prisoners have tamed mice and lavished affection upon them. St. Francis, lacking other audience, addressed the birds of the air. Mrs. Tallet, deprived of a fuller life by her own plainness and Miss Ada's demands, had, by sinking herself into her service, lost her own soul and gained Miss Ada's world. She drove Emmie quite mercilessly in Miss Ada's interests. That was Emmie's second discovery — that life here was no easier than life at Fincham's. True, there was no dairy work, and less scrubbing. The inmates of the Corner House did not drop cakes of mud from their shoes. But they did need silver polished and glasses shone, and tables laid and ashtrays emptied, and hot-water bottles filled. Washing up and sweeping and dusting in that house could have kept one person busy all day: but there was answering the door, waiting at table, cleaning shoes, polishing floors, preparing vegetables and making beds to be considered as well.

Mrs. Tallet did all the cooking, helped with the beds, waited upon Miss Ada, and unless the weather was too bad, washed in addition. The laundry, she said, not only charged prices fit to ruin you, but deliberately destroyed stuff into the bargain.

Every morning Emmie rose at six and raked out and lighted the boiler so that the water should be hot to meet the needs of the wakening house. Then she did the step, swept the pavement and polished the knocker. Indoors again at a trot she swept and dusted the dining-room and hall, cleaned out the grate of Miss Ada's room and lighted the fire in it. On good mornings she managed to sweep and perhaps half dust in there too. Then she laid the breakfast in the dining-room and switched on the gas fire. Back in the kitchen she prepared the tray for Mrs. Begbie, who breakfasted in bed, while Mrs. Tallet cooked the breakfast and took up Miss Ada's tea. By that time it was eight o'clock and the first of the breakfasters was down and ringing the bell. Between that time and nine o'clock she spent in serving the breakfasts, snatching hasty mouthfuls of her own and trying to "get forward" with the vegetables.

After breakfast she washed up, made beds, clumsily at first under Mrs. Tallet's impatient eye, but more neatly and speedily as she learned Mrs. Tallet's methods. Then there was the sweeping and dusting to do upstairs and the bathroom to be made spotless, lunch to be laid and served. More washing up and then the special things ... silver cleaning, household mending, shopping, getting in coal and sticks. Teatime. Washing up again and more vegetables, a little lull and then dinner. The last wash-up of the day, beds to turn down and curtains to draw. Mrs. Begbie's hot milk to be carried upstairs. And then at last, in the farmer's words to his wife, in the old song, "The rest of the day is your own". It was about this "rest of the day" that Emmie and Mrs. Tallet first had words.

On her first half-day Emmie had gone to see Miss Trappit and asked her the way to the Public Library. Miss Trappit had obligingly, in the rôle of a ratepayer, signed the card that Emmie brought back, and by running like a hare she had managed to reach the library before it closed and secure her allowance, one fiction and one non-fiction book. With these under her arm she had returned to the Corner House at nine o'clock, though she was not officially obliged to return until ten. Mrs. Tallet was seated in the kitchen when Emmie entered; there was no washing-up to be seen, and Emmie found, when she went up to her room and peeped into the others in passing, that Mrs. Tallet had honourably performed the duty of opening beds and drawing curtains. There was a good hour, then, for reading. She thought of the old armchair by the boiler and the book and the hour with the pleasure of a miser telling over his gold. She settled down opposite Mrs. Tallet who was turning a sheet "sides into middle", one of her schemes for saving Miss Ada's pocket.

"Oh, so you're a reader, are you?" asked Mrs. Tallet unpleasantly as soon as she had opened *The Babyons*.

"Yes," said Emmie, without looking up, and then, thinking that this lack of attention and brief answer might annoy, added, "Aren't you?", and looked up, grudging the moment, but waiting for the answer.

"No, I am not. I've no time for nonsense of that sort, and I shouldn't have thought you had, either."

"Well," said Emmie, "you've done all my jobs, thank you, and it isn't time for Mrs. Begbie's milk yet."

"Don't thank me. It's your day out and you're entitled to it. I didn't mean that. I meant that I should have thought that you could have found something better to do than fill your head with a lot of twaddle. There's a hole in your stocking at this minute."

Emmie said guiltily, "Is there?" and looked. There was, a large one.

Mrs. Tallet pushed towards her a large scarlet biscuit tin that served her for a workbox. That was actually a gesture of consideration, if not of friendliness, for Emmie's mending things were naturally at the top of the house. Emmie had dropped her eyes again and was already deep in the story.

"Well, aren't you going to mend it?" The harsh voice wrenched her back across the centuries. Glamour faded. She said, almost irritably, "No, not now, another time."

"Yes, and I know when that will be, upstairs, afterwards, wasting the current."

Oh, blast the woman, why must she nag just now? "I shan't mend it at all tonight," she muttered.

"No, that's just it. That's how readers are. Reading saps the senses. It's just another form of laziness."

Emmie gave a loud, deliberate sigh. Mrs. Tallet was quite undeterred. Another angle of the business had struck her.

"I suppose you'll read in bed. Well, let me tell you that I won't have Miss Ada's bill, that's quite large enough as it is, made larger by such foolishness."

"I've six candles that I brought from my last place. They felt the same about reading there."

"Indeed. Well, you can give up that idea. There'll be no candles burned in this house, dirty drippy things. And you'd drop off to sleep as like as not, setting the place on fire. No, if read you must, you'll pay sixpence a week off your wages for the light."

That was just the sort of bargain that Mrs. Tallet loved to strike. She was too short-sighted to see that it was minor persecutions like this, and her habit of charging a shilling for a breakage, that made girls so prone to get away from the Corner House as soon as possible: then Miss Ada had to pay for an advertisement in the paper.

"I would gladly," said Emmie coldly, "pay a half-crown now for half an hour's peace."

Mrs. Tallet's mouth closed with a snap. She drew back her box. Something in that gesture made Emmie realize that it had been offered. Her heart smote her.

"I'm awfully sorry I spoke like that. If you don't like reading I can't explain. Only . . . you'd hate it, wouldn't you, if I kept shouting up the stairs to you when Mrs. Clarkson was telling you something. It's like that."

Mrs. Tallet stopped in her stitching to consider this startling comparison. Was it possible that any one could feel about a few printed words as she felt about Miss Ada's voice? And, moreover, how did it happen that this chit of a girl after a week in the house, knew how she felt about that morning interview that inspired her for the day. It was either a good shot in the dark or else this Emmie was clever. She considered that possibility. Certainly she was well spoken and her manners were nice and she wasn't afraid of work. Perhaps, after all, a little reading at night . . . better than hankering out of the window after a boy. Perhaps a sixpence was too much. Yet there was Miss Ada to be considered. Every wasted penny impoverished her. Mrs. Tallet waited until Emmie, at five minutes to ten, reluctantly closed her book and rose to put on Mrs. Begbie's milk. Then she said:

"If you were keen to earn that sixpence you could wash Mr. Wykham's socks when you do your own things. I'd take them out of his laundry for you and put them back."

Emmie said, "Oh, thank you, Mrs. Tallet, that's a marvellous idea. Thank you so much for thinking of it." Then she turned quickly to the milk that wasn't nearly boiling, to hide her blushing face. She had been in the house just a week, and already there was nothing that she wouldn't have done for Mr. Wykham.

156

On that first morning when she arrived in time to wash up the breakfast things, Mrs. Tallet had taken her into the front of the house as soon as the last cup was dry and on its hook, and said, "This is Mr. Wykham's room. You'd better do it out now. You have to watch your time for this, he's sometimes in nearly all day. Dreadful nuisance."

Emmie had collected dustpan and brush and duster and entered the narrow slip of a room that contained only two armchairs, covered in scratched, worn leather, a sectional bookcase and an untidy desk covered with papers. Dust and cigarette ash lay thickly everywhere, a very dirty cushion occupied one armchair and a small typewriter with a piece of paper in it was tilted in the other. She swept the floor and did the grate carefully, raising as little dust as possible because Mrs. Tallet had warned her that the papers on the desk must on no account be touched, even in dusting. The books of the shelves, however, she might dust, and she lingered over them, recognizing one or two and wondering about the rest. She had never seen so many books in private possession before. Many of them, judging from the covers, were in foreign languages. French she recognized, but there were others, not French. And at the end of one shelf there was a group of thin books, dully bound, and under each title the name, "Murray Wykham". Wykham! Duster in hand Emmie dashed to the mantelpiece where a number of letters were pushed behind the clock. "Murray Wykham Esq." Then it was the same. Heavens, she was actually in the room of a person who wrote books. What kind of books? With fingers shaking from excitement she drew them out, one by one. Let it be poetry, oh, let her know a poet!

The Press on Trial. All about newspapers. The familiar names leaped up at her from above the long quoted passages and the columns of figures. She put it back hastily. *Money in Action.* Worse. Full of long words and figures. Four others, much the same; and then, at last, one called *In Rhyme.* She turned the pages quickly searching for something short enough to sample now; but most of the pages were almost as closely printed as prose, until suddenly there came a page, empty-looking and white, and in the middle the thin lines —

AT THE ROMAN EXCAVATION

I'd bury this deeper and sow it over
With a close green crop of beet or clover.

I'd bury the hearths where the fires were laid,
And the tiles and drains the dead hands made

I'd bury it deep and forget that we
Shall one day reek of antiquity.

That some day a digger will exclaim, "Ah,
This was a garage or cinema."

Or say of this shilling laid bare by the picks,
"I'd place it at nineteen twenty-six."

For dig, and think, "These too were men
Whose now has turned to a fabulous then."

And what becomes of our solid town?
No. Bury it deeper and stamp it down.

She read it twice, urging her brain to mould the impression of the shape, the rhyme, the metre, so that she might remember it and ponder the meaning at her leisure. Then she laid the book in place, dusted the lower shelves and was at the door with the brush banging against her legs when Mrs. Tallet appeared. "Haven't you finished in there yet? I thought you'd gone to sleep."

Shortly after that when she was laying the table in the dining-room and had returned to the kitchen for the bread and water-jug, Mrs. Tallet said, "Mr. Wykham wants his lunch on a tray. He's got some work to do." Emmie judged from her voice that she considered Mr. Wykham and his work as unmitigated nuisances. When the tray was ready, she regarded Emmie distrustfully, and said, "Carry this carefully, now, and don't forget the step down into his room."

Emmie heaved up the heavy tray and set off blithely. She was going to see, with her own eyes, a poet. The thought carried her up the stairs and across the hall, and then, just outside the door, left her. She was going to see a poet, and how? Wearing an ill-fitting print dress, and the cap and apron of servitude, with her hair roughened and her face shiny with heat and her shoulders bowed down by the burden in her hands. Not thus should one approach. Stupidly, since advance was inevitable, she hesitated for a moment; and courage came, some tag end of classical lore, a memory, a quotation came to her. "Ganymede was cup-bearer to the gods." What more could one ask?

She straightened herself, lodged the tray on her out-thrust hip and with the hand thus freed, opened the door. Carefully she felt for the descending step with her foot — and stood in the presence. He had moved the typewriter on to one corner of the littered desk and was rattling away merrily. A brown-and-white mongrel lay curled on the muddy cushion in the armchair. Mr. Wykham did not look up, but went on typing with his back towards the door and the rest of the room. Emmie said, in a voice made small by nervousness, "Where shall I put the tray, please?"

Still without looking up he said, "Oh, anywhere. Here, look," and with his left hand swept together a sheaf of papers, baring a corner of the desk. Emmie rounded the corner carefully and set down the tray. Then she recognized him, the man who had told her about Louis Napoleon and the Corner House steps. He slipped out the paper at that moment and looked up. "Hullo," he said, "*another* new girl. I've seen you before somewhere . . . yes, gaping at old Freeman's house, weren't you?"

Emmie nodded, quite speechless.

"I suppose you came and gazed at the steps I mentioned with that same air of abandon and old Tally pulled you in before you came to yourself. Was that it?"

"I was coming here that morning," she said in that same small voice.

"Really? I wish I'd known. I'd have warned you."

"Of what?"

"You haven't discovered? Never mind, you will. In the meantime it'll be very nice seeing you around."

Half rising he dragged the chair along under him until it was opposite the tray and picked up the knife and fork. Emmie stood for a moment regarding him with critical interest, and then becoming conscious of her position, fled precipitately. She stood for an instant in the hall to steady herself, but her breathing was still uneven when she regained the kitchen where Mrs. Tallet was waiting with an enormous soup tureen on a small tray and a pile of plates on a larger one.

"Now listen. For today and perhaps tomorrow, since you've never waited at table, I'm going to do it. You just stand still and watch me. And try to learn quickly, for it's no part of my duty either to do it or to show you how. Begin by learning that plates are always passed from the left. Bring the plates and come along."

Mrs. Clarkson, in a mauve knitted suit today, sat at the head of the table. On her right was an elderly woman with a soft loose face, soft drifting hair, and a soft untidy frock with a good deal of fringe about it. This, Emmie learned during the meal, was Mrs. Begbie. She was Mrs. Clarkson's star boarder, for she was both wealthy and well connected. She might have

161

travelled, lived in hotels, had friends; but she was so timid of strangers and so distrustful of herself that she preferred to seclude herself at Mrs. Clarkson's, coddling the delicate health that she cherished as an excuse for complete physical and mental inertia.

Opposite her at the table was the girl who had opened the door to Emmie on the previous morning. Her name, Emmie learned quite soon, was Coral Bavister. "Coral" perhaps, or did the birth certificate read "Caroline" or "Catharine"? For what a sudden, unprecedented foreknowledge was otherwise lavished upon the parents of all the lovely "Ambers" and "Eves" and "Cherrys" who seem to be so appropriately named. Coral was a pretty but typical blonde, with wide eyes, rather grey than blue, brushed-up eyelashes and a row of curls at the back of her head. Coral was "standard". She had the right voice and the right clothes and the right kind of lipstick and nail varnish. She was the only child of well-to-do parents who, in her eighteen years of life, had never denied her anything that it was in their power to obtain for her. However, in her eighteenth year she had set them a poser by desiring to go on the stage, preferably in the West End. Mrs. Bavister, true to her principles, wrote to a great many people, explaining at much length Coral's beauty, accomplishments, and ambitions: and she had thoughtfully added that "money was no object". One such letter fell into the hands of a well-known and serious actress who had once worked at the Petersbury Repertory Theatre. She knew that that theatre, once a flourishing concern, was now often hard put to it to find clothes for its actors. She wrote to

Mrs. Bavister, telling her that she herself had received valuable training at Petersbury and recommended that Coral should apply to the manager there. She would write to him herself. She wrote — "Look out for Coral Bavister. Have never seen her, but hear that she's pretty and clever! Has money anyhow, and will probably lend her clothes about. Might be worth an occasional walk-on."

Coral, however, was actually clever, and she was shrewd. She was always ready, in that impoverished community, to lend money, clothes, a sympathetic ear; but she always received full value for them. Forty pounds, "lent" for a bit of wiring, brought her the lead in a show for a week. She was sick with nervousness, and more sick with the knowledge that she had obtained her chance with vile cash; but she knew that she could do it, and she did. The limited little public of the theatre liked her; the local press was kind, if restrained; people began to point her out to one another in the street. And although her shrewdness informed her that the reputation of Petersbury as a forcing-place for talent had dwindled, still she was young, and strong, and determined, and tomorrow was another day. Mrs. Clarkson and Mrs. Begbie vied with one another in spoiling her.

The fourth person at the table that morning was the one of most interest for Emmie. For one thing she had never seen a woman doctor before, and had expected to find a man at the table when Mrs. Tallet said, "Dr. Mason has just come in." She was a pale thin woman who looked very old beside Coral Bavister and very young beside Mrs. Begbie. She had smooth black hair netted in a knob on her neck and an oval face, spoilt by a high-bridged nose, and redeemed by dark eyes, deeply set and bright. She wore a neat black suit with a striped blouse showing at the neck and wrists, and beside the older women's ringed hands and the girl's varnished finger-tips, her hands, long and pale and dry-looking, seemed oddly naked and clean.

Conversation at the table was spasmodic and uninteresting. Only one bit of it gave Emmie any clue to the relationship existing between the four women. Miss Bavister refused potatoes.

"I simply *must* consider my figure," she said in her high emphatic voice.

"Child, there isn't an ounce of flesh on you," said Mrs. Begbie.

"Didn't we remark the other evening, Mrs. Clarkson, that she is slimmer now than when she came?"

"We did. And anyway potatoes aren't a bit fattening." Mrs. Clarkson felt bound to add that, for when people are eating potatoes they are not eating anything else, and potatoes are cheap.

"They *are*. They're simply full of starch, aren't they, Dr. Mason?"

"Now that is a professional question which I am sure Dr. Mason will ignore." Mrs Begbie spoke teasingly but there was an undercurrent of something in her voice that convinced Emmie that at some time or another one of her questions had gone unanswered.

"They're starchy, I believe, but no more fattening than sweets," said Dr. Mason disinterestedly.

164

"You're *always* knocking my sweets, J. M. I believe you're jealous because I get them given to me and *your* patients don't give you any." That was teasingly said, too, but there was just that same sting in it that there had been in Mrs. Begbie's remark.

"The word 'patient', my dear girl, implies one who suffers under. I trust you have none. Will you excuse me, Mrs. Clarkson? I have an appointment. I shan't be in to dinner." She rose rather stiffly with a cracking of knee joints and ankles, and walked with a brittle kind of uprightness to the door which Emmie hastily opened. She paused in the doorway as though conscious of Emmie for the first time.

"You're new, aren't you? What's your name?"

"Emmie."

"Emmie. I must remember that." A brief smile softened the severe lines of her face and set Emmie's susceptible heart throbbing for the second time within the hour.

"That was a smack right in the bonnie blue eye, wasn't it?" Miss Bavister was saying gaily as Emmie turned back.

"A trifle waspish, certainly," Mrs. Clarkson admitted, but added justly, "Still she was up most of the night."

Conversation turned to the curious things that women did for a living nowadays.

Emmie had quite a lot to think about as she cleared away and washed up. She had seen everybody in the house now and her mind was filled with strong impressions. Mr. Wykham and Dr. Mason are my favourites, she thought. Why? Miss Bavister is pretty and has lovely things, just the sort of person I should like to be, to look at. But there's something about the other two. As though they had a story behind them, or ahead of them. I wonder. And her initials are J. M. I wonder what the J. is for. Janet. Jennie, Jennifer. Anyway they're the two that I should really like to talk to, really know. I wonder shall I ever? For a little while, for as long as it took to dry ten plates and put them in the rack, she let her imagination run riot. "Loved, gone, proudly friended . . ." But with the eleventh plate reason resumed its sway. Nonsense. They'd speak to her nicely, no doubt, but after all — she was a servant, a low, scrubby kind of servant, and J. M. was a doctor, and Murray Wykham was a poet.

She discovered during that first month, the month had seen most of her predecessors grow sulky and tearful and rebellious and ready to give notice, that Murray Wykham was many things besides poet. He half-owned and wholly ran the *Petersbury Press*, for instance. He wrote articles for other papers and for magazines. He was something to do with a "Student" movement, and through the spring and summer, gave lectures and conducted tours for foreign students who were visiting places of historic interest in England. Nor did his interests end there. Queer people would call at the back door in the evening.

"Mr. Wykham in? I want to see him about getting me a Council House."

"Ask Mr. Wykham if he can spare a minute to come and see that drain we was talking about."

Emmie, who had ordered her copy of the *Press* as soon as she discovered his connection with it, would pore over each page, and frequently, in a column headed "The Watcher", found an echo of those evening voices. The column frequently served as a topic of conversation at meals, acrid in his absence, inquiring in his presence.

Mrs. Clarkson, for instance, who at lunch had remarked, "I see that our Mr. Wykham has been letting himself go about Town Terrace again. He'd better by far inquire into the state of the Council houses' bathrooms. I'm told on good authority that they're used to store coal and onions in," would ask him at dinner on the same day, "Do you really think anything will ever be done about Town Terrace, Mr. Wykham?" To see him set about earnestly answering questions like that made Emmie's blood boil.

All of them, except Dr. Mason, made desperate efforts to engage his attention, to show off and to appear intelligent in his presence. That was, perhaps, inevitable in that over-feminine atmosphere; but they were so spiteful afterwards. "Such language," Mrs. Clarkson would say sorrowfully, after a conversation through which she had hung upon every word. "I do think that . . . er . . . lavatories should not be mentioned at the table."

It was through a comment of this kind that Emmie discovered a flaw in the person who was rapidly assuming an almost saintly aspect to her.

"Did the disturbance wake you, last night?" Mrs. Clarkson inquired of Miss Bavister at breakfast one morning.

"I did seem to hear somebody walking about; but I was very sleepy. What was it?"

"Mr. Wykham," began Mrs. Clarkson, and Emmie, who had set down the dishes and the hot plates and had reached the door, turned at the sound of the name and opened a drawer of the sideboard and stood there as though searching for something. "That terrible Major Spiller, you know, the one whose wife divorced him, brought him home last night, thoroughly drunk."

"No?" Miss Bavister's voice betrayed more interest than horror.

"They made such a noise getting in, blundering up against the door and singing and shouting. It was really disgraceful. I put on my dressing-gown and came on to the stairs. When I saw who it was, of course I went back. Major Spiller is not a person by whom one would wish to be seen in a dressing-gown. But I saw enough to know that they were both thoroughly drunk. Oh, good morning, Mr. Wykham. You seemed to have had a very merry party last evening."

"Oh. Did we disturb you? I'm so sorry. Poor old Spiller had just heard about his wife's new marriage. He was very low. So I joined him on a blind. Most efficacious."

"I don't see why he should be low about it," said Mrs. Clarkson coldly. "He'd been flagrantly unfaithful to her for several years, apparently. I shouldn't think he can care much what happens to her now."

"No, that's just what no virtuous woman, nor perhaps any woman ever would see. Some men are just naturally polygamous. But that doesn't always mean that they are tired of, or unkind or even indifferent to, the woman they're married to. Anyway, she was a cold marble female. I don't think he robbed her of much."

"Mr. Wykham!" exclaimed Mrs. Clarkson, but her voice, though shocked, was no longer cold, there was a kind of rallying tone about it. "In front of Emmie, too," she said in a half-whisper.

"Oh, Emmie . . ." said Mr. Wykham, looked towards her with a smile.

Emmie shut the drawer with a little squeak of terror at having attention thus riveted upon her, and went tumbling down the kitchen stairs.

He hadn't denied it. In fact he had admitted it. He had been drunk.

Drunk.

Dread word to one of Emmie's class. Men drunk. Quarrelsome. Or with a dreadful gaiety that could change suddenly to dangerous rage. Being sick all over the place. Knocking the wife and kids about. Women drunk. Screaming, laughing, swearing. Tearing one another's faces. Knocking the kids about.

Dread word to one of Emmie's class.

Drunk.

It was not associated with writing books, or reading them, or caring how the poor lived, or being fond of dogs as Mr. Wykham was fond of Stumpy. It was associated with roughness and poverty and brutality and degradation.

She was very unhappy about it until she discovered that Mr. Wykham, even drunk, was quite unlike her

169

father, or Ted Gibson, or the other habitués of the Pot of Flowers.

6

One evening, just as Emmie was about to follow Mrs. Tallet up to bed, the third of the metal bells that hung in a row above the kitchen door rang loudly. That third bell was his, and with the alacrity and pleasure with which she always answered it she ran up the stairs and into his room. He'll see me without my cap and apron, she thought: and then despised herself for the thought. What difference could it make? The narrow room was blue with smoke and stiflingly hot. Murray, in his shirt-sleeves, was sitting before his typewriter with his head in his hands. At his right an over-crowded ashtray spilled over on to the table; at his left stood a whisky bottle, an empty siphon and a glass. On the corner of the table was a pile of letters, stamped ready for the post.

He raised his head as she entered, and she stared with alarm at the drawn white face and the eyes with the fiercely contracted pupils. She wanted to run away, partly from fear of what he might say or do, partly from shame at seeing her idol like this. But she was rooted to the floor, and his first words banished fear and shame alike, for it was his own voice speaking.

"Oh, thank God it's you. Directly I'd rung I was afraid that Tally might come. Emmie, have you been sufficiently put upon today?"

170

"I don't know . . . I'll do anything," she offered doubtfully, for though the voice was his there was a subtle uncertainty in it, and he held his head as though he had a stiff neck.

"Then be a perfect angel and just take these to the pillar-box on Abbey Hill for me. And let Stumpy run with you, will you? These letters must go tonight, and he must go out. And I'm simply not capable."

"Do you feel ill?" asked Emmie, snatching at straws.

"God, yes, or I wouldn't ask you. I expect you've been up since dawn. Do you mind? Are you frightened?"

"Not a bit." Just to be asked that gave her a feeling of protection that she had never known before. "Come on, Stumpy."

The mongrel looked at her with luminous yellow eyes and wagged his tail but made no effort to rise.

"Go on, stupid," said his master, "go walk with Emmie."

Slowly, as if under protest, Stumpy rose and allowed her to fasten his lead to his collar. Murray Wykham rose too, caught the edge of the desk for support and lowered himself carefully into the armchair. Emmie led Stumpy out.

The letters in her hand told her why people treasure letters from people they love. The words may be known by heart, but the very paper is sacred. The writer's hand has lain upon the sheets, the loved eye has travelled the pages. One of the envelopes was handwritten and Emmie, under the street lamp, feasted her eyes upon the straight lines of irregular scribble. It was only a short walk to the pillar-box and the cool April air with a scent of soil and growing things in it was refreshing and exciting. The Abbey Gate loomed solidly, its lower walls grey in the light of the lamps, its top black against the faint light of the sky.

How many nights had it seen? Spring nights like this; hot nights lit by the harvest moon; nights when leaves whirled past it; nights of snow. Years and years of them. And the people too. Every one of them passing it with a sense of his own importance, which only the years could prove of no importance at all. Saddening thought, reducing her present pleasure and excitement to nothing.

But a thickly budded hawthorn tree overhung the path a little farther on, and Emmie, looking up, could see stars through the knotted branches. Something unnamed and indescribable took her by the throat. It was all to do with the Spring, and with being alive, and knowing that there was beauty in the world, within touch if out of reach; and with the having just seen Murray Wykham in his shirt-sleeves and having his dog here, and with the knowledge that she would see him again in a few moments. Tears filled her eyes for no reason that she knew, and the salt of them in her throat as she choked them back was more delicious than anything she had ever tasted. Why try to describe it? All who remember the first days of their first love know it all. And who forgets them? Feet light, head held high, happy voice chattering to the dog, dear for itself and doubly dear because his, she sped back to the house. The door was ajar as she had left it and the atmosphere

172

had cleared a little. He was sitting where she had left him, with his hands hanging limply over the arms of the chair. Stumpy ran to him as though he had just returned from a month's absence, and at the touch of the cold nose on his ear Murray opened his eyes and rubbed his hand across them before reaching for Stumpy's head.

"Hello," he said, "you're back then. Bless you."

"Do you feel better?"

"No. I dunno. Yes, I think I do."

"Would you like me to call Dr. Mason? She's in."

"Merciful Heavens, no! I'm not ill. I'm just dead beat and half sozzled: the soda gave out. I'll be all right."

As though in proof he pulled himself up in the chair and moved his stiff gaze slowly from Emmie to Stumpy and back again. An expression of comical surprise dawned on his face. Was he farther gone than he'd thought, or was it a fact that they were both looking at him with exactly the same yellow eyes with exactly the same expression of dumb worship in them? His own eyes dropped and fell upon her little work-reddened hands hanging beside the skimpy folds of her afternoon dress. He reached out and took the one nearer him.

"Like a frog," he exclaimed, and dropped it to pick up the poker and stir the red embers of the fire.

"Kneel down there and warm them."

Glad to stay, yet reluctant to expose to view those hands from which the winter's chilblains were only just beginning to fade, Emmie knelt down and held her hands straight down in front of her, by her knees.

He leaned back again in his chair and sat watching her with the speculative curiosity that most people could arouse in him. It was a curiosity as easily allayed as aroused in most cases; for he had the not-altogether-enviable gift of being able to read a great deal from a few remarks and movements. Coral's hard-headedness, hidden from so many people by her youth and prettiness, was quite obvious to him. His versions of Mrs. Clarkson and Mrs. Begbie would have moved both those ladies to anger had they known them, but they would have recognized the unadmitted truth in them, too. He brought what was left of his consciousness to bear upon the child by the fire. She was very young and rather pretty. There was something very attractive in the way that her hair grew in a peak off her forehead and curled over her crown and ended in soft little whirls on her thin white neck. Why didn't she hold out her hands to the reluctant blaze as anyone else would? Was she hiding them? Why? They were surprisingly clean with short well-kept nails. Red, of course, and she'd had chilblains badly.

"Is your home in Petersbury?" he asked.

"No," and to forestall the inevitable next question, she added, "I haven't a home at all."

"What do you do with your spare time? I suppose even you have *some* spare time."

"Sometimes I go to Miss Trappit's, sometimes I walk and look at things. And I read a lot."

"Do you? What are you reading at the moment, for instance?"

174

"A book called *The Martyrdom of Man*. It's by Winwood Reade. I believe he's *The Cloister and the Hearth* man's brother."

"Can you understand it?"

"Of course. Why not?"

"Why not indeed?" And why do you say *The Cloister and the Hearth* in that reverent tone?"

"Because I think it is the best story that I've ever read."

"I'm not sure that I don't agree with you. Did you ever read the other. *It's Never Too Late to Mend?*"

Emmie shuddered, "I've never touched a pail of cold water or pulled my belt in tightly without thinking of it ever since."

He leaned forward in his chair.

"Do you know, some things take *me* so. I once read a book called *Human Livestock* and there was a bit in it . . . well, a bit about a negro . . . who was scalded . . . I've never really enjoyed a hot bath since. The moment the water gets nicely stinging hot I think . . . And that's a thing I've never told any one before. Look here, I must get to bed. I shall be babbling presently." He pointed to the bookcase.

"Any time you want a book, just help yourself. There must be some there you haven't read."

"There are," said Emmie, scrambling to her feet. "I've looked at some, when I was dusting, you know. You're a poet, aren't you?" The last sentence was hushed with awe.

"Lord no! I once thought, long ago, that I might be, but it needs clean hands and a pure heart."

He walked unsteadily to the shelves and tugged *In Rhyme* out of its place. He tapped the title with his first finger-nail. "Where, my young literary friend, would you guess that that title came from?"

"Keats," said Emmie a trifle doubtfully lest this obvious answer should be wrong. He nodded slightly, looking at her, approvingly? mockingly? drunkenly?

"Go on, say it."

"To know the change and feel it,
When there is none to heal it,
Nor numbed sense to steal it,
Was never said in rhyme."

"Pass friend," said Murray delightedly. "Here, you can have this if you like . . ." He held the book towards her.

"Could you," began Emmie, remembering the books that Miss Stanton had given her, "*would* you write in it? Some time, it doesn't matter now."

"Oh, certainly, now. Let's finish it off." He reached for his fountain pen and leaning heavily on the desk wrote across the front page, "For Emmie, who knows a good book, but accepted this. M. W."

"There you are. Now hurry along and leave me to stagger upstairs unobserved."

Clutching the book to her chest Emmie came out into the hall wellnigh staggering herself. The impossible, the miraculous had happened. She held the concrete proof of it in her hand. Hand. The hand that had written the verses had written her name, had closed on the book's cover, had rested on the page. And it had reached out, that hand, and taken her own in a brief clasp. It floated before her dazzled eyes, thin, knotted at the knuckles and stained brown with nicotine at the fingers. She was aware that as she entered the hall from Mr. Wykham's room, Miss Bavister, back from the theatre, entered it from the front door. She knew that on any other evening she would have said, "Good night, miss," and asked whether there was anything she could do. But tonight that was impossible. No other face must blot out his remembered face, no other voice sound in her ears. She made her way to the back stairs with carefully averted head, and so missed the look of sharp interest and deep suspicion that Coral directed first at her retreating figure and then at Murray's half-open door. If Emmie had been carrying a tray it would have been different, but a book!

That one half-hour of light was worth the week's sixpence. Blasphemous thought, it was worth all she would ever earn, and more. She closed the book and pattered barefoot across to the switch at the door after she had found nine lines that were, to her, deeply significant. They were headed with a very old line. "O Mistress Mine!" and read —

Christ, not content with the old sins,
Indicted adultery by lustful looking;
And since I first laid eyes on you
The Recording Angel has been busy booking
That sin to my account.
But here is comfort, no amount

Of thought can make adultery partnerless.
So every time we meet, cold Puritan,
He blots in your page too. "Mistress, mistress."

That appeared, to her unformed taste, to be a very wonderful verse, and to imply that Murray had suffered from unrequited affection at the hands of some "cold Puritan". Combined with the evening's happenings and conversation it established him as most lovably human. He was "Murray" henceforth in her thoughts.

7

That evening ushered in the happiest period that she had known, and indeed many a lover has been more unfortunately placed. She was under the same roof, bound naturally to see him, hear him speak every day. She had managed to say, quite casually, to Mrs. Tallet one morning when they were making Mrs. Clarkson's bed and the butcher's boy had come for the orders,

"Don't bother to come up again, Mrs. Tallet. I can manage Mr. Wykham's bed alone. It's the smallest."

And there was the bed, tumbled from his sleep, and the pillow with the hollow where his head had lain. There were his crumpled pyjamas that she could almost imagine were still warm from his body, and the book just as he had dropped it before he turned to sleep. Holy things, every one of them. And despite the open window and the morning air that fluttered the curtains there was a definite scent of him in the room. She breathed it in greedily; it might have been incense. Scent of cigarettes and hair cream and shaving soap, and something else that was none of these, something that was just himself. Ten minutes out of her long, hurried day could be devoted to the reverent handling of his things and to making the room as tidy as a shrine; for Mrs. Tallet, never happy out of the kitchen, was only too glad to fall into the habit of going downstairs when Mrs. Clarkson's bed was made.

When the work upstairs was finished she began to count the hours to lunch, if he were coming in, and after that there was the evening to look forward to. Perhaps because that first talk took place between ten and eleven she always found herself looking forward to ten o'clock. And often enough ten o'clock found her with nothing to do but to follow Mrs. Tallet up to bed. Even then there was tomorrow to long for, and so the circle again.

It was more than a week before he next noticed her as an individual. It was becoming more of a custom, to Mrs. Tallet's annoyance, for him to lunch from a tray when he came in, and on a Tuesday when Emmie carried it in he said, "Oh, by the way, do you ever go to the pictures on your night off?"

"I haven't done yet." She might have added that her experience of pictures had been going in a crowd from school to see "African Pathways" and "Steering West" which were supposed to have some bearing upon history.

"When is your free night?"

"Tomorrow, it's always Wednesday."

"Well, there's a good picture at the Orient this week. If you like to go I can let you have a pass. I get them because of the paper, you know. I'll remember to bring one home. Look in here tomorrow after seven some time and ask me."

He returned to his book and appeared not to hear Emmie's whispered "Thank you". But that did not stop her heart from singing. He had noticed her, remembered her, and some time during this afternoon, or tomorrow, he would think of her again when he put the "pass", whatever that might be, into his pocket.

She tried not to think of the real reason why she had never yet sampled the pictures for herself, which was that she was shy of approaching the wide, brightly lit entrance by herself. There were always such a lot of people there, queues of boys getting tickets while the girls who were with them stood about gossiping and staring, or smoothing down an eyebrow with a wetted finger, inspecting the photographs, or powdering an already powdered nose. They all looked so assured, they knew which side of the vestibule to go for their tickets, they knew which door to approach when they had obtained them. Emmie, who had never attempted an exploration, never guessed how easily obtained such knowledge was, and she shrank from the risk of making a fool of herself. Tomorrow, of course it would be different. She would take courage from the thought that *he* had wanted her to see the picture, that he had handled the pass, that he might ask her it she had enjoyed it. Tomorrow would certainly be different.

She had intended to spend Wednesday afternoon poking round the shops to discover how best she might lay out the forty shillings handed her at the end of the month by Mrs. Clarkson; but while she was washing up it began to rain in a gentle, determined manner, and by the time she was ready it was a settled downpour. It would be silly to get her only coat and her shoes and stockings soaked before the evening, so she went up to her room and spent what remained of the afternoon mending and reading. She supposed that she would have to go out if she wanted any tea. On other free afternoons she had had tea either at Miss Trappit's or at the Woolworth café. However, it was still pouring at teatime, so she decided to dispense with the meal though her stomach cried out for the transient warmth and comfort that two or three cups of strong sweet tea could give it. She read on. Presently from the stairs below she heard Mrs. Tallet's voice.

"Emmie, Emmie. Aren't you coming down?"

Tea for two was laid on the end of the kitchen table and there was a delicious scent of toast in the air.

"Tea's been made ten minutes," said Mrs. Tallet crossly, sitting down at once and picking up the teapot.

"I'm sorry. I didn't think I'd get tea today."

"Well, you musta been in a curious place before. Thank Heaven we're not as close as all that." She leaned sideways and drew a plate of toast from the open oven where it had been keeping warm. Emmie settled down to the hot tea, thinking — this is my lucky day.

"I'll wash up," she said.

"There's no need," said Mrs Tallet shortly. "I shan't wash up for you tomorrow, even if I stay in, as I expect I shall. Fair is fair."

"But I'd like to," said Emmie. She looked at Mrs. Tallet almost fondly. She stared round the bare clean kitchen, thought of the rooms upstairs, of the completed mending in her drawers, of Murray whom she would see in two and a half hours' time, and she felt that she loved the whole world. Wash up! Why she would have scrubbed the kitchen if Mrs. Tallet had given the word. She did wash up, despite Mrs. Tallet's warning.

"Take my advice and stick up for your rights. It doesn't matter here, because I hope I'm just. But anywhere else you'd stand a chance of being imposed upon."

"Oh no I wouldn't," said Emmie happily. "I can be werry fierce."

"Well, maybe you could. You can't always tell. I didn't think you'd be a mite of good that morning when I saw you there," she jerked her head at the stair door, "looking like a schoolgirl."

"Oh, did I? Do I?" asked Emmie, hurt by the comparison and ignoring Mrs. Tallet's implied compliment.

"Well, don't look so sorry about that," said Mrs. Tallet sharply, "far better to look like a schoolgirl than a tart, which is what most of the rubbish nowadays do."

Mrs. Tallet seems to like me this afternoon, thought Emmie, and forgot the five toilsome weeks of aching bones and haste and grim mastering of strange duties that had won her that approval.

Mr. Wykham wasn't in at seven, nor at half past when Emmie, idly hanging about the kitchen, helped

182

Mrs. Tallet to dish up dinner. It was almost eight o'clock when she heard the shriek of his brakes outside and the sound of Stumpy's feet in the hall. She gave him time to get his coat off and then went up the stairs into the hall and knocked gently on his door.

"Oh, there you are," he said, and went on reading the letters that had come for him by the afternoon post. "Get your things on and I'll run you down. It's raining cats and dogs."

Utterly overcome, Emmie embarked on protest. "No, really, there's no need. It isn't far. And you haven't had your dinner."

"It's quite far enough to get wet in, and not far enough to make all this fuss about. Get your things on quickly."

Emmie started, thought of something and came back.

"I'll go out at the back and come round."

"What is this? An intrigue?" he said, without looking up. "Oh, all right. I'll wait in the car."

It was dusky in the car, for the hood was up and she could only see him when they were directly under a street lamp, or passing another car, but all the time there was the block of his solid body by her right arm and every now and then the sight of his profile and his hand on the wheel. He stopped outside the cinema and leaned across her to open the door. Then, with his arm still outstretched, he peered through the opening made by the outswung door and said, "Does that poster say Laurel and Hardy? There look, under the big picture."

Emmie looked, and at first could see nothing on account of the blaze of lights and her own confusion. Then she saw it and said, "Yes."

"That decides it. I'm coming too, if you have no objection. I can never resist Laurel and Hardy."

"What about your dinner?"

"What about it?" he asked, starting the car forward again and turning into the parking place.

"You haven't had it."

"I know that. And I haven't had my lunch either. But I can't stand being tied down to meal-times. I can get something later on."

He rounded the queue of youths and unattended women, pushed a way through the attendant damsels, and with Emmie at his heels walked straight into the place. Nobody asked to see his "pass", but a man in a much-buttoned uniform said, "Evening, Mr. Wykham, nasty night it's turned out." He answered with a brief "Foul", and then they were inside, seated at the back with a hanging curtain between them and the gangway. All the lights, except some faint rosy-shaded ones along the walls, were darkened. There was a stealthy rustling as the audience settled down to two hour's happy oblivion. Arms crept around neighbouring shoulders, hands stole into hands. A haze of blue smoke ascended and hung. The enchanted hours passed.

Sudden brilliance of lights, the National Anthem, a rush for the exits as though the place where they had all been so happy had suddenly become unbearable. Just at the entrance, where the marble step gave way to the common pavement, somebody pushed against Emmie and she fell, rather than stepped over the edge. Mr.

184

Wykham caught her arm and threw an indiscriminate "Clumsy pig" over his shoulder.

And just at that moment Emmie saw Dr. Mason step on to the pavement a yard or two to the left. She looked at Emmie in what she privately thought was a "funny" way and aimed a muttered "Good evening" over the heads of the people between herself and Mr. Wykham who called, "Hi. Can I give you a lift? We're coming straight along."

"No, thanks. I'd sooner walk," she called back, and jerking up the collar of her raincoat, stepped briskly away.

"Well, did you enjoy it?" Murray asked as they turned off the car park into the glistening wet streets.

"Awfully, thank you," said Emmie, whole-heartedly.

"Yes. It was a good show. Here, look, while I think of it. Shove this in your bag and they'll let you in any time."

"Oh, thank you." She took the piece of cardboard that he dug out of his pocket and put it into her bag.

There was silence until a sharp turn and a bump and the glare of the headlights on yellow doors told her that they were at the garage, one of twelve that had been made from some stables behind the Dean's residence.

"I'll open the door," she cried, fumbling ineffectually to let herself out of the car. He laughed and leaned across to do it for her. "You'll have to get out first. There you are. Just pull sharply to the right and it'll run back." It ran back smoothly. Within five minutes they were letting themselves into the Corner House. It was just half past ten.

"Now," he said, "would you like to do something for me?"

"Yes, I would. Anything."

"Then make me a pot of coffee and a sandwich of some sort. Anything will do. I've just got a letter to finish. I'll be ready as soon as you are."

She flung off her hat and coat, lit the gas, put on the milk and the kettle and then sat down on the edge of the table to wait while they boiled. She was conscious that ever since they had left the cinema happiness had been seeping away from her, like air from a punctured tyre. She folded her arms and tipped back her head as though seeking the answer to the puzzle upon the ceiling. It had begun, this descent from ecstasy, at the moment when her eyes had met Dr. Mason's. But why? Why had that cool, half-appraising, half-pitying look made her feel that she shouldn't have been there, that she wanted to shake the hand from her arm (and Heaven knew it had dropped quickly enough), and hide herself? Why? She was still puzzling when the milk came to the top of the saucepan. She made the coffee, laid a cloth on a small tray, reached down a cup and saucer and set off up the stairs.

"Ah, beautiful," he exclaimed, and then, "No sandwich?"

"Oh dear, no," she cried. "I forgot it absolutely. I'll get one."

"No you won't. I don't really want one. No, honestly. I'd rather you just perched down here and waited while I drank this."

"Let me pour then."

"Yes, do. And if you don't mind I'll take my shoes off. I had to walk across Button's Common this afternoon."

He kicked off his shoes and wriggled his toes. "Old Mother Tally darns better than she did," he said meditatively. "She used to put a sickly green wool into my socks to punish me for having blue ones, I think. Not so cobbled either." He lifted a foot and surveyed it critically.

"I've been doing them since the week after I came," Emmie said quietly. It sounded like boasting, but she could not resist it.

"No. Have you really? Why?"

Emmie explained Mrs. Tallet's method for raising sixpence. "And since I'd washed them it was quite easy for me to darn them too."

"Easy? Do you like darning then?"

"Some things I do," said Emmie cryptically.

"Well, you shan't have any darning for a long time. I'll go out tomorrow and buy me twelve pairs of the stoutest socks I can find."

"Why?"

"Because you've got eyes exactly like Stumpy's," he said, smiling. "And now you run along to bed."

8

Quite soon after that evening there was a letter from Miss Stanton, to whom in her first week at the Corner House Emmie had sent her address. It was a long letter, closely written, and she did not have time to read it until just before teatime.

187

"DEAR EMMIE,

"Thank you for your letter which was sent on to me here, see above." (Emmie looked and saw the London address.) "I've left Swything after one of the stormiest scenes I've ever been in. It's all rather complicated, but may interest you, since you know all the people concerned.

"It began with this business of supplying milk for children at playtime. I objected to it at first because only those that can pay a ha'penny can have it, which is another case of to him that hath, &c. However, Mr. Gannet, and he one of the managers, wanted to supply it, so I had to pipe down. Then the roof leaked like mad in January and I applied for it to be mended, and since I'd obstructed his milk he obstructed my tiles and we paddled about like ducks for a week and then I said I should write to the County Director if it wasn't done over the week-end. It was done. But ever since then Johnny Gannet, who was fourteen in January but wasn't allowed to leave until March, started to make a nuisance of himself. He systematically started rows, defied me, and bullied any children who were willing to behave. After about three weeks of it I saw that it wasn't just a phase, but a put-up job, so I wrote to his father who sent back a message, *by* Johnny, that I was paid to keep order and that it was up to me to do it. Oh, I forgot to add that four or five times during this time the milk was sour and I sent it all back, and threatened to complain. Well, after that message from Mr. Gannet I said to J. one afternoon when he was amusing himself by thrusting his compasses into Frank Bailey's stout little behind,

" 'If I have any more bother from you I shall give you a thrashing, big as you are.' He replied, 'Corporal punishment ain't allowed.' All the kids laughed. I said, 'All the long words and bad grammar in the world doesn't make that true.' And I dragged him out and gave him six good ones on the rear. Pa Gannet then brought an action. There was a frightful stink. The other managers, except the clergyman, whom may Heaven reward, sided with him, and I was asked to resign. I suppose if I'd had a union behind me I could have fought it, but I'd always thought that if you knew your job and did it properly you didn't need unions. However, here I am, staying with Miss Frome who has been an angel throughout, and who will, I think, find me a job with her firm. I don't suppose any other school would look at me now. I rank with Herod as an oppressor of the young.

"And that brings me on to the matter of the money. It was a vast sum and I'd love to know how you amassed it. I wouldn't take any of it if my future were more rosy and settled; as it is, I'm very grateful to keep thirty and send you twenty back. Bank it or buy some clothes. I still think I'm in your debt. Whatever I spent on you I spent on myself, just as if I'd backed horses with it. So don't send any more, or give it another thought. I mean that.

"I hope this new job is nice, and easier than the old one. St. Petersbury sounds delightful. One day I hope to come and see you: and you might let me know when you have a holiday. If I have found a niche by then I'd love you to spend it with me. There isn't room in this place for another gnat. Ella is most kind, but I think I am too old to take easily to this sort of kindness. And I loathed leaving my cottage. I wonder shall I ever see it again. I used to think that I should end my days there. I suppose that was wrong and dull of me. One should seek and welcome new people and new things. This is the whale of a letter, but I'll end it now, if for no better reason than that it is the bottom of a page. Good night, dear. Take care of yourself and write to me soon.

As ever, HELEN STANTON."

There was a cheque for twenty pounds with the letter. "Buy some clothes." Emmie stood in the kitchen with the sheets of the letter in one hand and the cheque in the other, and before her eyes there passed the vision of all the clothes twenty pounds could buy. A yellow silk dress for the warm days that were coming, and a wide straw hat with a brown ribbon: the winter coat and the velvet hat that she had wanted on the day she bought her uniform: silk stockings and soft suède shoes. And then suddenly the vision was swept away in a wave of overwhelming shame. That had been her first selfish thought, clothes! — when she should have been burning with indignation at the injustice with which Miss Stanton had been treated. Miss Stanton who had sent her twenty pounds and bidden her forget the rest of that enormous debt. Miss Stanton who had saved her from her dreadful home, and given her the

190

education so that she could at least speak to Murray without shame at her own voice. Miss Stanton who had been so very dear, the light of every day. Miss Stanton who was like something remembered from a dream.

Tears of rage and shame filled her eyes and ran down her burning cheeks. Turning back her apron she fished in her pocket and drew out her handkerchief and dabbled at them. She would remember, she would recall Miss Stanton. She tried to imagine her with the cane in her hand, giving Johnny Gannet "six good ones on the rear"; or storming about the flooded classroom. But it was useless. There all round her was the scrubbed and shining kitchen with the queer half-light that came through the high window making it somehow secret and cosy; and there were the unconnected legs passing on the pavement outside; and there in the distance the noise of the traffic passing on the other side of the house. And the kettle was on the stove, beginning to sing, and the teatray was ready set. All these were real. Miss Stanton stood against the unknown background of London, and to feel for her with your mind was like feeling for something with your hands in the dark. It was dreadful, it was shameful, but it was terribly true.

But at least you needn't take the money. The cheque was puzzling, but some one could tell you what to do about that. That twenty pounds was not going to be spent on clothes for a selfish little bitch who was justifying the worst thing Ella Frome ever said about her.

She hoped intensely that Murray would ring and ask for coffee that evening as he had done once or twice since the time when she had first made it. If he did it would give her a good opportunity to ask him how she could use the cheque to Miss Stanton's advantage. If he didn't, she would have to go and knock on the door and chance any one's wondering what she was about. She was aware that what she meant was that she must chance meeting that funny look in Dr. Mason's eyes again. Twice, since that night at the cinema, Dr. Mason had been in the hall when she had come out of Murray's room and though each time she had given her a brief smile and murmured her easy "Good night, Emmie", there had been something disconcerting in her expression.

He did not ring for coffee, and directly Mrs. Tallet set off on her evening's attentions to Miss Ada, Emmie slipped up into the hall and knocked at his door. There was no answer, and as she stood there, disappointed, the front door opened and Dr. Mason came in. Emmie felt her face redden, though she could have given no adequate reason for her confusion. Dr. Mason paused at the foot of the stairs and said, "Emmie".

"Yes, madam."

"Were you wanting Mr. Wykham for something?"

When in doubt, tell the truth. She had seen that on a poker-work calendar somewhere.

"I wanted to ask him something about a cheque."

"Anything I can tell you? I know quite a bit about them."

"I don't like to bother you."

The deep-set dark eyes dwelt on her for a moment. Why, they asked, are you willing to bother him about something that you hesitate to ask me? There was nothing of rebuke in the glance, but there was a penetrating kind of pity that gave Emmie the uncomfortable feeling that her thoughts and hopes and little subterfuges were all exposed beneath its scrutiny.

"Not a bit of bother," said Dr. Mason briskly. "Just come up to my room. No, come up this way, it doesn't matter." Inside her neat bare bedroom she pushed the door to, pointed to a chair and flung her coat on the bed.

"Now tell me, while I wash my hands."

"It's quite a long story."

"Never mind, I like stories."

Emmie told it succinctly, not wasting a word, saying that the money was lent her and that she had paid back fifty pounds and had had the cheque for twenty returned to her. "I want to know what to do about it. I've read of cheques being torn up," she finished, "but I daren't do that until I was quite sure."

By this time Dr. Mason had washed and dried her hands and was sitting in the other chair with her elbows on her knees and her chin in her hands.

"So long as you don't take the cheque to the bank the money will stay in your friend's account," she said at the end of the story. "But are you sure that you can afford not to take the money?"

"I won't take it. I can't," said Emmie passionately. "It's her money . . . and anyway I don't deserve it."

"Then tear it up." She unlinked her fingers and stretching out reached for and lighted a cigarette. Emmie got up.

"No, don't go for a minute, Emmie. There's something else I want to say to you. It's a bit difficult. I don't want you to be annoyed, or to think me interfering."

Something to do with Mr. Wykham, thought Emmie, and steeled herself for what was coming.

"Anyway, I'll say it. How old are you, Emmie?"

"Seventeen."

"Well, look here, you must take it that I'm saying this because I'm so very much older than you. And also because I do think that women should stick together in this rough world. It's about you and Mr. Wykham."

Foreknowledge and her utmost efforts could not keep the blood from mounting into Emmie's face, blinding and scorching; but she said with the same sudden dignity that had surprised Ella Frome,

"What about us, Dr. Mason?"

"Two or three times I've seen you coming out of his room, late; and you were at the pictures with him. I know there's nothing in that, and I know I sound like Mrs. Grundy . . . but I do wonder whether it's *wise* of you. Mr. Wykham is an unusual person, and some of his notions are very odd — but still —" Dr. Mason appeared to have lost her composure and the sentence trailed off.

The hot blush receded from Emmie's face, leaving it white and curiously hard.

"I suppose you mean that even his odd notions wouldn't extend to being friendly with me?" Because I am a servant, she added to herself. And Dr. Mason is trying to warn me that there is only one construction to be put upon any intimacy between him and me. I must make an effort to explain.

"I go to his room," she began steadily, "because I sometimes take him coffee, late. And then we talk, mostly about books, and he lends me books and sometimes papers. And that night we *were* at the pictures, but it wasn't planned; he drove me down because it was raining and then there was something he wanted to see himself. And he had hold of my elbow when you saw us because somebody had just pushed me and I had fallen off the step. That's all."

Something new was creeping into the expression of the eyes that were watching her so closely, something that was neither appraisement nor pity.

"And you . . . are you in no danger of succumbing to his fatal charm?"

"I'm afraid I'd done that before I knew him at all. The breach was made long ago, before I came here, when I first began to read poetry."

"Because he writes, is that it?"

"I suppose so. I used to read things people wrote, you see, and wonder what they'd be like to know, and whether they'd be different from other people. And I think Mr. Wykham is."

"I agree with you." She paused, stubbed out her cigarette and folded her hands together again. "You know, Emmie, you're an unusual person, too. Perhaps that is why I risked being thought officious and spoke to you like this. I was going to say that I thought you'd be much wiser to find somebody — well, of your own age, and spend your time with him, or her. And now that seems impertinent. But to be quite frank with you — Mr. Wykham hasn't much respect for conventions, and he does drink rather much, and people aren't always as responsible as they should be when they're drunk."

"I've seen him when he wasn't very steady," said Emmie, smiling. "But he was quite intelligent, and quite himself, even then."

"Strangely enough, I believe you. You know, Emmie, I think you're the funniest square peg in a round hole I've ever seen, but I believe you're going to square the hole. Look here, how about talking to me sometimes. Doff that ridiculous cap and apron as I doff my overall, and come in here and talk to me . . . about books and things."

It was a suggestion made on the spur of the moment in response to a sudden burst of insight that showed her Emmie as an exile. How very lonely her life must be. How much those talks "about books and things" down in Murray Wykham's room must mean to this romantic, susceptible child. And how dangerous, or at least fraught with potential danger they were too. She knew all about the charm that Murray's natural, outspoken, haphazard manner held — but she knew more of him than that. And yet now, looking at Emmie, seeing that transparent innocence and also that reasoning, clear-sighted judgment, "the breach was made long ago", and "quite himself even then", she wondered whether Murray might be, quite legitimately,

196

interested in the child's character. She felt like an interfering fool.

But Emmie, suffused again with crimson, was saying, "I'd love to do that. May I ask you something?"

"Certainly."

"What does the J. stand for, when they call you J. M. downstairs?"

"Java. My father was there when I was born and mother would name me that. I've often found it rather —" The telephone that stood by itself on the small table beside the bed began its urgent clatter. She rose stiffly from her chair and picked up the receiver. "Speaking. Oh yes. I'll be there in ten minutes."

She lifted her coat from the bed and began to struggle into it. For a moment she looked desperate and hag-ridden, Emmie could see that she was entirely forgotten.

"I'll fill your bottle again," she said, "then it may be warm when you come in."

"Thank you so much. Then you nip along to bed. Good night, dear."

She hurried away, dropping jerkily down the stairs two at a time, and leaving Emmie with a great deal to think about. However, the long day's work and the strain of the last half-hour prevented her from staying awake a moment once her head was on the pillow, and then almost immediately it was morning and there was no time for thinking on Tuesday, which was Mrs. Tallet's day for washing. And before the next bedtime a great many things had happened.

9

Mrs. Tallet set off up the back stairs with Miss Ada's jug of malted milk and called her usual, "Remember the lights", to Emmie who had artfully taken to raking out the boiler overnight. That gave her an excuse for lingering behind for a perilous ten minutes in case Mr. Wykham should come in and demand coffee.

He had been out all day. Miss Bavister had said at lunch-time, with a lightness that did not quite hide a certain discontent, "Mr. Wykham hardly ever seems to be at lunch now." And Mrs. Clarkson had said with a gentle air of patience, "And when he does come in he almost always wants something on a tray. I'm afraid he isn't very considerate." She spoke as though she were obliged to load and carry the tray herself. Emmie thought — bosh! It's far easier to carry a tray in than it is to stand here watching whether any one needs potato and remembering that though it's quicker to pile plates it's all wrong to do so. I wish they'd all lunch off trays. "He's probably hanging about to discover what decision they have come to about those new town buildings. If the meeting this morning passes the idea he'll have a red-hot article in the *Press* tomorrow."

"All about Town Terrace, Ferny Court, and the New Cut, I suppose," said Miss Bavister. She seemed to gain a perverted kind of pleasure, Emmie had noticed, in siding with Mrs. Clarkson and Mrs. Begbie in criticizing Murray's activities.

"He'd be a far more popular person and carry a great deal more weight if he didn't get so excited," said

Mrs. Clarkson. "After all, people have lived in Town Terrace for a great number of years, without taking much harm. In fact they must like it, you never see a house of that sort empty for a day. He defeats his own ends by his violence. His father, who had the paper before him, had far more influence, the *Press* was a guide in those days. I've heard my husband say many times that the *Press* always voiced the right opinions."

"Because they agreed with his, perhaps. Personally I think it always voices the right opinions now." Dr. Mason's voice was as gentle as Mrs. Clarkson's.

"Yet you never seem to get on very well with him," Coral Bavister said pointedly.

"That doesn't mean that I don't think his opinions are right. You don't get on very well with me, personally. Yet you took my advice about your laryngitis, didn't you?"

"That's utterly different. After all, you are a doctor. It's your job to give the right advice."

"So it is Mr. Wykham's job to give the right advice, as he sees it, in his paper."

"I must disagree," Mrs. Clarkson spoke quite sharply. "A paper's job is to report the news of what has happened, not to offer opinions about what is, or may be, going to happen."

"Oh, Mrs. Clarkson, what an upheaval there must be at this minute, in all the places where old newspaper men are buried. Will you excuse me? Clinic afternoon."

"Unusual for her to stick up for him like that, isn't it?" asked Coral as the door closed behind Dr. Mason, "What did happen there? They used to be quite matey when I first came."

The soft pink on Mrs. Clarkson's cheek deepened a little. "I'm not sure, so perhaps I ought not to say, but it was something to do, I think, with that Caxton girl from a dreadful little shop in the Saltgate. I think J.M. went for him about it."

"What! 'Carry On' Caxton?" said Coral incredulously. "I can't believe it. No wonder she went for him. How absurd." And how unnecessary — her mind added — with me here ready and willing, and quite experienced enough, and clean at least.

"Well, Emmie, if you'll come out of your trance," said Mrs. Clarkson, becoming aware of Emmie's presence and posture, "the plates are ready for you."

Emmie came out of a state of mind extraordinarily like Coral's and removed the plates.

"Carry On" Caxton lived only two doors from the Trappits' and a love of gossip, tempered perhaps by a little commercial jealousy, had led Miss Trappit to talk about her to Emmie. A dreadful girl who would sleep with any man who paid her. A dreadful draggled painted girl. What could he want with her? What was known, oddly enough, as the "usual" thing, she supposed. And her whole being melted in a flood, not of disgust but tenderness. The idol fell a little lower until his place was no longer in her head but in her heart. And lodging there, he could fall no more.

He hadn't been in to dinner either. A boy from the office brought Stumpy to the back door at six o'clock and asked that Emmie should let him run out some time between eight and nine. That she had done, and was now waiting as eagerly as Stumpy was waiting in the untidy room upstairs for the slam of the door and the familiar step.

Patience and hope were rewarded. The door slammed and a moment afterwards the third bell swung, sounded once and went on gently swinging. She was up the stairs, across the hall and into his room in half a minute. He had his hat on the back of his head and beneath it his hair strayed wildly over his forehead. His coat was unbuttoned, his tie streaming and his eyes horribly bloodshot. But worst of all his face seemed to have changed, to have become aged and flaccid, with pouches under the eyes and chin.

"Evening, Emmie," he said, normally enough, "can I have some coffee?" And then, as she turned back to the door, he added in a loud, truculent voice, "What do you think they've done? They've decided to borrow twenty thousand pounds to build a new Municipal building so that the Mayor can have a parlour, by God, and the Watkins china can be properly housed."

Emmie stood dumb. Why should this concern her? Or him?

"You don't know what that means? Or are you dumbfounded, as every right-minded person should be by such monstrous folly — such barbarous stupidity? The office of Mayor is an old and honourable one, God forbid that I should decry an office that my fathers held with honour." He raised his hat and replaced it crookedly. "But so are the privies and drains in Town Terrace old, if not honourable. Why should the one demand a two-shilling rate and the other be passed by with averted nose?" He laughed without amusement, and at the sound Stumpy retired behind a chair and Emmie took a step backward.

"I don't think you should make such a noise," she said timidly.

"Make such a noise? I'll make a noise tomorrow, if it gaols me. Do you know, Emmie," he leaned both hands on the desk and bent over towards her, "there are scores of women in this town who haven't got a parlour and hundreds of children who aren't properly housed. But the Mayor must have a parlour, and the china that frowsty old Watkins left to the town because he knew that any right-thinking heir would smash the rubbish, that must be properly housed. Dear God, and I've worked and worked and talked and talked, all for this."

"Perhaps they'll build some new houses as well."

"Not they. They'll have done their building now for fifty years. And they can't stick any more on the rates, anyway. And they never pass more than one resolution in five years. Blast their thick heads."

"Do you really want any coffee?"

"Yes please, I do. I've had nothing since breakfast." He took off his hat and threw it into the corner and snapped his fingers to Stumpy. Emmie vanished.

When she returned he was standing with his elbows on the mantelpiece, staring at the ashes of the fire.

"Why haven't I a fire?" he asked crossly as she set down the tray.

"Mrs. Tallet said it wasn't to be kept up when you didn't come in for lunch."

"Exactly," he said bitterly. "That's logic, that is. Because she saves the grub she grudges the coal. If I'd

202

sat here all day stuffing myself and using light I'd have had a fire."

"It isn't my fault. I did put some dust on after she'd said that."

He sat down suddenly, and some of the glare went out of his eyes.

"My sweet, I know it isn't. I must be going crazy. You're the only person in this house worth a damn, and here I am going for you like a pickpocket. Do forgive me."

"That's all right," said Emmie. "Shall I pour?"

"Will you? Can you bear with me for ten minutes? I don't know. I think perhaps you ought to be in bed. Anyway sit down." He stretched out and flicked Stumpy's cushion to the floor. "I've got to go back to the office in a minute or two and get my little piece in. Lomax is holding the space. But what is the good? I might just as well agree with the damn fat fools. Why should I care whether the Mayor sits in his parlour making silly pompous speeches, or whether the people in Town Terrace queue up for the one privy? No, it *isn't* a W.C. After all the W. *does* stand for something, and they don't have it. And it's no use pretending that I don't care, because I do. And I can't be the only one who'd rather see a few council houses than a great ugly barrack with the town arms over the door."

Emmie sat still and watched as he stirred his coffee with increasing violence until the saucer held as much as the cup. Strange man to upset himself so. What would he have done or said if he had seen the Bacon cottage? Still, this was the stuff reformers were made of, she thought, and adoration leaped within her. He drank about half the coffee that was left in the cup and then jumped up. "This is no good," he said, and opening the cupboard by the fireplace he took out the whisky bottle and glass that always stood there. He poured a stiff drink and swallowed it quickly.

As though immediately revived he said, "Well, use or no use, I'll let them know what I think. I'll ask them how many children are worth the Watkins china. I'll sting them somehow. I'll show them that one person in this rotten place isn't dazzled with red robes and flat hats and twenty thousand pounds' worth of brick." He paused and looked at her dully.

"What was I saying? Oh yes, I know . . ."

He reached for the bottle again, but Emmie was quicker. With it in her hand she said breathlessly, "You're too excited now . . . and if you've got to go out again you'd better not."

"Give me that bottle," he said, advancing towards her.

She put it behind her and started backing to the door. He followed and laid his hands on her arms, high up by the shoulders. Emmie bent backwards and her eyes widened with terror, but she kept the hand with the bottle in it behind her and pushed the other against his chest. Even at that moment, something deeper than terror or doubt whether she was doing the right thing registered a shattering joy at that contact.

He began to shake her, gently at first and then with gathering force. Her fingers opened and the bottle fell into Stumpy's chair. He did not notice it, or the fact that he had only to lean over her to pick it up. He went on shaking her as though the mere exercise of violence released something in him. Suddenly the floor beneath her feet tilted, the room was full of furious faces rocking wildly from side to side, her head fell loosely forward. Everything was very still.

Then a voice said, "My God, what am I doing? Emmie, don't faint. Hold up. I've got you."

The hard punishing grip of the hands had changed, they were kind now and supporting. They held her up and then gently lowered her into the chair on top of the forgotten bottle. She raised her head. Her neck wasn't broken then, after all. As he met her eyes he said slowly, "I'm mad. I've often wondered, now I know. To go for you of all people. I ought to be kicked for a mile and then put behind bars."

"It's all right," said Emmie. "It was my fault, I shouldn't have annoyed you."

"You didn't, Emmie, you couldn't. Look here, you go to bed now and leave me to wallow in my mire. I'll apologize tomorrow. I'll do anything if you'll only forget about it till I can make it right with you. Will you try to do that?"

Emmie nodded and stood up. He went with her to the door where he paused, tilted back her head and dropped a light kiss on the peak where the hair grew off her forehead. The room swayed again, and then up went her two little red hands, one on either side his face and she was kissing him as she had never kissed any one in her life.

For just the briefest moment the situation swung in the balance. She felt him stiffen and breathe hard. His arm went half round her and she pressed closer to him. Then he withdrew his hands, took hold of hers and drew them down. Holding them firmly in front of him he said in a queer staccato voice, "This won't do, you know. We don't know what we're doing. I'm half lit and you're . . . over-excited. Go to bed now and forget it all. Or remember that I'm not a bit of good." He opened the door, gave her a firm push and slammed it to again.

Emmie leaned against the wall outside and tried to regain her breath. It would never do to faint here. He would be coming out presently to go to the office and Miss Bavister would be coming in at any moment. She dragged her shaking limbs to the stairs and began to mount to the top landing. The top stairs were lighted, which was unusual, but she was too preoccupied to notice. She rounded the last twist in the stairs and then, with a gasp, tightened her clutch on the banister rail to save herself from falling. Mrs. Tallet sat on the top stair.

The fear that she had been watching, overhearing, and was now waiting to make a row flashed through Emmie's mind and was gone. For Mrs. Tallet's face was paper-white, etched with black lines, and her mouth was closed so tightly that it looked just like another line. Her skirt was turned back over her knees, revealing a petticoat of grey flannel and striped knickers buttoned below the knee. She was clasping both hands round her ankle — and a trickle of dark blood had run over her knotted fingers and was gathering in a little puddle on the stair below.

"Where have you been?" she said. "I thought you were never coming. This vein in my leg has burst. Is Dr. Mason in?"

"I think so. I'll see. Oughtn't you to put your leg up?"

"I couldn't hold it then, silly. Go and get the doctor."

Veins, dark blood, varicose veins. Not so dangerous as arteries. Should be held farthest from the heart. Leg up or down? Emmie wondered as she tumbled down the stairs again. Anyway, it was only for a moment. Thank God there was a doctor in the house. Dizzily she skidded over the lino and literally fell against the door of Java's room.

"Come in. What is it?" cried the calm voice. Oh blessed calm. She drew enough control from it to say quietly,

"It's Mrs. Tallet, a vein in her leg has burst."

Dr. Mason threw back the bedclothes and leaped to the floor. While she was grabbing her slippers she said, "Hold me that dressing-gown." Emmie snatched it from the bed foot and held it open. Dr. Mason tied the girdle and picked up her bag.

"She's sitting at the top of our stairs," said Emmie, and dashed on ahead.

Within fifteen minutes Mrs. Tallet, bound and bandaged, having already submitted to the indignity of being carried to her room, was enduring the further ignominy of being undressed by Emmie and the doctor.

"You're not to tell Miss Ada and spoil her night," she said when her head emerged from the top of her old-fashioned frilled nightgown.

"And you're not to try getting up tomorrow not to spoil her day," Dr. Mason said sharply.

"I shall be quite all right tomorrow."

"You will if you stay in bed. I mean that, Mrs. Tallet. If you fool about with that leg it may never get well."

Outside the door she laid her hand on Emmie's arm: "Will you knock on my door first thing as you go down? Then I can go in to Mrs. Clarkson and really make her understand that this is serious. Mrs. Tallet is quite hopeless. I can remember when she had 'flu. She simply kept about and gave it to us all."

"I'll knock," said Emmie.

"Good night, then."

"Good night."

Tomorrow there would be the breakfast to manage alone. And what about the lunch? And it was Wednesday when she was going shopping. There would be no half-day for her with Mrs. Tallet in bed.

But he had called her "my sweet"; he had held her; he had kissed her. She would see him tomorrow and show him that she bore no grudge. She fell on her bed utterly exhausted and utterly happy.

10

Next day Emmie came closely in contact for the first time with Mrs. Clarkson: and long before the day was ended she saw that life without Mrs. Tallet would be unbearable at the Corner House.

Mrs. Clarkson's day had started badly with Dr. Mason coming into her room with the news about Tallet's leg. She had begun to get up soon after that because goodness knew what that ignorant child would do with the breakfast, and anyway there was no hope of getting tea. In that she was wrong, for Emmie, who had been astir since half past five, presently appeared with a tray of tea, the outward and visible sign, had Mrs. Clarkson but seen it, of her determination to carry on for Mrs. Tallet, who, she dimly believed, would have done the same for her. And then, of course, it was that vile Indian tea that Mrs. Clarkson loathed. She struggled down five minutes before her usual time to superintend the cooking of the breakfast which Dr. Mason was already eating.

She followed Emmie into the kitchen when she cleared away the breakfast things, and said, "Open the window wider, Emmie. I loathe the smell of bacon to hang about."

"It won't open at the bottom, madam, the cord is broken."

"Mrs. Tallet should have seen to it."

She strolled into the pantry and lifted the lid at random.

"Good gracious. When did you last wash out this bread crock?"

"I always do that on Saturdays."

"I think it should be done twice a week. It's full of stale crumbs. They all turn the bread stale."

Emmie overlooked this remarkable piece of information and began to wash up.

Mrs. Clarkson left the pantry and came over to the sink.

"Do you usually use as much soap powder as that?"

"Yes, madam."

"Very wasteful. Half the amount would do."

Perhaps Emmie's silence informed her that this was not exactly the moment for such criticism. She reached down a cloth from the line that hung within range of the boiler's heat and dried two cups.

"It's very sad about Mrs. Tallet," she said, and her voice was no longer querulous. "However, it won't be for long and I think that if we all put our shoulders to the wheel we shall manage. I'm sure you'll do your best, won't you, Emmie?"

Acutely embarrassed, Emmie muttered something into the wash-up bowl.

"I'll go up now and see if she has eaten her breakfast and have a little chat with her. Then I'll do my bedroom. That will be a help, won't it?"

She put down the cloth and walked gently out of the kitchen. Emmie finished washing, wiped and wondered for a moment whether Mrs. Clarkson would bring down the invalid's tray. But it seemed unlikely so she ran up for it. Mrs. Tallet was alone, looking very woebegone.

"Miss Ada has been in to see me," she said to Emmie. "She's really dreadfully upset. She's so tender-hearted that it's almost worse for her than it is for me."

You are a besotted old woman, thought Emmie as she heaved up the tray and then stood back to let the doctor enter the room. I'll bet Mrs. Clarkson made her own bed and then shut herself away. And that was exactly what Mrs. Clarkson had done.

When Emmie went up to ask what order for the butcher, she said, "None, I really can't cook today. I'm far too upset. You'll have to run out, Emmie, and buy some cooked ham or something."

Emmie's heart sank, there just wasn't time to go out this morning; she never went shopping in the morning even when Mrs. Tallet was about.

"I could cook chops, or something like that," she said. Anything, oh anything that the boy could bring to the door.

"Oh no, Emmie, it's very nice of you, very nice indeed, but I won't let you bother. We can manage with some cooked meat."

As Emmie sent the boy away she was not far from tears. The thought of all those rooms, all those beds, weighed on her like a tangible load. She shut the back door just as Mr. Wykham gained the bottom step of the kitchen stairs. Her heart gave a jolt. She had not seen him at breakfast, for he was not there when she took in the food and had gone before she cleared away.

"Hullo," he said, quite at his ease, "I've just heard the sad news about old Tally. How are you managing? Going to get somebody in?"

"No," said Emmie bitterly, still ruffled over the meat question. "We're all Going to put Our Shoulders to the Wheel and Carry On. And that means that instead of having chops delivered I have to find the time to run to the cooked meat shop. And there's never time to shop in the morning. She's so *stupid!*"

"Unanimously agreed. But why must you run out for the cooked meat?"

"Cooked meat shops don't send boys round."

"Nor they do. Still, I might be able to spare my bright boy for half an hour. How much cooked meat do you need?"

"Will you be in?"

"No."

"Three quarters of a pound, I should think. I don't really know."

"Right. I'll tell him three-quarters. Anything else?"

"No, thank you. You are good to me."

"Rot. Well, I must fly. Mind the wheel doesn't run back on you. Good-bye."

No, there was no one like him in the world. He might be queer and he might get drunk, he was still unique and splendid. Her love for him rose in sheer physical pain in her heart as she hurried upstairs to attend to the bedrooms. And there she had another surprise. Dr. Mason came, dressed for the street, from her door just as Emmie came from Miss Bavister's room.

"You needn't go in there, Emmie," she said, "I've done all that was needed. And can I bring you anything in?"

"No, thank you, that's arranged for," said Emmie warmly. "And thank you for doing the room."

Really, people were good, some people. And they were the two that she had picked on on that first day. I must be psychic, thought Emmie.

The cooked meat arrived after about an hour, borne by the boy who sometimes brought Stumpy home in the evenings. He bore also an enormous sheaf of yellowy bronze tulips, done up in a cone of stiff paper.

"'Ere's the meat," he said cheerily, "and these are for yourself. And Mr. Wykham said I was to say that I was at your dis . . . dish . . . well, you know. I can go anywhere for you."

"Thank you, but there isn't anywhere. You might say that I'm grateful."

"Righto. Sure there're no errands?" He whistled himself away.

Those were the days when it seemed to Emmie that she did not draw a full breath during the whole day. Perhaps that accounted for the state of heat and breathlessness in which she was always finding herself. She began to long for the night to come simply that she might at last go to bed and be still. The mere waiting upon Mrs. Tallet at the top of all those stairs became a burden.

It was a pity, too, they were such lovely days to be lived through unseeing, and wished away. Even the air that blew into the sunken kitchen was heavy with the early summer scents of growing things and dust and newly tarred roads. From the windows upstairs she could catch glimpses, isolated as flower studies, of the beds in the Close Gardens full of tulips and wallflowers and hyacinths, of flowering cherry and lilac and pink almond, of laburnum just ready to break into gold. The loveliest time of the year. Sometimes as she swept and scrubbed and dusted, scoured and cooked and served, a few stray words would haunt her —

How the young wind was crying on the hill
And the young world was breaking into flower.

Let them go as they will, too soon,
With the beanflower's boon,
And the blackbird's tune,
And May and June.

Too soon.

They are not long the music and the laughter.

Hurry, hurry, hurry, upstairs and downstairs and into Mrs. Begbie's chamber. "Had we but world enough and time." Hurry, hurry, hurry.

At the end of three weeks Dr. Mason struck a blow for her. She invaded Mrs. Clarkson's sanctuary one evening after dinner and "spoke to me as I suppose doctors talk to panel patients", Mrs. Clarkson said next day to sympathetic Mrs. Begbie.

"Mrs. Tallet isn't going to be of much use for some time. You simply must find somebody who can give Emmie a hand. The child is going to pieces and if you're not careful she'll have a breakdown."

Mrs. Clarkson sighed pathetically and gave her gentle smile.

214

"I'd noticed that too. Though I do what I can, Dr. Mason. She's never had to lay a hand on either of my rooms since Tallet went to bed."

"Nor on mine, but that's neither here nor there. Whom can you get?"

"That is the trouble. When Emmie came she was the only applicant, and every week the paper is full of places for girls."

"Isn't there a woman?"

"I'll try to think of one."

"Think now," said the relentless woman. "Where's that old Kate you used to talk so much about?"

"Oh, my dear old Kate. Yes, well of course she might come in, if her husband could spare her. She was very much attached to me."

"I know," said Dr. Mason dryly. "Would you like to come and ask her now? I'll drive you to her house."

Mrs. Clarkson rose reluctantly. She detested being driven into decisions.

"Very well," she said, "it would certainly be a burden off my mind."

Kate's husband, as it happened, was away from home on a job and Kate was only too ready to oblige. So Mrs. Clarkson was able to go into the kitchen where Emmie was belatedly cleaning the silver and say, "Emmie, there's going to be help for you tomorrow, an old maid of mine is coming in. She was much the best maid I ever had, absolutely devoted, and I'm sure things will get back into their usual swing with her about."

Emmie was glad to hear the news of impending relief, but Mrs. Clarkson's method of imparting it left

215

her with the strong impression that she herself had let things down very badly and that had the devoted Kate been in her place she would have managed far better. She laid her head on the table beside the uncleaned silver and shed several tears of weariness and irritation.

And even after this unprecedented activity upon Mrs. Clarkson's part Dr. Mason had the audacity to interfere again.

"I hope that now the remarkable Kate is in charge and Mrs. Tallet is able to get downstairs again, you'll manage so that Emmie has every afternoon off, for a week at least."

"My dear J. M., that must be a case of telepathy. I thought of the same thing myself, not five minutes ago."

Not five — or any other minutes ago, you old humbug, thought Java, but aloud she said, "Emmie could come out with me to Fen Willow this afternoon. The air would do her good and she could open those stupid gates along the old Turnpike for me."

11

Sun, and little opening leaves almost transparently green; meadows gilded with buttercups and silvered with daisies. The willows beside the old Turnpike dipping their green hair in the water, and the cuckoo calling and calling from the shelter of the hawthorn trees. Intelligent conversation; brief bitter comments of Dr. Mason's that opened hitherto unnoticed windows of the mind. A farmhouse tea at a place on the way back; the pleasure of eating something that you hadn't thought about and slaved over. A pleasant afternoon, a golden afternoon to be gathered up, moment by moment, and treasured and stored away.

But the best part about it was the uprising of something that the grinding three weeks just past had trodden down; the longing for ten o'clock to come, not for the cessation of toil that it brought but for the possibility of seeing Murray again and of seeing him when she felt normal and alive and less as if she had been pulled limb from limb and then steam-rollered. But Murray Wykham had not heard of the reform in the kitchen and would have died sooner than ring his bell at any time during the day.

Emmie spent three of her five holiday afternoons with Dr. Mason and discovered on one of them that Murray and Java had one thing in common, the capacity for raving about something that did not concern them personally. This was a thing new to Emmie. Miss Stanton could rave, but it was generally about a personal matter; Mrs. Fincham could moan, but always about something that affected or afflicted her; but Murray had raved about the new Town building, and on the second afternoon Java had a bout of indignation over some woman and her baby.

She had called at a cottage, stayed a long time, during which Emmie had had a private, imitative struggle with a cigarette, and came out looking white and furious. She drove for quite a while in silence, and then said in a low bitter voice as though she had

217

forgotten Emmie and were talking to herself, "It makes me utterly sick."

"What does?"

"Seeing these miserable strings of brats that ought never to be born. Eight in that family under twelve. Three completely simple and the whole brood just ready to catch anything. The mother is pretty feeble-minded too, but even if she weren't how could she cope with them all? And even if she were bright, what can I or anybody do about the number of them? All very well to say she's had too many too quickly, but you can't show her how not to."

"Why not?" asked Emmie, and added, "If there is a way", because she wasn't herself very sure.

"You're not supposed to. The population must be kept up, even if it's kept up by masses of simple-minded people who never have enough food when they're children, and never have a job when they're grown up. Politicians yap about numbers, and parsons yap about souls, and we go on trying to bring up people that would have been drowned if they'd been pups."

"I would probably have been drowned," said Emmie quietly.

"Why?"

"Well, there were an awful lot of us, and Freddie was simple and we all had runny eyes and noses and no shoes. And my father drank, though he was kind enough, and mother drank too and had an awful house. But you see, if you'd had your way I wouldn't ever have been alive at all."

218

There was a brief silence, during which Emmie tried to imagine the thing that to the human ego is almost unimaginable — the possibility of its own non-existence, while Java pondered over the problem presented by Emmie's simple admission. At last she said, "That gives food for thought. Because after all you are glad to be alive, aren't you, Emmie?"

"Very," said Emmie, and thought of all the joys she had known, books and flowers and weather and the hope that there was something awaiting her, and knowing things about history and the world, and meeting people like Murray and Java.

"What happened to you, to make you so different, I mean?"

"I was saved," said Emmie bluntly.

"You mean religion?" asked Java, to whom the phrase called up Salvation Army meetings at street corners, and who thought, Good God, there must be something in religion that I haven't reckoned with.

"No, not religion. Somebody, my school teacher, just took me away and showed me things and sent me to school. I think, you know I often think this, that the State ought to take children away from homes like mine and bring them up properly. It would save an awful lot of misery and time and trouble too."

"I agree with you. I believe they are doing something like that in Russia. We may live long enough to see how it turns out. But people will argue that even a bad mother is better than no mother at all."

"I don't believe it. Look at the N.S.P.C.C."

"I know," said Java hastily, "don't let's look at it. But you see, I believe half those women hate their children long before they're born. They don't want them, they've nothing for them. They hate them." She broke off suddenly at the sight of Emmie's face. "Look, let's scurry into Gigglesworth and have tea there. We can't come out tomorrow afternoon because I'm at the clinic. I hope you'll find something nice to do."

"I shall buy some clothes," said Emmie, who had been deducting five shillings from her hoard in the interests of the N.S.P.C.C. and was satisfied with the remainder.

"Good. What shall you buy?"

The talk drifted away to that absorbing feminine subject.

12

That evening, just as she had finished washing up and was hanging the teacloths over the line, Murray's voice sounded from the back stairs.

"Emmie, could you spare me a moment? Up in my room, bedroom." The voice was retreating even as it sounded and Emmie hurried after it.

He stood in his shirt-sleeves in his bedroom. Every drawer and cupboard was open, two suitcases partially filled lay on the bed.

"I know you tidy everything away very nicely, but can you tell me where you ... Good Heavens, child, whatever is the matter?" For Emmie was standing in the doorway with both hands pressed to the bib of her frilly yellow apron and such an expression of horror and dismay upon her face that he jumped to the conclusion that she had had a heart attack from running upstairs.

"You're going away?" She could hardly force the words from her whitened lips: the shock was too great: she had never imagined, prepared for this.

"Emmie, are you ill?"

She hastened to relieve his anxiety.

"No . . . just taken aback."

"Why? About my going? I thought you knew. Everybody knows. I always go away from now until the end of August. Every year."

"You'll be coming back at the end of August?"

"Of course."

"Eleven weeks."

"Is it? I hadn't counted. I only know I've got a hell of a lot to do."

"What?"

"Oh, heaps. Go abroad for one thing. And see people and learn how the world wags."

"I see. What was it you wanted to ask me?"

"Whether you'd tidied away a couple of my shirts, and a checked coat of which I am very fond though it doesn't deserve I should be. Oh, and there's a swim-suit missing too."

"I've got the shirts," said Emmie; "I was turning the cuffs."

"You were what?"

"Turning the cuffs."

"What kind of procedure is that, may I ask? And why do you do it?"

"Because the cuffs were all frayed. I'd seen Mrs. Fincham do her husband's. They're like new afterwards."

"But, dear child, there's no earthly need. I've masses of shirts and if I hadn't there're shops. Still," he added, for her face was stricken, "I'm very partial to those shirts, and it'll be very nice to have them as good as new. Will they be ready when I come back? Good. Then just have a look for that coat, will you?"

Emmie went straight to the coat which was hanging under another for lack of a hanger of its own. She folded it and laid it on the bed. A blue woollen object on the floor among the shoes she rescued and identified as the swim-suit. She folded that too.

"You know," he said, "when I called you up I rather hoped your heart would melt at the sight of my plight and you'd help me. I've driven it a bit late. I want to get to London tonight."

"Tonight!"

"I hope you don't object to that."

"I thought tomorrow."

He looked up again, opened his mouth to speak, thought better of it and went on throwing things into the bags in silence.

"What happens to Stumpy?"

"Goes to the kennels."

"Does he like it there?"

"He loathes it, but it's the only thing for it."

"Couldn't he stay here?"

222

"I'm afraid not. The Tragic Mu — Mrs. Clarkson wouldn't like it."

"I'll go and see him every day some time."

"Will you really? Could you? It'd be awfully good of you. Cheer him up no end."

He slammed down the lid of one case, clicked down the catches and swung it on to the floor. It was coming, the last moment when he would go, vanish into an unknown world where people would greet him and be pleased to see him, where he would be busy, wanted, caught up in a whirl of activity of which she had no knowledge. "A shadow in which I have no lot or part."

"Oh," he said, pausing in the act of closing the other case, "camera please, on the peg behind the door."

To reach it she was obliged to push the door almost closed. He rammed the camera into the corner of the already well-filled case and slammed down the lid.

"There, that's done. Thank you so much. And Emmie, you may sit in my room and play my gramophone, do what you like; that is unless she lets it for a spell. And I'll send you a postcard from time to time if I go anywhere interesting. Look after yourself. Good-bye."

He held out a hand. She put one of hers into it, and then, uncontrollable as a blink, her other hand shot out and clutched at the back of his, so that she stood for a moment hanging on to him as though she were drowning. His eyes met hers — just like Stumpy's again, he thought, and he glanced aside with a certain discomfort. For just that moment the air seemed to grow dark with tension: then he put out his other hand, loosed hers, and with a little pat, dropped them.

"Good-bye," he said again, "bless you."

He picked up a case in either hand and Emmie pulled the door back and held it while he went through.

Miss Bavister was on the landing. "Hullo, just off?" she said lightly. "Have a good time."

"Without a doubt."

Emmie came through the doorway, closing the door slowly on the empty room behind her. She did see this time, as she turned towards the back stairs, that Miss Bavister was looking at her with a hard bright gleam in her grey eyes. And she saw, just as she turned, that the firm pointed chin flew up and the painted lips curved. She heard the clear voice say, "Any chance of your being in Town when I'm at home? If there is and you give me a ring I'll sock you a dinner."

"Kind lady. I'll see if I . . ."

The kitchen stairs gulfed blackly and she closed the door on the rest of the speech. Oh to be Coral! To be pretty and free and to have that assurance of manner and that supply of money. Coral, quite plainly, liked Murray too. She should have felt drawn to her by that, known a fellow feeling. But instead she hated her.

She could hear through the open window of the kitchen the sound of the slammed car door and the whirr of the starter from the road at the side of the house. The kitchen was warm and full of the fading scent of food. Kate was putting on her hat and exchanging a few parting shots with Mrs. Tallet. There was a deep irreconcilable enmity between the two of

224

them, enmity bred of jealousy and their competition to serve Miss Ada. Emmie tidied the sink which she had abandoned when Murray called down the stairs and then slowly and dully began to rake out the boiler. There was no point in leaving it late tonight. Nor would there be for seventy-seven other nights. It was like having the Sahara to cross.

13

Meanwhile Murray Wykham, having left St. Petersbury by the South Gate, was speeding along the quiet road that ran across the flat country to join the busy Watford by-pass. It was the old Roman road, narrow by modern standards but straight and level, and hardly busier now than in the days when the legions marched along it. Driving needed only perfunctory attention and he found his mind drifting. It was a lovely evening, with the sun low behind pearly banks of cloud. The hedges were covered with the white blossom of hawthorn and there were tall daisies opening in the meadow grass. He thought at first of his errands, the people whom he would see, and the places. Then, as the light faded and couples began to appear by stiles and gates and under the hedgerows, he found himself thinking about Emmie. Had he been blind in the past, or was he fancying things now? That was the question. He recalled and weighed over several things that he was evaluating now for the first time — from her stricken look at the sight of his packing to the careful mending of his clothes.

Suppose she was in love with him.

What nonsense, she was only a child.

No, that was the nonsense.

Emmie belonged by birth if not by nature to an order that matured early. Returns proved that several scores of girls in England were married at the age of sixteen. Besides, there was always the evidence — acceptable to one of Murray's kind — of literature. From Juliet to Tessa in *The Constant Nymph* they ranged, all witnessing that love needed neither age nor experience. And they proved, too, that first love, early love, was the hardest kind to endure.

He dived back through the mixed experiences of his thirty-nine years and dragged up the memory of his first love — his stepmother's sister, Winifred. Gosh yes, he could see her now, playing tennis in an embroidered white frock with a tight waistband and her hair puffed out over the temples and turned up into a "door-knocker" on her neck. He'd been just seventeen at the time and she was nineteen. That was the year the War broke out and in the next year she'd married a young officer. The bitter blow that that had been! He remembered almost with shame, after all these years, how he had searched the table of prohibited degrees of relationship in the Prayer Book to find out whether stepmother's sister was ranked with grandmother as a person man must not marry.

Suppose she had loved him, and they'd been married and shoved into bed together. Merciful Heavens, what a prospect. What ignorance, what bungling, what shame.

Yes, but a girl at seventeen is older than a boy, or so it was believed, and ignorance didn't matter in a girl.

He pulled himself up short. Was he contemplating marrying Emmie? Of course not. But he was arguing as though he were. That set him thinking about his one brief and disastrous excursion into matrimony. Where was Myra now? He neither knew nor cared; and yet once she had had the power to turn all his flesh to water and to draw it towards her as the moon draws the tides. He thought of that for quite a long time while the sun melted into gold behind the lilac clouds and the moon came up unnaturally wide and red from beyond the scented meadows of hay.

Once was quite enough. He'd never marry again. Because you liked tomatoes it didn't follow that you wanted to shut yourself in a greenhouse and eat tomatoes all the time, and think about how the greenhouse was to be kept and furnished, and offer an explanation every time you went out, or came back late, or looked at any other comestible. Besides, there were always plenty of tomatoes on wayside stalls, and after one experiment in the greenhouse line the wise man was content to depend on them. His thoughts veered again. Wayside stall. Emmie.

He felt suddenly the convulsive clasp of her small work-roughened hands. And behind that the crisp spring of her hair on that night when he had been drunk and shaken her. And behind that the thin warmth of her shaking body on that same evening. Of course, he'd been a frightful fool. He had all his bright theories for setting the world straight: he raved against stupidity and cruelty and meanness. But he had been stupid and thoughtless to the verge of cruelty. And there wasn't much he could do about it now.

And there was no doubt at all that the child was very unusual and attractive. And anyway he was probably bothering himself about something that would adjust itself. He did not credit himself with much fatal attraction.

14

Two nights later, Emmie, on her way to bed, turned aside, crossed the hall and stole into Murray's room, closing the door gently behind her. She dared not, of course, play the gramophone as he had told her to. Somebody would hear her and ask what she meant by doing so and to have to explain would take all the charm out of the permission. She wanted to think and she wanted to be in his room, to be able to see the bare desk left as he had cleared it, and the shelves with his books on them. She could just see them in the last of the long twilight. She curled up in his armchair with her feet under her and her head on the arm and stared round the shadowy room.

Java, speaking in all kindness that afternoon, had upset her so that her mind seemed flayed. What had she said?

"Emmie, you're a little minor this afternoon. Is anything the matter?" She had said "No" to that.

"Do you feel well? I think perhaps you need a real holiday. Couldn't you go away somewhere?"

"I don't want to go away."

"I think that if I were you I would look for a job at the seaside."

"Why?"

"It'd be good for you. And you'd never get a harder place than you have. Kate goes tomorrow, you know."

"I'd rather be at the Corner House if —" Began Emmie vehemently, and then, fearing the perception of the woman beside her, she snipped off that sentence and said, "I don't want to go away. I like St. Petersbury, for one thing."

Java cast a side-glance at her and thought — Murray Wykham, of course, as I thought. Poor little devil. Presently she said inconsequently, "Do you ever think about space, Emmie?"

"No. No, I don't think I ever have."

"I do. When I get up against something I can't have, or can't alter, I just think about the space out there, beyond the farthest star, beyond the sun. Going on and on, so vast that the planets are specks of dust compared with it. And then I think of time, too, going on and on and on, beyond imagining. Then I think that on one of those specks of dust, for a fleeting moment, there is a person, a lump of protoplasm that calls itself Java Mason and thinks that its little affairs matter. And then I laugh."

"Do you find that that helps?" asked Emmie, and her voice was hard.

"I do. Because I realize that even if I got what I wanted I couldn't keep it. My greatest happiness wouldn't leave a trace. My profoundest thought is less than the fall of a leaf, so what can my feelings matter?"

Emmie thought — and shuddered.

"I think that that is a terrible idea."

"Is it? It helped me over one of the biggest trouble I ever had."

Emmie dared not ask what that was, but she looked up questioningly.

"And that was wanting somebody who didn't want me."

And that, Java Mason, was a lie told for Emmie's benefit. For your man loved you completely until a little nick in his finger ended his useful life nastily with blood poisoning.

"It denies hope," said Emmie.

"And forestalls despair. If you spend your life thinking that your completion and fulfilment lie in another person's arms and you can't ever be there, life is a poor affair. But if you realize that even if you were there every beat of your heart would be a step nearer a state where there are no arms or kisses or hearts, well then you are at least fitted to get on with your job. 'He that layeth down his life', you know."

"How long did it take you to get to that state?"

"Just as long as it took me to see the facts — less than a second."

That was the conversation that Emmie, curled in his chair, with her cheek on the place where his hand had rested, remembered. There was truth in Java's ideas as there is truth in any idea that denies self-interest and the claims of the poor human flesh, but it was beyond Emmie to accept it.

Here in this room he sat and wrote and ate, smoked and drank whisky and patted his dog. He was tall and thin, and his shoulders were broad but he slouched a bit: and his nose jutted in a curious fashion, and his cheeks fell in: and his hair was often untidy and a little grey over the ears. Her memory of him was so vivid that it seemed he must be present.

"I love you," her mind cried. "I wouldn't care about the space outside or the passing of time, or the fact that I was only a speck of dust if you were here, and could hold me, and I could kiss you. But if I think of space and time and being a lump of protoplasm this room isn't real any longer and I'm not real and you're not, either. And I shall go mad. I shall go mad. I shall go mad."

She twisted round in the chair and fell into a furious fit of crying that lasted until she was exhausted. And then suddenly she was asleep with her head on the leather that her tears had darkened.

She woke stiff and cold, and with a sense of shame that gathered as she remembered last night, when the first milk-cart rattled past the far side of the house.

And that morning there was a postcard for her.

15

The Wednesday half-days began again. It was lovely to walk in the sunshine past stalls laden with delphiniums and stiff with heavy bunches of Madonna lilies, eloquent of country gardens. It was lovely to find a seat under the heavy foliage of a tree in the Abbey Precincts and let the scent of the roses in the borders blow over your face. But there was a draw-back for Emmie, in those long light evenings, when, returning from the library or from a walk, she was obliged to pass the corners or the ice-cream stands, where the youths of the town spent their leisure in the warm weather. She hated the ice-cream stands especially, for as well as forming a meeting place for cheeky cat-calling boys, they spoilt the look of the streets she had come to love.

Even the Abbey Hill lost its dignity when a motor-cycle with its accompanying stall drew up in front of the massive gateway and dozens of papers with "Icyo" printed in bright scarlet across them were tossed down the moment the Icyo they had wrapped was devoured. And the devourers in their pale flannels and canvas shoes lounged about, making remarks, and strange lip-smacking noises, calculated to attract attention from the passing female. Even when the voices said, "Some peach!" or "Kid, your hat is swell," they evoked a curious shame. And in a way it was all to do with being a servant. Other girls who were neatly dressed and who walked circumspectly could pass the groups without being annoyed: but there was always one of the number who knew Emmie, the butcher's boy, the baker's boy, the milk-man's son.

"Whatcher, Emmie! How's the dragon?" appeared to them to be a most promising opening. Mrs. Tallet might be a dragon, thought Emmie, crimson-checked from embarrassment, but you daren't call after *her* in the

232

street. Queer that there should be a single aspect of Mrs. Tallet that one could envy.

Emmie would pass them, her knees stiff with self-consciousness, her grip on her book or parcel growing harder and harder, the pretty colour flooding her face and neck. And the papers would flutter, even on a windy day brush up against the walls of the gate and catch in the niches where the saints had stood; and personal and impersonal feelings would mingle in Emmie's strong conviction that This Ought to Be Stopped. Murray's "pompous red Mayor" ought to do something about it . . .

But anyway the Gate would probably still be standing in dignity when ice-cream was made in every house. After all, water used to be hawked through the streets and most people now had taps. Thoughts like that were handy and comforting; if you could think them hard enough you were slightly armoured against "Hullo, stuck-up, aren't we grand this evening!" "No, Bob, she looks nicer in a cap." And so forth. Her indifference to the bright flannels, so unlike the reaction of most of the town girls, made the calls the more malicious. Still they could be passed. Those summer half-days soon brought forward another problem, not so easily overcome.

Miss Trappit, one Wednesday, was especially pressing with her tea invitation.

"You haven't stayed for the last three weeks, and I'm sure all this walking in the sun isn't good for you, you're looking very peaked. You take your book and a chair and sit in the garden and then have tea with us. We've got strawberries! And that isn't all." Lowering

233

her voice to a note of mystery, and sparkling with the delight that the nicer kind of spinster takes in match-making, she added, "There'll be somebody to tea who'll make a nice friend for you." Not recognizing the significance of Miss Trappit's expression, and too shy to ask any more. Emmie carried out a chair and seated herself in the green shadow of the chestnut tree, hoping rather that the proposed friend should be a girl, a pretty girl with congenial tastes, if possible a girl who did housework for a living. To such a one there would be much to confide, little comments and grievances, which offered to either Java or Murray would savour of grousing. But Mrs. Meadows, following into the garden with her inevitable basket of mending, soon put an end to that hope.

Lifting her eyes every now and then to where Carrie and Alfred were engaged in weeding the crazy paving, she began to bid for Emmie's attention.

"We've got a new lodger," she said. "Such a nice young man and clever too. He's got a scholarship at the Technical."

"How long has he been here?" asked Emmie, closing her book.

"A fortnight on Saturday. Meggie took him cheap for a permanency. She liked his face. And really, you can't wonder. He's got such a nice, open, country kind of countenance. And his name is Jimmy Hawke."

Some altercation now arose between the gardeners, and Carrie blundered up to Mrs. Meadows. "'Tisn't fair," she complained in her thick childish voice. "He snatched. I want to do something else."

"So you shall," said Mrs. Meadows soothingly, "there's a basket of peas on the kitchen dresser. You may shell them."

Babbling her thanks Carrie went off kitchenwards.

The shadow of the chestnut grew until it covered the whole of the little garden. Mrs. Meadows looked at her old-fashioned watch. "Time for tea," she said. "Alfred, you'd better stop now and begin washing your hands."

Jimmy Hawke was already in the sitting-room when Emmie entered rather shyly behind Mrs. Meadows. He blushed a bright scarlet when the old lady setting down the tea-tray, introduced them across the table. He held out an enormous hand, a ploughboy's hand that projected too far and too suddenly from the sleeve of his coat, and the sight of the raw young wrist and the furious blush set Emmie at her ease. In the bustle of Miss Trappit's entrance from the shop, and the settling of Alfred and Carrie to the table, and the passing of large cups of tea and plates of strawberries, she studied him with interest. He had won a scholarship, so his face evidently belied him. For it was indeed a "nice open country kind" of face, wide but not fat, high-coloured, lit by grey eyes between bristly sandy lashes and surmounted by a thatch of rough sandy hair, ineffectually plastered with grease that left dark tracts upon its fairness. She thought of Robert Burns.

"What do you do at the Technical?" she asked.

"Draw," he said with a smile. "I'm going to design engines . . . for aeroplanes, one day." His voice was thickly Suffolk but he spoke carefully.

"Do you like St. Petersbury?"

"Not much. I've never lived in a town before. I miss the open."

"I come from the country too."

"Do you? Now you don't look like a country girl to me."

"Compliments already," cried Miss Trappit gaily, and maybe her tactics were sound, for the young faces opposite coloured simultaneously and their mutual confusion broke down more barriers than many hours of careful conversation could have done. Alfred gulped the last of his tea and rose to deal with the clock. That drew Miss Trappit's attention to the time.

"Why don't you two young people trot along to the pictures?" she asked. Jimmy Hawke swallowed hastily and turned to Emmie.

"Would you care to do that?" he asked primly.

"I can't," said Emmie. "I want to take Stumpy for a walk — Stumpy is a dog, and he's been left in kennels. I try to see him every day."

With far more enthusiasm than had coloured his forced inquiry about the pictures the boy said, "I'd like to come too, if I may. I'm fond of dogs, and I like walking."

"All right," said Emmie, with less enthusiasm. "Perhaps we'd better go then."

And something in her mind complained — I'm being jostled into this. This is going to make a muddle. I want to walk with Stumpy alone and have time to think. But something else countered — this boy is lonely, lonelier than you could ever be. And he's so young. He may be nineteen, and he may have got a scholarship, but he's a baby compared with you.

Emmie thanked Miss Trappit for her tea, and with her unspoken but more-than-hinted-at blessing the pair set off.

The folly of her weak behaviour was amply demonstrated within ten minutes of collecting Stumpy. The boy made a great fuss of him, soothing who knows what nostalgia for the things that ambition had made him leave.

"He *is* a nice dog! Good old boy! And what funny coloured eyes for a dog. Like marmalade. They remind me . . . yes . . . they're the same colour as yours."

"They are *not*," Emmie said sharply. Oh, unbearable words, intolerable situation, to have to listen to a repetition of something that had been said in such different circumstances, in such a different voice. ("Why? Because you've got eyes exactly like Stumpy's. Now you run along to bed.") And it was April then, with the magic of night in the air: the hawthorn tree and the stars: the hopeful prophecy of the Spring. Now it was July and this earnest, pathetic, but real and solid and nice, oh so nice boy was blundering in upon a stretch of country that had been virgin to Murray.

"I'm sorry. Maybe that was rude." The voice rose to a question. Pity wrung Emmie's heart.

"Well, who would like to have their eyes called marmalade?" she asked with an effort at lightness.

"You're not cross, are you? Don't be cross, because I've never liked anybody so quickly in my life before."

Not to be borne.

Oh, why in relief at finding him informidable and the atmosphere of tea-engendered liveliness had she ever spoken to him, looked at him, smiled at him?

"Tell me about your life," she said quickly.

And she had been right, in a way, to think of Burns. For this boy had a gift too. For all his slowness and apparent solidity he managed in a very short time and without a wasted word to lay before her a picture of a small farm in the remoter part of Suffolk, out by the Breckland, run by his father, his brother and himself. He told of the schoolmaster, who, after his fourteenth birthday, had made him a "working man", had gone on teaching and encouraging him and had finally forced him to sit for the Frampton Regional Scholarship, of which Emmie learned for the first time now. How she would have liked one herself.

He told of early pokings into aged motor-cycles, cranky cars, newly imported tractors. He spoke with a kind of cool passion, reasonably, as though used to arguing things out to himself. "Of course, I know it won't be easy . . ." "Of course, I know I'm starting late . . ." but there was obviously no trace of doubt in his mind as to the ultimate outcome of his efforts.

Conviction was in him. For a little while all Emmie's muddled feelings fused into envy — his path seemed to lie so clear before him, his life to be so little dependent upon the behaviour of other people. But, acid test! would she be willing to change completely? To be a boy with big protruding wrists and a passion for mathematical drawing: not to know that Murray existed? Not for a moment.

238

They took Stumpy back to the kennels and Emmie said, "I must go back now. I live in the Close." She was prepared to say good-bye to him then, but he turned and walked along beside her. In the street that led on to Abbey Hill there came towards them a girl dressed in a floating dress of chiffon patterned in several shades of crude green. An "Alice band" of yet another green confined a multitude of bobbing henna-ed curls. Green toeless sandals showed grubby toes with tinted nails. She combined, with enviable art, a cheeky smile for Jimmy with an insolent up-and-down stare for Emmie, as she drew level with them.

"Good evening," she said.

"Evening," Jimmy mumbled, and Emmie could see his ears blazing. "That girl always speaks to me," he grumbled when she had passed. "I can't think why. I suppose because we're nearly neighbours."

"She'd speak to anybody — any man," said Emmie bitterly. "That is 'Carry On' Caxton." The conversation at the table came back. Murray and that girl. With real spite she added, "She makes me think of that old song, 'They're hanging men and women too, for the wearing of the green.'"

Jimmy Hawke gave a great bellow of laughter.

"Oh very good," he said. "I shall think of that every time she calls out to me. I shan't mind any more." He looked at Emmie adoringly from between his bristly lashes and Emmie, who had been caught in the infection of his mirth, stiffened suddenly. However on Abbey Hill she was glad of his presence, for by some unwritten law of conduct the gathering around the ice-cream stand never called or hooted after couples. Curious glances followed them but no sound.

In the lane at the mouth of the opening between Numbers Five and Six, Emmie halted. "I go down here," she said. Jimmy Hawke halted beside her and shuffled his feet in his thick shoes.

"Do you come to Miss Trappit's often?"

"Almost every week."

"Then I'll be seeing you. Come next week if you can," he said in a rush and hurried away.

That queer, infallible, female register recorded. "He likes me", and for some reason the verdict made her feel a little sick, a little ashamed. It would be quite impossible to go regularly to the Saltgate shop after this. And yet why?

On the next Wednesday afternoon she went to the library early and then took Stumpy for a long walk in the country. On the Thursday morning when she gave the post a brief hopeful scrutiny she discovered a letter addressed to herself. For a second her heart raced, but even in that second she realized that it wasn't Murray's writing and that the envelope of cheap blue paper was as unlike his as possible. She opened it quite roughly with a thrust of the thumb.

"DEAR MISS BACON," she read, "I was so sorry not to see you this afternoon. I wanted specially to see you because I wanted to ask you something. Some of the fellows here are getting up an outing to go to Cambridge on the river on Sunday week. I wondered whether you'd come with me. (Several girls are coming.) I've never seen Cambridge, though I've been on the river at Brandon, so I wouldn't drown you! Please try to come. Yours sincerely,

J. HAWKE.

"*P.S.* Miss Trappit gave me your address. I trust you don't mind my writing."

Well that was easy. Sunday outings were out of the question. Wednesday was her half-day. Thank God, she added. And Thursday was Mrs. Tallet's, so she would have to write her refusal at bedtime and post it some time tomorrow. That was settled. But that evening, while she was washing the dinner things in the darkening kitchen, a light, almost timid knocking sounded at the back door. Cloth in hand she opened it and was confronted by Jimmy Hawke, breathless and sweating from nervousness. Oh, thank God that Mrs. Tallet wasn't here. Never, never must he do this again.

"Did you get my letter?"

"Yes. I was going to answer it tonight."

"I just couldn't wait to know. Can you come?" Earnest, humble, beseeching, sickening.

"No, I can't. I'm sorry." She spoke with more than usual energy.

"Oh!" Flat, a burst balloon. Immediate pang, hasty, apologetic explanation.

"You see I simply can't get away on a Sunday. I only have the afternoon on Wednesday."

"Couldn't you manage just for once?"

"I daren't even suggest it."

"What a shame." And now, of course, he had the wrong impression entirely. He thought that she would have gone had it been possible.

"Never mind, I tell you what I'll do. I know a fellow who'll lend me his old bus one of these Wednesdays and we'll go by ourselves. That is if you will. How'll that be?"

"I . . . I simply can't talk about it now . . . you see Mrs. Tallet will be back in a moment . . . lucky for me she's out now. And do you mind not coming here any more . . ." Her voice trailed off. Instantly his face was flooded with sympathy, he looked at her through his sandy lashes with the utmost understanding and pity so that she was literally sickened with shame.

"I get you," he said quickly. "I'm so sorry. And you might write to me all the same." There was just a gleam of impudence in his eyes as he said that, and he was conscious of it too, for his retreat was hasty and without dignity.

She felt very badly about the whole thing all that evening, but she did not write; what could any letter do but render more false the situation? And in the morning, after the postman's second round, she had something else to think of. There was a parcel for her; untidily wrapped and bespattered with foreign stamps. This was indeed the writing, and at the sight of it her heart beat so jumpily that her fingers could hardly unfasten the knotted string. There was a sheet of note-paper between the brown paper and the box it wrapped. She did not, for a time, probe beyond it.

"DEAR EMMIE,

"Stumpy wrote to me the other day and told me that you had visited him on every day but two of his exile. (How I should love to know what happened on those days!) And he said that you had taken him for walks and given him several indigestible but very pleasant things to eat. So he wanted to buy you a small token of esteem. Since I have charge of his hoarded wealth and anyway my taste is superior, he left the shopping to me. I hope you and he approve of my choice. I was walking down a little street in Frankfurt, talking to a friend very wisely on this and that, when I suddenly saw these which reminded me of Stumpy and of you. (You'll know why.) I broke off the conversation and darted into the shop. The friend, a very earnest young man, now suspects that I am more frivolous even than he had feared.

"I shall be home for certain on the twenty-seventh of August and hope to find you flourishing.

"Yours M. W."

Inside the battered box was a string of amber beads, warm to the touch, light as air and the colour of marmalade. Like Stumpy's eyes and mine, thought Emmie. I wonder how he knows that I've taken Stumpy biscuits; he must have written to the man at the kennels.

She slipped the beads over her head, tucking them down inside the neck of the print frock. She would wear them always, night and day . . . like a rosary. Queer how Catholics, and they alone, had translated into religious practice the ordinary earthy instincts of human beings. She indulged in a moment or two of half-mystical, wholly sentimental thought and then with a wrench returned to the polishing of the oak of the hall and stairway.

The twenty-seventh — she had a definite landmark now. And the days slipped past, incredibly crowded and satisfactorily swift. Kate had left as Dr. Mason had predicted and Mrs. Tallet set to work to "Clear the mess that that slut had let the house get in", which really meant that she took advantage of Mr. Wykham's absence to indulge in a belated bout of spring-cleaning. Her leg was still troublesome if required to support her for very long at a stretch, but with indomitable courage which in other circumstances might have approached the heroic, she would wash and iron curtains and covers or scour paint with the faulty limb precariously supported upon a hard little stool.

By word and example she urged Emmie on, and the Wednesday breaks which marked the weeks' passing seemed, now that they were less welcome, to succeed one another with extraordinary rapidity.

They were less welcome because Jimmy Hawke was showing some of that persistence and blindness to obstacles that was to carry him so far in a hard and obstructive world.

On the very next Wednesday but one, when Emmie emerged from the railed-in pathway she found a large, battered, brightly-painted car drawn up on Abbey Hill as near Freeman's passage as it could be. In it sat Jimmy Hawke, glazed with heat, patient, hopeful.

"Gosh," he said, when he saw her, "I began to be afraid that you'd gone out the other way, round the Cathedral. Are you doing anything this afternoon?"

"Going to the library," said Emmie, glancing at the books she carried.

"Well . . . come on, get in and I'll drive you there."

"Oughtn't you to be at a class?" she asked a trifle ungraciously.

"I cut it. I thought perhaps we could go to Cambridge today."

"I had thought of going to see Miss Trappit," said Emmie with that elusiveness which is supposed to be so enchanting, and which is so easy when you don't care and so difficult when you do, explaining why almost any day you can marry a man you don't love and can hardly ever marry one you do. The realization of all this mixed up with thoughts of Murray and feelings of shame that the very sight of Jimmy was beginning to raise in her, caused her to climb into the car quickly and say,

"All right, let's go to Cambridge then. I don't care if I don't change my books."

"I've got a first-class story at home that I'll lend you if you don't bother about those."

"What's it called?"

"*Death Draws a Blank*. Of course, maybe you don't care for thrillers."

"I haven't read many."

Literary conversation died a natural and not untimely death.

"Jolly good of that fellow to lend me this, wasn't it? It's a shocking old bus though. There's a dreadful drag to the right all the time. I think the . . ." He became highly technical but he seemed quite happy talking more or less to himself, so Emmie gave herself up to the scenery.

At Cambridge the river was crowded, and when Emmie heard the cost of hiring a punt she was dreadfully, and vocally, eager to abandon the idea and to do a little sight-seeing on foot: but Jimmy Hawke had conceived a picture of himself wielding a pole while Emmie lay back, lazy and luxurious, upon the cushions, and nothing was going to come between him and the actuality. So they pushed out upon the river and merged with the gay, musical crowd. Jimmy punted with just sufficient skill and a good deal of superfluous vigour. He grew warm and shed his coat. Emmie with sensitive antennae a-quiver, was not blind to the fact that his striped cotton shirt and Woolworth braces failed to hide the active beauty of his arms and shoulders. Now and again he turned his moist warm face and gave her a happy smile.

The flat fields with their tapestry embroidery of little flowers stretched away into the heat-shimmering distance: the plaintively merry music from the gramophones hung on the air: the sun was warm and the smooth movement of the punt delightful. If only, if only, if only it hadn't been Jimmy. Base, false, treacherous thought which made every one of those happy smiles pierce her with an arrow of self-disgust.

246

Tonight, no later, she must make it perfectly clear that this kind of outing must never be repeated.

Presently Jimmy drew in under the shade of some low trees that overhung the water and drove the pole firmly into the mud of the river-bed. Then he sat down, wiped his hot face and reached for the little cardboard attache case that he had brought with him. "Miss Trappit packed us a picnic. She's a nice woman, isn't she? Really she was as eager about what we'd like to eat as if she'd been coming herself."

Yes, thought Emmie, she would be. It was easy to imagine with what pleasure Miss Trappit had thrown herself into Jimmy's plans. There was tea in a cheap but ancient thermos flask, milk in a bottle that had contained Mrs. Meadows' medicine, sugar in a screw of paper. There were three kinds of sandwich and four slices of solid brown cake. And it had all been thought out, packed, carried and unpacked to be eaten in such a different state of mind.

And nothing happened to help Emmie. The scenery, the situation, the picnic, and having Emmie there where he had pictured her worked upon Jimmy's feelings so that the glances he threw her grew more and more sentimental. Not to reply in kind grew more and more like snubbing a nice exuberant dog's advances. Heaven send that he wouldn't finish up the day by wanting to kiss her. She should scream, have a fit, be hysterical — was, in fact, almost hysterical now.

However, Jimmy, sentimental and persistent, was no thruster. He repeated again and again how glad he was that she had come, how he was enjoying the day, how he was able to talk to her as he wasn't to any one else, but that was all. All until they were half-way home again and the slight chill of the evening made him stop the car and reach for his discarded coat. He pushed one arm into a sleeve and then, in the act of pulling it up, stopped, drew out the arm and said, "I say, you'd better have this."

"I'm all right, really, thank you," said Emmie, belying the gooseflesh that had been steadily creeping along her bare arms for half an hour.

"No. Go on, have it. I'm quite warm, feel my arms compared to yours." He laid one hand on her thin childish arm. True the big red hand was warm — and in a queer way, comforting, even in a brief touch.

"I'd never forgive myself if you took cold." He held open the coat invitingly, and again, against her will, Emmie snuggled into it.

It was as definitely *his* coat as Murray's things were *his*; it had a faint scent of hay about it, and petrol, and Woodbines. He did not start off immediately, but began, shyly though with that same conviction with which he discussed the future, to tempt the gods.

"Have you really enjoyed the day?"

What answer but "Yes" could there be to that?

"Good. I'm glad of that, and I wanted to know because I want there to be more of them. I've never been very friendly with a girl before — and I doubt whether I'd ever have started out that night with you if it hadn't been for Miss Trappit suggesting it. After that it seemed quite natural. And you're so different. Most girls frighten me, they're so loud and bright. So you will be friends with me, won't you — Emmie?" The name came out tentatively.

"I d ... I don't know."

"Why not?"

"It wouldn't be any good, really it wouldn't."

"Why not?"

"Because I don't feel right about it."

"Why? Don't you like me?"

"Well yes, in a way I do. I think you're a very nice boy, and kind, and clever too, but —"

"But what?"

"Oh, don't let's go on, please. Just take me home and then forget all about me. After all you've only seen me twice; well, three times counting that minute at the back door."

There was a brief tense silence, then he said heavily, "I'm sorry."

"I'm sorry too," said Emmie eagerly.

"I guess I spoke too soon. I ought to have worked up to it a bit more; but you see I wanted to be sure. I wanted to think that we'd be sure of meeting every Wednesday evening — I can't get off every afternoon. Are you sure we can't?"

"Quite sure. I'm sorry."

He let in the clutch and the car jerked forward. They sat in a silence that was uncomfortable, but neither dared break it. Once she stole a timid glance at him. What she expected to see she did not know, but it was with faint surprise that she saw him looking quite ordinary with his lips pursed in a soundless whistle. But how ridiculous, why should he look different, and why shouldn't he whistle? For one brief moment she saw that there was no need to pity him — it was self-glorification indeed to do so. She was the one to be pitied, for she had flung away something pleasant and sound and safe and ordinary — why? And for what?

On Abbey Hill he stopped the car and she got out, slipping the coat from her shoulders.

"You'd better put it on. It was awfully nice of you to let me have it."

He put it on obediently.

"Say thank you for me to Miss Trappit for my tea, will you? And thank you a thousand times for a lovely day."

"That's all right," he said awkwardly, fidgeting with the hand brake. Once he looked up at her and again she thought of a nice dog.

"Good night," she said quickly.

"Good night."

There, well at least she had nothing on her conscience: she wasn't pretending an interest that she didn't feel. There'd be plenty of girls who'd be glad to go about with him and listen to him, who'd relish his sentimental glances: girls who weren't comparing and wishing all the time; plenty of girls whose hearts weren't fixed.

After that Wednesdays were devoted to Stumpy and were very pleasant until the moment of separation came. His desire to go back to the Corner House was so obvious, and had to be countered with, "You wouldn't like it, Stumpy. He isn't there and it's no sort of a place. But there're only forty (or thirty or twenty) days more to wait."

16

On the last Wednesday in July Emmie put on the yellow linen frock and the wide imitation leghorn hat with the brown velvet ribbon that had at last become hers and fetched Stumpy out for a long walk as far as the old Turnpike. It wasn't farther than they had often walked and the road was shady, but she found herself growing unaccountably hot and "muddled" as she described it to herself. And her usual optimism seemed to have deserted her: depressing thoughts would come uppermost. Even Stumpy's delight in the long walk set her thinking of the chained dog at Fincham's, and there must be hundreds like him. And the fields of ripening corn with their sudden bursts of poppies made her think of the rabbit massacres and the horses. The trouble was, she decided, as she heaved herself on to the stile beside the main gate, that once you had begun to think like that you were never free again. You went on and on. You even began, after all these years, to wonder about things at the cottage at home. Where was Freddie? And the two that had been such miserable little babies at the time of her exodus. And had mother had any more babies, and if so how did they fare? She had a sudden pang of conscience. Ought she to have done anything about them? Sent money, instead of spending it on this frock and hat, for example. But what

251

was the good? Her mother would only have spent it at The Pot of Flowers. Life was altogether too much.

She walked back with Stumpy to the town where they had tea at the Woolworth café, Emmie drinking the tea and Stumpy eating the bread and butter. Then after the usual wrangle about direction she pulled him into the kennels yard and left him in his enclosure. She would go home now and get her book, pay a visit to the library, and then, if she could banish this lassitude, go to the pictures.

Mrs. Tallet was in the kitchen, slicing cucumber. She looked at Emmie rather coldly and said, "Mrs. Clarkson asked me to send you to her directly you came in."

"Now?"

"She said directly."

An errand perhaps.

Without taking off her hat she went straight up to Mrs. Clarkson's room and knocked at the door.

Mrs. Begbie was seated with Mrs. Clarkson on the massive soft that was in its summer position near the window that opened over the Close Gardens. She rose as Emmie entered and with a little confusion said, "I think I'll leave you." She went out and closed the door.

"Come here, Emmie," said Mrs. Clarkson. "I've something rather unpleasant to say to you."

Unpleasant! What was it? Emmie raked through the immediate past and could think of nothing that she had done amiss . . . except of course running out after tea to see Stumpy. That was it. She looked at Mrs. Clarkson calmly. After all she had never been late with the dinner, or left anything undone in order to snatch that twenty minutes or so. And she would not be frightened. She would say so straight out.

"When Miss Bavister came to pack for her holiday today," said Mrs. Clarkson in a mournful voice, "she found several of her things missing. I have the list here. Four pairs of stockings, a ring and a little fur tie. Do you know anything about them?"

"No," said Emmie.

Of course, this was just what would happen: the moment anything was missing the maid was suspected. How unfair.

"Think of what you say now. We are not anxious to suspect you, but after all we can't have things disappearing, and Mrs. Tallet is above suspicion."

"And I hope I am."

"Now, impertinence isn't going to help us." Mrs. Clarkson held up a plump hand. "If you have made a mistake — and you're very young — it will be much best for you to return the things and admit your wrong. I dare say then we might take a lenient view."

"But I haven't got them."

"I'm afraid I shall have to look through your things before I can accept that."

"You're perfectly welcome to look through my things. Go now, please. I'll stay here."

That meant only one thing to Mrs. Clarkson, the things had been disposed of. Unfortunate experiences in the past rose up to prejudice her against Emmie, who after all must have some faults. And since she was neither lazy, rude, nor dirty, her fault was probably dishonesty.

She eyed the girl more closely. That looked a good frock, and the hat wasn't the kind of hat that the average housemaid wore. Of course you could never tell, these cheap stores sold such marvellous imitations. Still, one could easily find out. In Mrs. Clarkson's limited mind the whole thing was falling together like a puzzle. Emmie was, in many ways, a superior girl, and superior girls unfortunately hankered after things that neither their position nor their means entitled them to. What more natural than that Emmie should have taken advantage of Coral's happy-go-lucky nature and the untidiness of her room to take something that might never be missed and sell it? She reached out and lifted the beads that hung down over Emmie's flat chest almost to her brown waist belt. Warm and light — amber. Not to be bought under four or five pounds.

"Before we go into the matter of searching your room," she said coldly, "perhaps you would tell me where you got those beads."

God grant that my face shall not redden, and that I shall manage to stand up through this.

"They were a present."

"Indeed; you are a very lucky girl to receive such presents. That necklace wasn't bought for ten shillings, you know."

"I don't know what it cost."

"Who gave it to you?"

Tell the truth? And start her off on another tack? No.

254

"Honestly, Mrs. Clarkson, these beads have nothing to do with the other matter. I could easily tell who gave them to me, but you either wouldn't believe me or you'd misunderstand. And you ought to remember that I work in Mrs. Begbie's room as much as in Miss Bavister's and Mrs. Begbie has far more valuable things and more of them; she hasn't complained of losing anything, has she?"

"Well, n-no," Mrs. Clarkson admitted. "At the same time, Emmie. I must say that your manner is not reassuring. You sound as if you had thought this all out. And your whole demeanour shows that you don't realize the importance of the things you are charged with."

"I'm being accused, not charged," said Emmie mildly.

"I'll go up to your room," said Mrs. Clarkson. "Wait here."

She returned after about a quarter of an hour. She had Emmie's one pair of good silk stockings dangling from her arm and three books in her hand.

"There were three books belonging to Mr. Wykham in your room, one under the pillow by the way. And I shall ask Miss Bavister to have a look at these stockings. What are these books doing in your room?"

"When Mr. Wykham went away he said that I might take any of his books, I've had lots before, and that I might use his gramophone, which I haven't done. The stockings are mine, the only good pair I have; but I don't suppose I can prove that in any way."

For some strange reason the more Mrs. Clarkson looked in vain for any evidence of guilt the more exasperated she became. If Emmie had broken down and cried she would have thought of what a good maid she was, and how these people never had any moral training and she would have talked about "another chance and things like that. As it was she became more and more convinced that Emmie was "deep".

"Put the books back in Mr. Wykham's room," she said at last, "and leave the stockings here. The whole thing is most unsatisfactory, most unsatisfactory indeed."

For the first time during the interview Emmie knew a pang of feeling for Mrs. Clarkson. Of course, she had to ask, Miss Bavister was a lodger after all. She said gently.

"I'm sorry, madam. But really I know nothing about these things. And it isn't very pleasant for me either."

Mrs. Clarkson resented Emmie's tone, she wasn't going to be pitied by a housemaid.

"That will do," she said curtly, "you may go."

Left by herself she tossed the stockings into a distant chair as though their touch contaminated her. It was all a stupid, sordid nuisance, and it was unfair that she, Ada Clarkson, gently born and bred, should be brought to a pass where she had to decide between the veracity of a careless lodger and a presumptuous servant. Not for the first time she toyed with the idea of selling the Corner House, adding its selling price to her diminished capital and retiring to a small house where Tallet could look after her in peace.

That would have its advantages. She would escape from bother, from the iniquitous rates and the competition for Tallet's attention. But it would mean parting from her furniture, and leaving the Close where she belonged. She thought of the Adam doorway, and the graceful sweep of the stairs, and the view from the front windows. Her heart failed her. Like the slum dwellers who pine in their council houses, she was the slave of her environment.

But even at that moment something was approaching that was to make the decision for her.

Emmie went up to her room and looked at her bed with longing. She would have liked to get into it, pull the covers over her head and shut out the world. The actual accusation troubled her less than the atmosphere in which it was made. She had known perfectly well that nothing would be found in her room, and surely in the face of the lack of evidence even Mrs. Clarkson's suspicions must die. But that instant assumption — I have lost something, therefore Emmie must have taken it — that did hurt. And so did Mrs. Clarkson's manner, and Mrs. Tallet's cold glance when she came in. Also there was the matter of the books. They were Mr. Wykham's books, Murray's books, and if he had lent them to any one else Mrs. Clarkson would never have ordered their return like that. If a lodger had been suspected of murder his books wouldn't have been interfered with. Anyway, the fact that the books were gone made it imperative that she should go to the library now. She put on her short woolly coat and picked up her book. At the door a thought suddenly struck her and she reached inside for the rusty key that had been there unturned for who knows how long.

If, and there was just that possibility, if somebody had tried to "plant" something on her there was a chance that they might try again and be more thorough about it. She dropped the key into her coat pocket and went slowly, heavily down the stairs.

Despite the utter weariness that had been troubling her all day, she lay for a long time awake and thoughtful after she was in bed. Ought she, in self-respect, to give notice and look for another job? Mrs. Tallet was being very awkward. She didn't say anything but she kept looking as though she were thinking, "So that's where you're like the rest of the rubbish is it? I might have guessed!" And Emmie would not open the subject so that they could talk it out.

But if she gave notice now she would be gone before Murray returned. Unbearable thought. Never to see that face, or hear that voice again. No. A thousand Mrs. Clarksons, ten thousand Mrs. Tallets, twenty thousand Miss Bavisters should not drive her away. Was that, could that be the idea? She thrust the unwarrantable thought away. It smacked of the penny dreadful. It was absurd. It just happened that Miss Bavister was careless with her things had mislaid some, and naturally suspected the maid. It would all be cleared up in the morning.

In the morning Miss Bavister, dressed for her journey to town, refused either to identify the stockings as hers, or to admit that they were Emmie's.

"I simply can't say, Mrs. Clarkson. They seem just the same colour and thickness, but one can't go by that. Stockings can be exactly the same, can't they?"

"You're willing to give Emmie the benefit of the doubt, then?"

Emmie, almost hysterical, not only at the present situation but also at the thought that within two hours Coral Bavister might be within reach of Murray, having him ring her up, going out with him, exclaimed with a shout.

"I don't want the benefit of the doubt. They're my stockings, and I want you to say so."

"Kindly control yourself," said Mrs. Clarkson, "and remember where you are."

The three of them stood silent after that, staring at the stockings. The silence grew uncomfortable. Mrs Clarkson cleared her throat. Emmie, who had discovered that she was standing with her arms folded, thought, I look like a fish-wife, and dropped them, and was immediately sorry because of the dragged-down feeling that came upon her. Finally Coral said, "Well, I must fly. Better let Emmie have the stockings, Mrs. Clarkson. I must be more careful another time, that's all." It was easy to see what she meant by more careful, more careful to lock her drawers, more careful to watch Emmie. There was poison in the speech.

Coral bent and kissed Mrs. Clarkson. "I'll write to you," she said, and was gone. Of course. Mrs. Clarkson liked her, they were friends, she would be believed.

Mrs. Clarkson pointed to the stockings. Innocent brownish stockings which Emmie had loved very much, selected with care, paid for with a pang at her own extravagance when there were so many other claims made by her heart upon her purse. There they lay on the chair and one would have thought they were serpents.

"You heard what Miss Bavister said, Emmie. Take them away."

She wanted to say, I don't want them; won't touch them. But they looked so limp, and somehow appealing, lying there despised and almost disowned. She picked them up without speaking and went into the passage.

After she had set the table for lunch Mrs. Clarkson appeared in the dining-room.

"I forgot to tell you, Emmie, that I want the extra leaf taken out of the table. There'll only be three of us for lunch. It unwinds here."

She went away, leaving Emmie to clear the table, unwind the stiff mechanism and drag out the heavy mahogany leaf. She had only just time to set the things back before Mrs. Clarkson and Mrs. Begbie appeared for the meal. Shaking and sweating she sped down the stairs for the dishes.

Dr. Mason did not appear for lunch. Emmie kept some food hot in the oven until three o'clock and then reluctantly turned out the gas. It would have been a relief to have seen Java, especially if she could have seen and spoken to her for a moment alone. She felt somehow that there would have been one person who would have tried, at least, to understand.

260

Mrs. Tallet was preserving a stony silence, broken only by the giving of orders, and that in the fewest possible words. Her eyes, when they met Emmie's, were as hard and cold as pebbles. Actually a great deal of her ill-feeling was generated by the fact that she had been on the verge of liking the girl. Emmie's behaviour while she had been ill had been commendable, and once or twice while Kate had been there Emmie had flattered Mrs. Tallet by siding with her during some incident in their interminable quarrel. And all the time she had been doing this. There wasn't the faintest doubt in Mrs. Tallet's mind. Emmie ranked now with all those others who had shattered Mrs. Tallet's faith (if she had ever had any) in servants as a class. There was a red-haired piece she remembered, who had systematically raided the larder and was actually caught handing a great parcel up the area steps. And there was that girl with the squint who had run up an enormous bill in Mrs. Clarkson's name and then left before she was exposed. Miss Ada had had to pay that bill, Mrs. Tallet remembered with fury. If ever she had the pleasure of laying eyes on that girl again! And then there was — But why pursue the subject? All girls were bad rubbish, and if there were any good qualities about any one of them, they were only a screen behind which vices might go the longer undetected. Oh if only Miss Ada would abandon the struggle to keep this great gaol of a house going, and retire to one which Mrs. Tallet could run unaided: say good-bye to the lot of the trash, lodgers and maids alike.

In the late afternoon Emmie was on her knees in Mrs. Clarkson's sitting-room, searching under the sofa for Mrs Clarkson's gold thimble that had rolled from her lap. Mrs. Clarkson's blood pressure would not allow her to bend and Tallet was stiff and awkward, so she had sent for Emmie. The thimble must be found immediately or it might be found by Emmie when she swept and disappear as Coral's things had done.

Suddenly the door was thrown open and Mrs. Begbie who had been to the hairdresser's, one of her few appointments, came stumbling into the room, her soft loose hair already adrift from its newly ridged waves, her face scarlet with haste and excitement, her eyes staring. She paused when she was within three yards of Mrs. Clarkson and said dramatically,

"Do you know, Ada Clarkson, what you have been sheltering in this house? An abortionist!" The dreadful word, never before used in that Victorian room, rang out, loud and vicious.

Mrs. Clarkson half-rose, thought better of it, and dropped with a scream into her chair, hands relaxed and eyes closed. Emmie scrambled to her feet from behind the sofa with the thimble in her hand.

"Here," gasped Mrs. Begbie, torn between concern and delight at the effect of her news, "get some water quickly."

Mrs. Clarkson half opened her eyes.

"Brandy," she said faintly, "in the cabinet."

Emmie, being nearest, opened the cabinet, took out the half-bottle of brandy and the medicine glass that stood beside it and poured a generous dose.

Mrs. Clarkson seized and swallowed it. Then she helplessly handed the glass back to Emmie and closed her eyes again.

"Here, give me those," said Mrs. Begbie. "I'm upset too."

Mrs. Clarkson regained full consciousness.

"No you don't, Emily Begbie. Not until you explain what you mean by dashing in here and frightening me out of my . . ."

Mrs. Begbie, with unwonted decision, poured out almost a glassful of the brandy, and then, coughing and spluttering,

"J.M.," she said.

"Dr. Mason! Have you gone crazy?"

Mrs. Begbie dropped down on one of the beaded footstools.

"I heard it in the hairdresser's. It's all over the town. She's been doing it for years, they say. Operations — you know. Now there's been an accident and an inquest and the police have got her."

"Are you sure?"

"Absolutely. The girl who told me is cousin to the woman . . . the woman who died and had the inquest."

"This is too much," said Mrs. Clarkson, forgetting her pose and leaping to her feet. "The maid yesterday, and this today. This is intolerable. I shall put this house in the market tomorrow. Why, I might have a murderer here next."

"You have. That's what it amounts to," said Mrs. Begbie. And then the full implication of Mrs. Clarkson's speech reached her fluffy mind. "But you can't sell the house, Ada Clarkson. What should *I* do?"

"I neither know nor care," said Mrs. Clarkson rudely. "Did you find that thimble, Emmie?"

"Yes, madam."

"Then send Mrs. Tallet to me."

Emmie dragged herself out of the room and as far as the top of the kitchen stairs where she shouted to Mrs. Tallet and stood collecting her senses while the old woman swept past her and along to Miss Ada's room.

She had not cried out, nor appeared to faint, nor demanded brandy, but she felt as though some one had dealt her a heavy blow over the heart. Java: the police: murder.

It sounded impossible, like something in a nightmare. And yet it sounded the kind of thing that might happen to Java. What had she said? — "Women should stick together in this rough world." That had probably been at the back of these unlikely doings. You could imagine it; some woman who had too many children or who had no right to be having one at all, appealing; something in Java that wasn't professional siding with her; and the deed was done.

She crept down to the quiet kitchen and found herself longing for Mrs. Tallet's reappearance. Mrs. Tallet would at least be somebody to talk and speculate with. Mrs. Tallet was old and might have known similar cases. She forgot that she had made up her mind that as

264

long as Mrs. Tallet seemed bent on silence she would do nothing to break it.

When Mrs. Tallet did come she was almost running. On her sallow cheeks, where even the heat of the oven had never been able to strike the faintest glow, there was a deep rose flush. Her eyes sparkled like coals and half the lines in her face seemed to have been smoothed away.

"Will they hang her?" Emmie voiced her coldest fear as soon as Mrs. Tallet set foot in the kitchen.

"Of course not," said Mrs. Tallet sharply. "They'll send her to prison as she richly deserves, and when she comes back she won't be a doctor any more. And now, Emmie Bacon," she continued in another voice, "it gives me great pleasure to give you a month's notice from tomorrow. That's the end of the month. And at the end of next month Miss Ada and me hope to be in a little house of our own, with no rotten lodgers and no rotten maids."

A dull thud answered her. The last blow had been the knock-out. Emmie lay senseless on the floor with her head in the stick basket.

18

From the first moment, when, in her anger and horror, Mrs. Clarkson had communicated her hastily-arrived-at decision to Mrs. Tallet there was never a chance for her to reconsider it. Mrs. Tallet was like a dog that has never been allowed to chase, or even look at, rabbits, and then is suddenly taken out to a common swarming with them and told to "Go to it".

The marvellous energy that she had always displayed in Miss Ada's service, even to purposes distasteful to her, was now redoubled. If Miss Ada would just sign the papers and pick out the house she would like. Mrs. Tallet would do all the rest. The ball had started rolling on that first morning after Emmie had been given notice, and it sped with gathering impetus through the month.

Emmie had waked, on that first morning, to the alarm clock's raucous clatter. She stilled it and then lay for a moment or two to find out, by thinking, why this morning seemed to be different from others. Three facts answered her.

Java was in trouble.

She herself had been given notice.

She had fainted last night.

She had never fainted before in her life, and had imagined that to faint was a painful process, preceded by queer feelings. But last night she had felt nothing at all. She had heard Mrs. Tallet speaking in that jubilant tone and then the floor had risen and she had heard and seen nothing else. She had come to in bed and been vaguely conscious of Mrs. Tallet handing her a glass and saying, "Pull yourself together." She had drunk whatever was in the glass, gone to sleep and here she was.

And it was time to get up. She scrambled shakily off the bed and began to put on her clothes which were lying about in unusual places. All the bad feelings that

266

she had not had last night were hers this morning. She felt leaden and quivery; her heart hammered and there was that old pain in her chest. Too much had happened suddenly. It seemed much more than two days since she had sat on a stile and watched Stumpy play — which reminded her that she had not paid Stumpy his usual visit yesterday. Would he have noticed it? And been disappointed? Did dogs know what a day, or every day, meant? Probably not. Anyway she felt too dull to worry much about it.

The knowledge that life at the Corner House was doomed to finish at the end of August filled her mind to the exclusion of everything else. The twenty-seventh, to which she had been looking forward so ardently, was to be, not the revival of life, but the beginning of the end. Murray would come back, but not to drink coffee, and talk, and prove that there was something in life other than washing dishes and sweeping floors. He would pack the rest of his things and find some new place to take them and go. While she, where would she be? Well, the answer to that was fairly simple. She would, because she must, remain in St. Petersbury. She would find out where he went and get a job as near by as possible. Then she would wait and wait until one day perhaps there would be a place for her in the house to which he had gone.

So there was no point in doing anything about it at present. She put the thought away and resolved to wait and work until the twenty-seventh. So side by side Emmie and Mrs. Tallet pressed on towards the end of the month. A board appeared above the door of the

Corner House, announcing that this desirable residence was for sale. Mrs. Tallet gave up all pretence of looking after Mrs. Begbie and had the additional pleasure of very haughtily turning away two people who came inquiring for rooms. She and Mrs. Clarkson went out to view small houses, and had interminable discussions as to which of the bulky furniture should be kept and which sold. During the third week of the month, a few days before the Corner House was to be offered in public auction, it was sold privately to an aged Canon with a wealthy wife. Next day, after a solemn session that lasted two hours, Mrs. Clarkson and Mrs. Tallet went out to engage a flat on Abbey Hill, since they must move now that the house was sold, and no suitable small house had been found. Mrs. Begbie, who had cried almost continuously since the night when she had brought the evil tidings from the hairdresser's, now realized that her tears were unavailing, and began to pack her things. She was going to Hastings on a long visit to a sister whom she privately detested.

Then Mrs. Tallet really went into action. She stood over Emmie as she scrubbed every inch of flooring and paint in the new flat. She packed glass and china and linen in small boxes that could be carried by hand through the August dusk up the area steps, along the lane by Freeman's house and so to the flat on Abbey Hill. Even the coal that remained in the shed went along that path, carried in a bath with Emmie at one handle and the determined old woman at the other. Emmie gasped and trembled and sweated: Mrs. Tallet grunted and gritted her teeth: but neither noticed either

her own plight or her fellow-toiler's. On the twenty-sixth, when the vans had driven away with the furniture that was to be sold, there remained in the house only the absolute necessities, the furniture that Miss Ada had clung to and the personal belongings of Mrs. Clarkson, Emmie and Mr. Wykham. These last now began to cause Mrs. Tallet acute anxiety. "He never has thought of anybody but himself," she grumbled. "He should have come, or written to tell us what to do with his stuff directly Miss Ada wrote to tell him about leaving. If he doesn't come tomorrow I shall order the van and dump the whole lot down at the *Press* office. Why should I be bothered? I've got quite enough to think about."

"If he doesn't come tomorrow . . ." I must go into the outer darkness without another sight or sound of him. But of course there is no "if" about it. Tomorrow he will come back. Tomorrow is the twenty-seventh.

And at last it was the twenty-seventh. A hot summer day with the sky deeply blue even as Emmie did the step and the knocker. Her low spirits had left her during the night and she found herself exchanging extravagantly cheerful greetings with the milkboy and the postman. There were four letters for him. That made it seem real that today was *the* day. Other people had been told and had timed their letters accordingly. By the time that broad golden sun had completed this day's journey the horrible period of waiting and indecision would be over. She would know where in this town to begin looking for a place. She must ask Mrs. Clarkson for a reference. It wouldn't, she felt, be a very good one. Mrs. Clarkson was not in the best of tempers these days, and there was the hardly-yet-forgotten business of Miss Bavister's missing things. Still, there were the ones before . . . and anyway, if she asked today it was bound to be all right. She was singing softly to herself as she lighted the boiler fire.

Mrs. Tallet had likewise risen in good spirits. She had decided that it would be a splendid idea to polish all the furniture that was going into the flat, and then, when it was unwrapped from the cloths and sacking that would protect it on its journey of an eighth of a mile, it would need no more attention.

She kept Emmie hard at work until it was time for Miss Ada's lunch. Nobody else, in times like these, was supposed to need food, but Miss Ada was not allowed to miss a meal. Emmie, half-swooning from heat and exhaustion, ate some bread and butter and drank some tea standing at the kitchen table. The kitchen chairs had been carried across to the flat under cover of darkness some nights before.

"What are you going to do?" asked Mrs. Tallet curiously, as she saucered her tea to save time.

"I expect I shall go to Miss Trappit's for a day or two, until I find a new place. I must ask Mrs. Clarkson for a reference."

Mrs. Tallet sniffed and said nothing. A bad sign perhaps, but one must ignore it.

Ten minutes later when she went to Mrs. Clarkson's room for the tray, she said, "Will you write me a reference, please, madam? I shall need one when I begin looking for another place."

Mrs. Clarkson looked at her coldly.

"I wonder at you," she said, "when you are well aware that it was your behaviour which in a great part caused me to decide upon this upheaval in my life."

"You mean . . ."

"What I mean is this. You would have been given notice for the end of this month in any case, and in these circumstances honest mistresses find it difficult to give girls references that would be very helpful in getting a new situation. You would be wise to have nothing in writing, and then when you have a place in mind your prospective employer can apply to me and perhaps I can explain tactfully that though there has been nothing proved against you, you must not be exposed to temptation."

"But you haven't any reason to say that," burst out Emmie passionately. "There was nothing proved against me."

"There were the stockings."

"Which you gave back to me. Miss Bavister didn't claim them. If you still thought they were hers you shouldn't have given them back to me. You should have fetched a policeman. I wish you had. I'd have been cleared then."

Large tears, as much due to anger as to sorrow, began to pour down her face.

Mrs. Clarkson raised her eyebrows. "I believe Tallet was right after all. If one is to be exposed to scenes of this kind, life is intolerable. Please take the tray and go."

But Emmie was beyond thought of trays. She stumbled out of the room, empty-handed, and began to make her blind way to the kitchen stairs. Half-way along the landing was the head of the main staircase and as she passed it a shadow loomed, a hand caught her arm and a voice said, "God Almighty, what is wrong with you?"

He was back!

For just one moment she fought madly for control . . . sniff . . . swallow, say "Nothing much" and go away, don't involve anybody else, don't betray yourself. It was no good. Crying, laughing, making incoherent sounds, she launched herself upon him, clutching his sleeve, his collar, the edge of his coat. He caught at the banister to steady himself, and tried to calm her. "All right," he said, over and over again. "It's all right. I'm here."

But she went on crying, in fact the hysterical noise grew louder and echoed along the empty landing and through the uncarpeted house. He backed down a couple of steps and tried to draw her with him, but except for the noise and the clutching hands it might have been a badly stuffed doll he was trying to make walk downstairs. He heard Mrs. Clarkson's door open, and quick as thought he swung Emmie up into his arms, ran down the stairs and into his room, and kicked the door to behind him. How light and thin, he thought, as he set her in the chair opposite the one in which Stumpy lay gloating; really, she was hardly heavier than the dog. And, he thought, except for the tears, she was behaving much as Stumpy had when he met him in the kennels yard.

"Now," he said, propping himself against the edge of the desk and looking down at her, "perhaps you'll tell me what all this is about."

Emmie snuffled and gulped.

"You know about everybody being turned out, don't you?" she asked at last.

"Well, you weren't crying about that, at this late hour, were you?"

"Not exactly." She hesitated and then said in a rush of words that went up and down and were sometimes loud and clear, sometimes drowned in sobs, "It was everything. Miss Bavister lost some things and they blamed me, and she didn't claim the stockings, yet they wouldn't say they were mine. And you were away, and then Dr. Mason went and Mrs. Tallet gave me notice and Mrs. Clarkson won't give me a reference and I've left it late to get a place because I didn't know where you were going and I've been dreadfully busy moving the things."

She paused from sheer lack of breath.

Murray Wykham took out and lighted a cigarette.

"And," Emmie began again, feeling that she had made a fool of herself and anxious to go into justifying details. He held up his hand.

"That'll do for one instalment," he said. "Let's go through them one by one. First — did you know anything about Miss Bavister's things?"

"No."

"I believe you. Skip the unowned stockings for a moment. I heard about J.M. It's a great pity, but she knew what she was doing, and I'll bet she hasn't shed a tear about it, so I don't see why you should. And you're looking for a job and haven't got a reference. That seems to me to be the real trouble, and that's easily fixed. If she won't give you a reference after I've had a word with her, I will. So mop up your face and let's see a welcoming smile."

But Emmie, who in a lifetime of troubles had cried very little, had just discovered the relief of tears, and now that she was happy again, now that he was here and the nightmare was over, she began to cry again from exhaustion and happiness. He watched her bony little hand unclosing and closing again on the sodden handkerchief, and remembered the surprise he had felt when he lifted her. It occurred to him that she might be ill, run down. "Dreadfully busy" had dropped out during her account of her troubles. And if she were ill who would bother about it? Not Mrs. Clarkson. And not Mrs. Tallet. For if Mrs. Clarkson were displeased with the child, Tally's attitude would be never a minute in doubt.

He looked round the room and thought of all the things he had to do, and arrange for, and pack, and swore softly to himself. But there was no doubt that if Emmie could have served him she would have done so, and he could not be less generous. Also it was useless to deny that there was a queer sort of link between them . . . all of her making, but no less strong for that.

"Listen, Emmie," he said, "I'm going up to see Mrs. Clarkson now, I was on my way when I met you. While I'm there you go and tidy your face and get a hat if you want one. You're coming out with me for a little while."

He opened the door and she could hear him going up the bare stairs two at a time. She went very slowly up to her room. Where was he taking her? She didn't

274

care, or even wonder very much. It was so marvellous not to have to bother any more. She held her face under the cold water that brimmed the bowl and combed her damp hair into order. She put on the yellow frock and the beads (she'd never thanked him for the beads, she had intended to do that first thing), and the hat with the brown ribbon. If Mrs. Tallet saw her there would be trouble, but she didn't care any more for Mrs. Tallet.

He didn't take her very far. The car slid along in the direction of the old Turnpike, but before the houses ended it turned to the right and stopped in a quiet shady street before a house that stood back a little from the road. Murray left her sitting in the car and went into the garden. Through the shrubs she could see him ring the bell and then go into the house. Quite soon he was out again and was holding the door of the car open.

"I want you just to let Dr. Finch have a look at you, Emmie. He won't hurt you, and he'll probably give you a bottle of something to stop your troubles getting on top of you the way they seem to. I'll wait for you."

19

"You may put on your dress now," Dr. Finch said at last.

She buttoned her dress and lifted the beads over her head again. The doctor was looking at her and pulling out his lower lip as though it were elastic and letting it spring back into place again.

"Where's your home?" he said at last.

"I haven't one."

"Relatives?"

"No."

"Come, come. Everybody has an odd aunt or so."

"I haven't. Why?"

He ignored that question.

"And you've been working at Mrs. Clarkson's. How long?"

"Since March."

He pressed a button on the desk and the door was immediately opened by the woman in uniform who had shown Emmie in. To her he said, "I'll speak to Mr. Wykham," and to Emmie, "Just wait in there, will you?"

Murray was sitting on the arm of a chair, fidgeting his feet and fingers impatiently. He jumped up and smiled at Emmie as he passed her to go into the consulting-room.

"Tell me, Wykham, what exactly is this girl to you?"

"Nothing. Nothing at all. Why?"

The door closed.

Emmie, stricken numb, went to the window and looked out, unseeing. After an age the door opened again and Murray, with a grave worried face, came through into the waiting-room. Without speaking he took her by the elbow and led her out to the car. They gained the old Turnpike again and stopped on the grass before the first gate. It was the place where she had sat in the sun and watched Stumpy playing. She shuddered, This was a place of ill omen. She had gone from here to face the accusation of stealing Miss

Bavister's things. And now she was here again, helpless and dumb with a sense of impending doom. Why had Murray rushed her to the doctor like that? Why had he brought her here? Why was he now fidgeting about, hesitating on the brink of speech?

He felt aimlessly in all his pockets, cracked his knuckles, pushed his nose from side to side with a nicotine-browned finger. Then suddenly he turned to face her, throwing one arm over the wheel and the other over the hood at the back. He stared at the fence over her shoulder and said quietly, "Are you as alone in the world as you make out, Emmie?"

Why, oh why was everybody asking that today?

"Yes."

That was true, wasn't it? Nothing should make her go back to Swything, even assuming that her mother was still living there. Miss Stanton was in London with Ella Frome. "There isn't room for another gnat here."

Alone? yes.

"You've been feeling ill, haven't you?"

"Sometimes. A little. Why? Did he say that I was ill?"

"It didn't need his saying so. I could see it. You've wasted almost away. Hadn't you noticed?"

"No. I've been tired, and a bit shaky and breathless, but I've been in a flurry so often." She paused and then added in a voice suddenly urgent, "What is it? You'd better tell me."

"Your lungs are touched. No, wait a minute. It isn't so awfully serious, yet. He says that you've got to have lots of rest, and nourishing food and air. He wants to send you somewhere where you'll have all these things."

"A sanatorium?"

He nodded.

"But I don't want to go there. I won't. Nobody can make me. It's for me to say, and I won't go."

"But, Emmie, it's the only thing to do. I'd do it, if it were me. There's nothing to dread about it."

"But I don't need to. If I feel ill nobody knows it, so it doesn't matter. I can still work. I'd be working now if you hadn't brought me out. I can have a week's holiday at Miss Trappit's before I get another job."

"Listen to me, Emmie." He put out both his hands and folded hers between them. "Unless you catch a thing like this in time you'll be very ill indeed — you might even die. And you won't be able to go on working, slaving about in dark kitchens for very much longer. You must be guided by me, since there's no one else. Now do be your good sensible self. Look here, I'll make all the arrangements for you and see you settled in before I go."

"Are you going away, again?"

"Yes. I didn't have time to tell you. I've sold the paper and I'm going away."

"Where to?"

"Abyssinia. Something's going to happen there before long and I want to be there to see it."

There was a long silence. The distant noise of a reaping machine came across the fields and in a nearby ditch a grasshopper chirped. At last Emmie said, "I wouldn't get a job there, I suppose."

"I'm afraid not."

"All right. I'll go wherever you say. Shall we go back now?"

"Perhaps we'd better. I've got a lot to see to."

This was the end then. The very end. Something had happened to her lungs; that was why she was always out of breath and shaky and had a cough in the mornings. And she was going to a place where they would try to patch her up so that she might come out and go on working . . . endless, endless floors, countless dishes. Another Mrs. Fincham, another Mrs. Clarkson, another Mrs. Tallet. Plenty of those in the world. And only one Murray Wykham whom she would never see again. "What is this girl to you?" — "Nothing. Nothing at all." What is this girl to anybody? Nothing. Nothing at all. And one day, when this girl can no longer scrub and polish and sweep, she'll die in the workhouse.

"Don't take it too hard," said the beloved voice. Awkward? Nervous? Sorry?

"I've been an awful nuisance to you. I didn't mean to be. I'd have kept out of your way if I'd known."

"No, don't say that. I shall always be glad that I noticed and we took it in hand in time. It's a wonder I did. Shows that there's something in Fate sometimes."

The car squeaked to a standstill in the road that ran past the end of the Corner House.

"You get out here. I'll see you when I come back for my things later on. I must go to the office now."

"Good-bye," said Emmie from the pavement. "You've been awfully good to me."

279

"Nonsense. You've been very brave. Cheer up now. There's a lot of life ahead, you know."

"I know," said Emmie.

He did not gather the significance of the two bitter words. He was being torn by the thought of his own inadequacy, the inadequacy of words and of comfort in the face of tragedy. He rammed home the gear fiercely and the car shot away. Years of underfeeding, he thought, and overwork and bad surroundings. Perhaps bad heredity as well, who knew? The result stood there on the edge of the pavement, doomed. But that wasn't all. There was a soul there too, and character, that strange thing known as a person: the thing that looked out from those yellow eyes, spoke with that tongue. Kind, intelligent, loving creature, being galloped into the grave and the everlasting nothingness by a faulty organism.

"Death's dolls are we, his marionettes."

He drove harder to escape his thoughts.

20

Emmie went up to her bedroom, shut the door, flung off her hat and sat on the bed. The part of her that had always done her thinking had been thrown out of order and could only turn over and over a few fragments of things that had been said before.

"Your lungs are touched."

"Abyssinia."

"Sanatorium."

She sat quite still, staring at the pattern on the wallpaper and waiting for her own identity to return and master the alien voices, After a time it did so.

I'm Emmie Bacon, it cried, I'm seventeen years old, I like books and flowers and animals and I love Murray Wykham. I'm all tangled up in a body whose lungs have gone wrong and those lungs are going to wipe Emmie Bacon out of existence after they have hampered her for the rest of the time she is alive. Mind over matter. Faith-healing. Will-power. What use? Didn't Christ Himself say, "Which of you by taking thought can add an inch to his stature?"

Of course there is the sanatorium. I can go in there and be patched up, and then there is the afterwards.

There is always the afterwards.

Suppose a miracle happened. Suppose that she were made really well, and that Murray changed his mind about her being "Nothing, nothing at all."

There'd be first the fierce mad pleasure of loving him and of being loved. But that wouldn't stop (she saw with clear, bitter sight) the gap that her seventeen years had made in her defences. It wasn't only her lungs that the years had devoured . . . it was her reason, her invulnerability, the happy indifference to time and conditions that most people carry with them to their graves.

Time. Even though Murray loved her, the years would creep and steal, dulling the senses, stilling the pulses, numbing and quieting, patiently and relentlessly preparing the way for death.

That was all life was, be it fortunate as hers was unlucky, great as hers was obscure, long as hers had been brief — it was all a prelude to death.

And it had to be lived in a world where every kind of cruelty and injustice flourished, so that it would never do to look either to the right hand or the left for fear of what might meet your shrinking sight.

People without imagination gloated over a plump new baby, not seeing in that innocent flesh the helpless sentient putty for the pincers of fate — war perhaps, pestilence, sickness or mere age.

A plump and lively horse pleased you, but where would it end? Crippled, driven, beaten and starved in Flanders as likely as not. And young lambs came on mint sauce by way of the bloody slaughterhouse.

"Look outside yourself." That was what the moralists advised for the unhappy. But there was no comfort there.

And there was none within.

Look carefully over your own life. Swything, mother and Ted Gibson, that was all clear in the light of later knowledge. Fincham's, Mrs. Fincham's miseries, the dog, the rabbits, the horses. Petersbury and the reward of working as hard as you knew how, condemned without proof as a thief and refused a reference.

It was all a tremendous booby trap.

Of course all these thoughts are made. Sane people would say, "Snap out of it, the old world's not so bad," or they would say, "You're morbid, and that's probably due to your health. You won't feel like this when you're cured."

282

But that wasn't true. You'd always feel this way. And always had. No, that wasn't quite true. She fumbled back. There must have been a day when she was exactly like Edna, only brighter, and the next day she had been different. And the difference was due, as far as it could be due to any one to Miss Stanton. Miss Stanton had opened a door that could never be shut again, and the fact that Emmie had strayed through that door in a different direction from the one that Miss Stanton had pointed out was the fault of neither of them. Miss Stanton, all unknowing, had made straight the path for Murray too. And now there was but one cure for the morbid mind, the touched lungs and the broken heart.

She rose, and leaving the hat upon the bed, went quietly downstairs and into the street, choosing the road that led in the direction of Fen Willow.

Evening brooded over the stretch of stagnant backwater bordered with willows and rushes and pink willow herb. No road ran near, no house or cultivated field could be seen. The grasses and flowers that Emmie had trodden to reach this spot were already lifting themselves again, covering her trail; and presently the parted waters closed over as silently, hardly rippled by her frantic struggles in the grip of the weeds far below.

Other titles published by Ulverscroft:

ESTHER

Norah Lofts

Artaxerxes, King of Persia, needs a wife. He picks the one girl who would have given anything to be passed over: a Jewish scholar, Esther, from the back streets of his capital, Shushan. To a King bored by the chattering of women wreathed in musky scents, this changeling is a breath of fresh air. But the new Queen of Persia is lost in a world of protocol, and soon loses her husband's favour. Worse, she has to hide her faith and deny her origins — for Haman, the King's favourite, is an Amelekite, an ancient enemy of the Jews, and determined to have revenge. Esther's only hope to avert a holocaust is to risk her own life and go, uninvited, before a King who has already disposed of one unpopular wife . . .

HOLY COW

David Duchovny

Elsie Bovary is a cow, and a pretty happy one at that. But a glimpse of something called an "industrial meat farm" shakes her understanding of the world to its core, and she decides to escape to a better, safer place. A motley crew is formed: Elsie; Shalom, a grumpy pig; and Tom, a suave turkey who can't fly but can work an iPhone with his beak. Toting stolen passports and slapdash human disguises, they head for the airport . . .

SUMMER AT LITTLE BEACH STREET BAKERY

Jenny Colgan

Summer has arrived in the Cornish town of Mount Polbearne, and Polly Waterford couldn't be happier. She's in love — with the beautiful seaside town she calls home, with running the bakery on Beach Street, and with her boyfriend Huckle. And yet there's something unsettling about the gentle summer breeze that's floating through town. Selina, recently widowed, hopes that moving to Polbearne will ease her grief, but Polly has a secret that could destroy her friend's fragile recovery. Responsibilities that Huckle thought he'd left behind are back, and Polly finds it hard to cope with his increasingly long periods of absence. So she sifts flour, kneads dough and bakes bread; but nothing can calm the storm she knows is coming. Is Polly about to lose everything she loves?

HAPPIEST DAYS

Jack Sheffield

It's 1986, and Jack Sheffield returns to Ragley village school for his tenth rollercoaster year as headteacher. It's the time of Margaret Thatcher's third election victory, *Dynasty* and shoulder pads, *Neighbours* and a Transformer for Christmas. And at Ragley School, a year of surprises is in store. Ruby the caretaker finds happiness at last, Vera the secretary makes an important decision, a new teacher is appointed, and a disaster threatens the school. Meanwhile, Jack receives unexpected news, and is faced with the biggest decision of his career . . .